That November Weekend

That November Weekend

A Romance Novel

BEVERLY WILDER

AuthorHouse™
1663 Liberty Drive
Bloomington, IN 47403
www.authorhouse.com
Phone: 1-800-839-8640

Published by AuthorHouse 04/22/2015

ISBN: 978-1-4772-9575-5 (sc)
ISBN: 978-1-4772-9574-8 (e)

Library of Congress Control Number: 2012922806

Print information available on the last page.

This book is printed on acid-free paper.

Chapter One

Kelly Gerard is a twenty two year old nursing student who is striving happily with the simple pleasures in life and working on her off school hours in Childress Bakery. Mark Scott is a twenty four year old young man, business oriented, uptight and unengaged in the thought of being in relationships. The two meet by accident one afternoon in front of the adjacent stores where they work. Mark wasn't watching where he was going and bumped into Kelly, tripping over her back pack and tearing the arm strap. Kelly was mannerly, understanding and laughed at him, knowing there was no harm done. Mark although embarrassed for his clumsiness doesn't really apologize but simply makes excuses for his clumsiness and becomes red in the face and just helps her pick up the items that spilled out onto the sidewalk. One of the employees peeks out of the door of the bakery to see what the commotion is and Mark explains that it was an accident and he is very busy in that he needs to meet a contractor and is twenty minutes late and everything here is fine, no problem at all. He acted it seemed to the witness that this incident was merely a disturbance in his busy schedule. Mark turned to the door of his store but looked briefly back at Kelly misunderstanding a sound she made for something she may have said. Kelly walked toward the door of the bakery and smiled and waved to Mark as she pulled a hair band out of her back pack and pulled her hair back with it. Mark walked ahead to the door of his store and reached into his pocket for the key. Mark had waited for three days for the contractor to make his appearance. He took possession of the store lease on Monday and there seemed to be an eternity of work to do because the place was a diner four short months ago. The whole store needed to be renovated, walls to be rearranged, appliances to be discarded and many new plans to be drawn out. Mark had a massive job ahead of him in transforming this diner into his hardware store. Twelve minutes had passed by when a truck pulled up; Burks and Sons contractors had arrived. Three men entered the store fixed with cameras, tape measures and planners. Mark extended his hand in greeting in agreement to get to work. Gary, the father, his son Ronald and hired hand Richard walked through the building with Mark advising him of the work order including the arrangements made with the electrician, carpenters, demolition crew and decorators. For four hours the contractors drew up the plans, phoned and made appointments and schedules were set up. Pens were flying, measuring tapes flipping in and out. These men meant business. Mark had lost track of time. "Listen there is a bakery beside me here, let me take a few minutes, I'll get us some snacks"

Gary and Richard stayed busy as Mark offered Ronald a choice of sweet or savory pastries. Mark decided "The bakery next store carries meat stuffed biscuits served warm with a smile. I'll bring a box full and we can all sit down and take a break. You know I want to sit down and let all these plans sink in and imagine how the place will take shape"

Childress's bakery was a family run establishment for ninety years and holding in the same location on West Front Street on the down town location of

Kingston. The large pitcher window was framed with detailed antique brick work built in the early nineteen hundreds by an Austrian mason. The building held

Childress's Bakery, Milesworth shoe store and the future hardware store. The upper two levels also with wonderful Austrian brickwork held apartments. "AWH!" Mark had to breathe in some fresh air of the early fall evening and paused to watch a couple store keepers across the street sweep the sidewalk in front of their stores and getting cleaned up for the end of the work day. He thought to his self "I better pick up food from the bakery and then wrap things up for the day myself."

The bakery was starting to fill up with people ordering desert either after eating at a restaurant or out walking after eating supper. Mark walked into to Childress's and to the right was a drink cooler, he reached into it and got four bottles of water. He reached into the pocket of his leather jacket and sat at a stool to wait to be served. Bob Childress dropped what he was doing when he saw Mark. "Hey Bud, you were some rude to my girl here in front of the store earlier today when she came in to start her shift!"

"Oh well it was an accident, she wasn't hurt or upset, smiled and waved when she entered your store. I'm sorry if it looked like anything different to you."

"You destroyed the poor girl's back pack, didn't even have the good will to help her pick things up or to pay for her bag. What gives with you? That seems really ignorant to me."

By this tangent, Mark feels embarrassed and quite taken back. "Well ok, I think you are over reacting and the bag didn't look expensive and I didn't see any damage or spill out onto the sidewalk."

"Oh no, you wouldn't see the damage; you were too caught up on how well she thought of you walking by here. If you come into this bakery again, I'll charge you triple for anything you buy."

"Hey Gary, I hope you all like cheese and bacon burritos and chocolate milk. Come on over to the counter and take a break with me.

By the time Mark had got back to the store the guys had forgotten what he originally went out for. Mark set a box filled with assorted burritos and chocolate milk on the counter and asked the men to help there selves. He even thought to get napkins and set them out for everyone. So the men sat around the counter eating and took a break from discussing renovation plans. Mark was referred to this contractor by the lawyer who handled the lease of the property. "I have waited four months to have the name of the store patented and for my business license to get put in place. The problem was zoning. I came close to being denied registration for a hardware store in the downtown core because of traffic conflicts for delivery and pick-ups. It turns out that I was applying for a permit for a lumber yard or so it seemed to the ministry. Someone mistook my application and it was placed before the board of business associates. If I hadn't opened a right for review, the assumed application would have been void and I would have had to pay to have the whole process started again."

Richard sympathized with Marks dilemma "You are with the program. You have knowledge of business, accounting, technology and guy you really know how to dress well. You are very well spoken and I'm not surprised with the thick mindedness of the Land Registry Office.

I know and have worked with some of the agents there" Gary added "The right hand doesn't know what the left hand is doing." The men chuckled and finished the food and drank their last sips of chocolate milk.

There was no pitcher window in the front of Marks store but there were three tall narrow windows. A large glass paned door was between two of the widows and the original brick was the front wall. Mark was standing between Gary and Ronald and across from Ronald when Kelly walked in with a tray of butter tarts, just made fresh. "Hi, excuse me, I hope I'm not intruding, I know you are busy."

Ronald recognized Kelly from college. "Hey Kelly. What brings you by?" He walked over to greet her and take the tray.

"I just came by with a peace offering"

Mark, red in the face came over to Kelly and interrupted. "Do you have business with me? I believe I told the man it was an accident. I have been very busy and preoccupied with mistakes made and problems in getting established here."

Ronald interrupted; Kelly was beginning to look nervous over Marks sudden concern.

"What's up Kelly? Is everything alright here?"

"I don't know, I brought these tarts over hoping matters would be smoothed over by now. I know that Bob Childress was quite offended but my Grandmother and I spoke to him."

"Mark, what happened? I know Kelly from College, she's good people. If there has been some sort of misunderstanding, I'm sure it is just that." Kelly set the tray of tarts down onto the counter beside the box of burrito rappers and empty milk cartons. By this time Mark and Kelly are both embarrassed and Kelly's glance met Gary's.

"Hello Mr. Burke. It's always nice to see you."

"Likewise Kelly, are you well? You look like you are working too hard, a bit thinner now aren't you? So what are you worried about here Kelly?"

"Well before I am deemed to be a coward here among all this concern for Kelly's wellbeing, if I may please explain! Earlier today I tripped over Kelly's back pack as I rushed to get to my door and apparently damaged it. I suppose a better gesture then just walking away would have been to offer to replace it and apologize for my clumsiness. You see I was late getting here and I feared that the contractors had been here and left. I have had so many stumbling blocks getting this venture under way and I have been preoccupied with it."

You know there's no apology needed, the strap isn't even broken. They just come loose from the buckle. My Grandmother spoke to Bob about getting over excited and I suggested bringing over these tarts in hopes that you would enjoy them. Please do indeed come into the bakery any time and pay the proper price for whatever you buy. So do you care for butter tarts? They are even still warm from the oven."

Chapter Two

Saturday morning came along like a welcomed first spring breeze for Kelly. She didn't have to work, the day was hers. She had reccntly moved into a very small bachelorette apartment in the basement of a house owned by a single mother who is a loan officer. She had one daughter and it was really a very quiet setting there. The apartment was simple, consisted of one big room with a bathroom. She slept on a pullout couch, picked it up every morning and transformed her bedroom into the living room. A small kitchenette with a counter and bar stool is where she cooked and dined. There were more shelves and books then there was furniture and a small wooden desk for her computer and a coat rack. Kelly lived on very modest means since she was only able to work part time at the bakery and had her student loan. She never even purchased new books but inquired on line for used books and items she needed to complete her courses. Kelly woke up to her landlord's cat pawing at the hair that lay across her chin. This was the usual manner in which she was awakened. She accepted it as her wakeup call every morning and thought it was quite a cute way to begin her morning routine. The next thing on the morning schedule was to share her cereal with Muffin but since there wasn't any milk; muffin got a pat of butter on the end of Kelly's finger. Not that every day was a regiment of steps, it was just that Kelly was getting used to a new routine since she recently moved to Kingston to finish her nursing coarse, but next on the agenda was to eat breakfast. Bob and Gene like to take care of Kelly by providing her with baked goods and she didn't mind taking the help. She chose a delicious multigrain bagel, patted it with butter and placed it into the toaster oven for a bit. She poured a glass of apple juice and gave thanks for all the many blessing she receives in her day to day happenings. Kelly's apartment though very humble was very well kept. She even folded her tea towels neatly on the towel rack. She always cleaned up after a meal and never left so much as a crumb on the counter and unplugged appliances and neatly wrapped the cords. The care that she took of all she had was because of the appreciation she had for all she owned. Kelly was about five feet ten, slender with jet black long hair. Her dark eye lashes and brows framed her face and her smile was the final touch to her perfect porcelain skin. Kelly didn't wear makeup, she didn't need to. Her cheeks were naturally rosy and her eye lids were blue tinged. She was fit and healthy, ran every morning before school. She did not run or exercise on Sunday. Sunday was her Sabbath day and she kept the Sabbath day holy. This however was Saturday and was the first free day she has had in over two months. It was a perfect day for a jog and she put back her hair and put on her jogging suit, patted the cat as she scurried up the stairs and out the door.

The weather man was at least correct one day that week; sunny with scattered clouds and 55 degrees. What a perfect day for a jog. Kelly would jog about five miles and it took about five minutes to get to the water front trail used mostly by joggers and it ran right around the whole river bank. By the time Kelly got to the trail, Mark ran up behind her and passed her heading home from his jog. He didn't recognize her but when he ran passed her she glanced sideways and greeted him. Kelly is a very friendly person, personable and a lady that people took an immediate liking to.

"Oh good morning, nice trail this river front. I wish there had been one like it where I come from."

"Oh you are new to Kingston too? I didn't know."

"Yes. I moved here seven months ago from Edmonton. I grew up in a small prairie town where fields were your back yards and farming was the main way of making a living. Anyway are you meeting anyone or running alone?"

"No I'm not meeting anyone, I'll run with you. So what are you building in the store next to Childress's?"

"I'm putting a hardware store there. I have plenty of space and plans are taking shape for the interior. So will you be looking for a full time job in retail at all?"

"I'm busy right now with nursing school and part time shifts at the bakery, they are my grandparents but I have only known that for eight months. They are the greatest people and we have really made up for lost time. They care so very much for me and I guess Bob can be a bit protective now of me. Again I am so sorry for his over reacting about our stumbling into each other the other day."

"Oh no that was my fault but I'm glad all is well and in the past now. I can see that your grandparents take good care of you, after all it's their job isn't it?"

"That's a nice way to look at it!"

"If you don't mind, how is it that you have only known them a short while?"

"My Mom, who was their daughter, went wayward and left home after getting pregnant with me—"

Mark interrupted at hearing of her misfortune and pleaded that she did not have to spill it. "You don't even know me, I'm sorry."

"It's no problem, I'm just happy I know them now."

"So your name is Kelly Childress?"

"No, it's Gerard. I was adopted when I was thirteen months old from foster care. I've always known that the Gerard's were my adoptive parents. I have five other sisters all adopted as well. Are you busy working today or do you want to go and sit down somewhere?"

"No, not working today. Let's go over to Starbucks, I think they have a variety of herbal tea there." Mark Invited.

Neither of them drank specialty coffees, beside they were filled with calories. Mark and Kelly left the trail and entered back into town to look for a more intimate place to chat rather than a jogging trail. She was kind of secretly attracted to him from the moment he bumped into her in front of the bakery. He is six feet three inches, slender with brown hair and eyes, clean shaven and darn good looking.

As well as being well dressed. Kelly accepted his invitation to tea even though she had planned on having a long jog to start her day off right. "So here we are; do you want to sit in or sit outside?"

"Oh let me check my running meter then I'll sit inside with you and we can chat. This shows that we jogged about two km. since we met. Where did you start off from, the store?"

"Yeah, so I only have a couple of block on you. We can finish in a while."

"Sure we can Mark; it's nice to just spend time chatting freely. I haven't had a free day to myself in weeks." Kelly complained.

"I know how you feel!" Mark concurred.

"So do you open hardware stores often or—?"

"No this is my first. I helped to run a farm equipment business with my father and uncle in Edmonton."

"So why did you move to Kingston Ontario away from your own business? I would imagine a farming equipment business would be very lucrative."

"Yes well you see—um, there was an accident. My father and uncle were crushed by fallen machinery."

Mark's eyes welled up and he got choked up as he tried to tell Kelly about the accident. Kelly was so sweet and showed much sympathy for her new friend.

She reached for his hand. "I'm so terribly sorry Mark. Please forgive me for prying."

"You are not, I guess we both have a couple of stories to tell don't we."

"Yes my friend. So let's enjoy our tea and try to keep each other's spirits up."

"Anyway, it's still all very fresh in my memory. I didn't see it happen but I did find them. My dad died instantly." He paused to catch his composure.

"My uncle—he died a few hours later. After the funeral my mother went into a rest home and is still not well."

"OH my dear Mark. How do you keep going?"

"I don't know but my faith sustains me and I need to be strong for my mother."

"Your mother, is she here with you or still back in Edmonton?"

"She is here. We couldn't stay there and continue to run the business after all that had happened. Mother has aged and she is sick all the time due to the depression, you know her immune system isn't even what it should be. I see her every day and try to take her out; you know to see different surroundings than her room in the home. She is able to stay at my house on the weekends now but still has nightmares and isn't coming around and able to enter into society as well as I would wish."

"Oh the poor dear. Is she faithful?"

"Yes but she is frail. My parents loved one and other more than I have ever seen another couple love. They worked, sang, played, did everything together and she doesn't want to live without dad. Am I ever rambling on, I'm sorry," Before Mark could finish apologizing, Kelly was offering her attention if he ever needed to talk or needed help with his mother in any way.

Kelly also had great faith in God and relied on Him for her every need. She counted on the blessings of the living waters promised to Heavenly Fathers children.

"Has your mother gone to church yet?"

"Yes, she just started about a month ago but only for the first hour. I then take her back to my house so she can rest and we have dinner together, read some scriptures before I take her back to the home. She is coming along; she even likes to wear colors other than black. That alone gives me hope; I almost gave up on ever seeing her smile again."

"Mark you are a wonderful son. I commend you for being the strength to your mother in her time of need. Good for you. It's very rare for a guy; I can see a daughter taking care of a parent. I admire you very much and I'm glad I'm getting to know you. Mark my offer stands, if there is anything that I can do for you, I would only be happy to help."

"Ok Kelly do you want to jog more or do you think you would come over to my house to meet my mother, she is there waiting for me."

"I hope I haven't been keeping you and that your mom is ok."

"Come over and meet her, it will be good for her to have another lady to chat with. If I know her, she is sorting through her fabric and trying to decide what to make a blouse from and what to make a skirt from. Here let me pay for the tea Kelly and we'll go."

"Mark, thank you. I'm a little nervous but I think it will be nice to talk to her."

"You are very personable; she'll be fine making your acquaintance."

Mark and Kelly made the jog back to his house. They didn't job back to the trail, it was easier to jog back north through town though a bit more busy with traffic. They made an easy jaunt down a hill then around the corner from the main street. They arrived at Marks house; the third brick and sided house in the subdivision. It was a newly built home in a growing subdivision. There were roughly six hundred new homes built up there in the past five years and twenty more going up on the same street where Mark lived. When the two jogged up the front walk, Kelly noticed a lady sitting by the window with a cat sitting on her lap and she wore a purple house coat. Mark unlocked the door and escorted Kelly into the front room where Marks mother was sitting. "Good morning Mom, nice to see you up."

"Hello Dear" Mark kissed his mother on the fore head and cheek and offered to get her some juice.

"Kelly this is my mother, Elizabeth Scott; Mom this is Kelly Gerard. She works in the bakery next to the hardware store. We have only known each other for a short time but have had a good morning jog and a visit already."

"Good morning Elizabeth. It's a beautiful morning and I see you are enjoying it with your cat."

The cat jumped off of Elizabeth's lap and scooted over to visit with Mark and Kelly. "Well cats know when someone is a good person and look at how she is greeting you Kelly. Here are some treats if you would like to give her some Kelly. You know you will be good friends with her for it."

"Sure Ma'am Kelly petted the cat while she fed Sandy her treats and the purring could be heard throughout the house.

Mark was so very touched by the kindness and interest that Kelly showed to his mother. He was so appreciative that his mother had someone to talk to even if it was for a brief few moments.

"Mom let me get you some breakfast, is there anything you favor this morning?"

"I think a fruit cup, a piece of toast and some apple cinnamon herbal tea please."

"Sure Mom. I'll fold a tea table down for you and you can sit in here by the window."

"Thank you dear, will you both sit with me and watch TV for a while after I eat?"

"Sure mom. We can unless Kelly has to be going. She can spend the whole day with us. It's up to her."

"I have the whole day free. Did you have cloths that you were choosing to make? I have good coordinating skill and can sew also."

"Mark I see that you two have been talking about things." Mark nodded and put his hand on his mother's shoulder and kissed her head. Elizabeth patted his hand and looked softly at Kelly.

"You know that I have been very sad than."

"Yes Elizabeth I know. I'm so deeply sorry for your loss and for the tragedy that has befallen your family. I see that Mark has been a constant strength for you. My heart goes out to you both. Please ask anything of me anytime."

"Thank you dear Kelly for your warm words. I have been gradually able to believe in the kindness and generosity of those close to us. I am finding hope enough that I can stand and get up in the morning and be grateful to breath. The parishioners here offer service and love to us in so many ways and we have been comforted here in our new home. God has blessed us with angels and he sustains us with his mercy."

Elizabeth began to cry as she often dose when loved ones offer their condolences.

She began to feel wearily in the memories of the tragic happenings and Mark recognized it. He suggested that she lay back in the chair to rest and covers her with a throw blanket. "Just rest Mom. Kelly and I will go into the kitchen and fix you your breakfast."

Elizabeth agreed, rested with her cat and closed her eyes. Mark escorted Kelly into the kitchen. He was very tender at this time and it was such a far contrast from their first meeting in front of the bakery. Mark made Kelly feel at home here and it was very easy for Kelly to feel comfortable with Mark because of the care and concern that he displayed for his Mother. Mark arranged the tray and fixed the tea. Kelly found a lovely china cup with a matching lid and quietly went to the chair where Elizabeth rested and placed it on the table beside her. Kelly noticed that the house was sparsely decorated with just a couple chairs and some side tables, a cat tree by the window and a foot stool and louvered desk by the side wall in the dining room area. There were window dressings but no art or pictures hanging on any of the walls anywhere and no plants to decorate the rooms either. The kitchen was fully furnished and stocked with food and appliances. Mark did all the work in there while his mother recovered when she came to visit on her weekend breaks from the rest home. All though the move from Edmonton was difficult for Mark and especially for Elizabeth, it was necessary given the tragedy that happened there. So much from the life the family had built together was lost and starting up a new business and trying to heal as well as the hard work in rebuilding and reestablishing seemed unbearable for both Mark and Elizabeth. Elizabeth nearly died of a broken heart. Mark lost thirty pounds in a month because of the stress of funeral arrangements, business closure; legal matters that needed to be dealt with that his mother did not have the strength to bear. All decisions and matters and the weight of the world was on Marks shoulders alone. All he had to hold onto was his religion and faith in God to lead and guide him through it all. He was only twenty four years old and he learned more about God, life and worldly matters in eight months then he had learned in his entire life.

Chapter Three

Mark and Kelly had an enjoyable morning talking in his kitchen as Elizabeth slept. Kelly is a beautiful young woman, a breath of fresh air for Mark. His distractions were many and focus strained by the responsibilities of the past months but making friends with Kelly allowed the burdens to be forgotten when he was with her. This new distraction that he had found in Kelly was a welcomed one. The softness in her eyes he saw as he poured out his agony, the spirit that touched his heart as she sympathized with him and the sweetness in which she used to interact with his mother caused Mark to desire and embrace in a friendship with Kelly. He had never felt such yearnings in his heart and he knew them to be true. The more he let himself ponder on these feelings the testimony of what was forthcoming in this relationship was very strong. Elizabeth walked into the kitchen as she was dressed then and carrying her cat. She inquired about going out for an hour or two. "Really mom, where do you think you would like to go? Do you want some lunch first?"

"Where did that cute china cup with its lid come from that you brought me the tea in?"

"I don't know Mom. It was in the cupboard so I must have unpacked it from the move."

"Oh well, it doesn't matter, it did cheer me up." Elizabeth smiled as she commented. "It reminded me of having tea with the Relief Society sisters back home. I must start writing to them and getting some communication going."

Mark looked very confused suddenly. "Mom, do you think you are up to that?"

"Well shouldn't I?"

"Oh yes, I'm glad you are looking forward to making contact again. I'll set up your computer, but for now, How about a walk around the mall. You suggested earlier that we should take a walk around the mall. Maybe we should stop for a snack and a salad at a nice little spot I have found there."

"Sure! Kelly would you enjoy being with us?

"Why yes, I would like nothing better. Anytime I have a couple free hours I would enjoy being company for you."

"Thank you. You said that you sew. I have had some fabric that Mark brought in for me to make some brightly colored clothes but I just haven't had the strength to attempt any of the patterns. Everything just sits in bags in my room. I look over the patterns and hold the fabric up to my skin but the ambition just isn't there. I have never in my life felt this desperate, I do appreciate your interest in me. Mark please, let's take a trip to the mall for a couple of hours."

Mark and Elizabeth with Kelly sitting in the back seat drove for ten minutes to arrive at the mall. Kelly held Elizabeth's arm as they walked into the mall while Mark parked the car. The two women waited at the front door and Elizabeth was quite taken by the size of the mall. It seemed to be four times the size of any mall in or near the small town in Edmonton. She was also pleasantly surprised by the festive decoration that had adorned the rafters since Christmas was just around the corner. Her eyes welled up with tears as it was becoming a happy day for her. Kelly beamed. Her radiant countenance was due to Elizabeth's happiness. Mark joined them and the three walked slowing taking in the festive surroundings of the season and exploring the possibilities of certain purchases. The first being a bag of candy cane flavored popcorn. Santa's village had not yet been erected but the excitement of the children could be heard as they marveled at the possibility of Santa's arrival. The second purchase was a pair of porcelain flower ear rings for Elizabeth to wear to church on Sunday then matched them to a mauve dress. Kelly supported her choice and what a grand day it was for the women. Mark reminded his mother that maybe she was over doing it, he didn't want her getting weary and that they should head for home so she can rest. Mark met them at the door with the car and drove them home to his house. After a short time at the mall, Elizabeth was tired and nervous because it was her first time being out and she began to shake. Kelly saw that she was happy but had too much excitement. "Elizabeth I'll start a nice warm bath for you. I find that that always calms me."

"Thank you Kelly" She whispered. She could barely put one foot in front of the other to go upstairs.

Mark was worried about his mother because he had not seen her that frail in weeks so he picked her up and carried her to her room. The cat was in Kelly's way and jumped up onto the rim of the Jacuzzi and watched the water fill the tub. "Good cat, you stay here. The bath is for Elizabeth."

The cat meowed and Mark came in to the bathroom. Kelly felt awkward but he left a cd player with some soft music for his mother to listen to. "I'm sorry if I made you feel uncomfortable, I wasn't thinking, sorry. If you wouldn't mind sitting up here with mom for a while, I'll make some dinner."

Kelly was sort of blushing, smiled and agreed to it. Kelly sat at the edge of Elizabeth's bed and suggested she help her into the tub and assumed she would be safe while Kelly sat in the bedroom.

The two women started talking first. "Elizabeth I see that you have a collection of bath oils. I used a combination of vanilla and chamomile."

That sounds delightful, that's usually what I use and I can't wait to soak in that. You are wonderful. Please stay acquainted with Mark. I can't believe he has only known you for a few days. How did you meet?"

Kelly told Elizabeth of their first meeting in front of Childress's bakery and they both had quite a chuckle. "I think Mark has been very preoccupied, my grandfather thought he was being stuck up. I think I understand his clumsiness now. It all fits with his story. I think he is attracted to me, at least I hope so anyway and I love the way he take care of you. It shows what a dear man he is."

"Kelly I know he is a dear and you see that because of your kind heart." The women held hands for a moment and Elizabeth got up with Kelly's help and proceeded to the tub.

"I told Mark I would sit up here with you; I'll just be in your room by the fire place with a book." Kelly took a book from the shelf in the hallway to read but instead, she sat and watched the fireplace. She thought it funny being there when she had only planned to go out for a morning jog. She sighed and smiles gently and she wondered what more surprises the day would bring for her on that November weekend. She was certainly soothed and the aroma from the kitchen was making its way up the stairs and into the room. She thought of Marks well groomed looks and his gentleness toward his mother and his attraction to her. She was quickened to his agony of the recent situations and she bowed her head in prayer for these two people and a change in their situation as well as success in rebuilding their lives.

Wonderful warmth filled her soul when she finished her prayer and she knew it to be a confirmation that her prayer had been heard and answered. Kelly sat back in the chair and listened to the sounds from the kitchen and waited patiently for Elizabeth to finish her bath. She opened the book and began to read until she was needed. Forty five minutes had passed and Elizabeth walked into her room wearing a bath robe and sat in the other chair beside Kelly. "How do you feel?"

"I'm rested enough to go down stairs but I am going to stay here for a while in my robe."

"Well sure, it's a very comfortable room. The house is fairly new is it?"

"Yes Kelly, we are the first owners. It's the new house I never had. The house in the west was built in the sixties and Gordon, my husband bought it after we got married. Ten years later he started the farm equipment business. Mark was five years old at the time; we were only blessed with one child."

"Elizabeth, you are shaking again, you don't have to speak of these thing if it upsets you."

"It dose upset me to talk but I'm getting well. It helps; I mean it was probably a good thing to move so far away."

"Do you have friends and family there that you can keep in touch with?"

"There are many people but I have been very ill and haven't been in contact with anyone. I'm only just beginning to be able to taste my food again."

"Elizabeth I'm so sorry."

"I mostly miss my friends, the sisters from church." Elizabeth began to cry and Kelly offered her a tissue.

"It's strange; I can remember their faces but can't even remember their names yet. I think there are picture of them that we brought but they're packed away."

"Oh I have noticed there are no pictures hanging anywhere."

"I have been in the rest home for six months and Mark bought this house a month later and was not able to move in until July. He had to stay at a motel until then. Mark inherited everything and I received insurance money which enabled us to begin life here in the east. Mark has plans to open a hardware store—"

"Yes I know; it is beside the bakery where I work. That's where we met. Have you seen the store yet?"

"No I haven't ventured there yet"

"Oh yes that's right, I'm sorry I forgot today was your first outing"

"So tell me, you have only known each other a few days?"

"Yes that's right, we met on Wednesday and then this morning on our jogging path. He ran right by me not into me." The two women chuckled. "I imagine he was very deep in thought. I thought at first impression that he was a bit aloof but I know differently now."

"Thank you. Mark is my life and my strength and all I exist for now. I want to be well again so I can be helpful to him instead of this hindrance." Kelly interrupted

"I know that you have been devastated by your loss. I wouldn't think that you are a hindrance to him."

Kelly hugged her.

"Well I am wishing to be well again, I still get exhausted from this depression,"

"Hey let's look through the collection of fabric that you have. I can help you coordinate."

"Well yes, let's do that. I love looking through my fabric. I think we got rid of or left most of my clothing home since I am in mourning and have lost a lot of weight anyway. I have been wearing simple cloths or not even getting dressed at all."

"Yes well let's see what we have here; there is a lot of flowered chambray, you are getting brave aren't you?"

"Yes, it's great for blouses and I like it with corduroy; I have burgundy, khaki and aqua."

"This chemise could be nice over something silk—"

"Oh ladies, did you want to come to dinner now or are you busy"

"Busy as can be Mark, I haven't had this much fun talking with some in a long time as I have had with Kelly today. I can't believe you haven't known each other all your lives."

"She's nice isn't she mom? Come Kelly you are welcome any time; do you like soup?"

"Sure Mark."

"I love making homemade soup."

"I can't wait to taste it Mark." Mark escorted the two ladies to the table, served them and then his self, then offered a gracious prayer of thanks for the food the company and their abundant blessings. The three of them enjoyed a soup and salad dinner with garlic bread, cheese and crackers. Mark and Kelly talked about how he made this scrumptious soup and even divulged some of his secret recipes. She offered to take some fabric and some of Elizabeth's patterns home with her along with measurements to create some wonderful Christmas fashions for Elizabeth. She also offered to show Elizabeth some of her beaded jewelry even though she does not wear dangly ornate jewelry, Kelly is very talented. She was raised in a caring Latter Day Saint family. She and her five other adopted sisters. Now there was a wonderful coincidence, Mark and Elizabeth were also Latter Day Saints. They never chanced to meet there because Mark was very busy with his mother and only started attending church about a month ago and would only stay for the first hour. Kelly was so pleasantly surprised with this; she couldn't stop talking about it. She had kept Mark and Elizabeth's attention so inattentively; Elizabeth forgot that she had to lie down. Kelly helped her into the living room to sit in her chair and Mark cleared the table to do the dishes. Once she had Elizabeth comfortable she joined Mark in the kitchen. By this time Mark and Kelly were very comfortable with each other, they did the dishes together and Mark put his arm around her shoulder and suggested that they go to church together tomorrow.

"Kelly I'm warmed by your concern for my mother and appreciate your attentiveness to her. I had been dating a girl back home but when my father and uncle were killed and my mother fell apart, she actually turned and ran. She didn't even turn up for the funeral. I guess she thought that life would be far from rosy if she stuck with me. You show up one day, smile at me and you become a breath of fresh air and turn around my dark winter night." Kelly is already very attracted to Mark in every way and is feeling a strong connection, then he puts his heart out on his sleeve like that and she melts.

"Come to church with us tomorrow, please say you will."

"I'll be ready Mark; will you be picking me up?"

"I surely will. Mom only stays for an hour. I'll take her back to the rest home, see that she's comfortable then come back and spend the rest of the time with you there. We will go back to the rest home and spend lunch time with her. Will you join us?"

"Yes I will."

"I would like to spend the rest of the afternoon and evening with you if you are free?

"Mark there no other way I would like to spend the day tomorrow. I like your mother and if there is any way I can just simply make her smile, I have done well in Gods eyes and if you favor me to, I'll spend the day with you."

"I appreciate you Kelly, you are so lovely, your parents must be proud of you."

"My parents taught all six of us girls that to be charitable is the most Christ like attribute; it's what we are here for, to serve one another we serve Him. Growing up, six girls in the family, we learned to share, show kindness and to solve problems and that was a big accomplishment for all of us, even for our parents. Both our parents lead the household but as individuals, we learned to function as a family should; to put charity first, family and God before ourselves. I feel so terrible for the tragedy that has befallen your family. The heart break you and your mother have been through must be unbearable yet you stand and carry on for the two of you."

The tears shot out of Marks eyes for about the first time since the accident. Having looked into Kelly's soft eyes as her words of love and sympathy caused Marks heart to finally morn; to feel the pain of his loss finally after eight months of carrying the weight of the world on his shoulders, he could cry. It was Kelly who helped to pull him out of his misery caused by the tragic loss. In an attempt to grasp hold of his strength again he failed. Mark reached out for Kelly for support and his sobs reached the pinnacle of his mourning. As she held Mark for what seem to be an eternity, her sweetness of spirit calmed his emotions and for what seemed to be an instant in time, his cry's healed his heart. They sat then quietly holding hands, Mark wiping away his tears thanks Kelly. "Thank you, thank you Kelly. No one has ever made me feel so cared for. Your tenderness; you are an angel you know."

Kelly was relieved for Mark. "Have you not cried once for your father since his death?"

"No Kelly, I know it's odd, but I have not been able to cry until now." He gasped for breath and tried to stable his emotions.

"Oh Mark you must have been in shock all this time over what had happened and being the only child to have to deal with all matters. I think you have been holding your breath and have finally had the opportunity to let it out."

"Kelly you are probably right. I don't know yet if I feel better or if I am going to be able to get up out of this chair." Mark was shaking and felt rather stone cold.

"Just breathe easily." She rubbed his arm and shoulder.

"Maybe you should sit back." He did and put his hands over his face to breathe deeply a few times. Then he looked up at the ceiling and Kelly stroked the side of his hair. He began to relax and could more calmly tell her about the past eight months.

"A shipment of equipment came and dad and my uncle Geoff had not released the guard on the safety clasp which held the machinery on the skid. The weight of the machinery shifted too quickly. The trailer tipped over and pinned dad and Uncle Geoff. I did not see the accident but I heard the crash. I found them and there was nothing I could do but wait for the rescue crew to come. They didn't have a chance."

"You're Mother; where was she?"

"By the time I located her at the church, she and the sisters were setting up for a service project or something like that. She had already heard about the accident and collapsed. Her heart was broken and became so frail; I thought she would die too."

"It sounds like she went into trauma induced amnesia or denial."

"It was a lot of both those. She couldn't go to the funeral and didn't really get out of bed for two months. I tied up loose ends and quickly as possible, sold the business and house. I was executor in my mother's absence. I took care of the funeral myself and moved here right after all legal matters were dealt with. Fortunately my father made provisions for us and we were well taken care of.

"Heaven knows the rest home must be quite an expense for you. It's all well that your father saw to looking after emergencies in his family, she may be there for quite some time. With Christmas coming, she may have a setback."

"She doesn't concentrate on the holidays at this time, but you are right. We believe; I mean her doctor and me that the best thing for her was moving away and starting fresh. To prevent draining the inheritance and insurance money, I am opening the hardware store. That will be a whole lot easier then running a farm equipment business and I'll have more time to look after mom. I have to do the best with all that I have had to deal with."

"Sure you do Mark, that's all anyone can ask of you. My goodness from what I have seen you have done well for yourself and your mother. You are strong willed and you are good. I pray that you will be all right." Kelly's sympathy had turned to admiration for Mark because of his strength in character and she knows his sorrow will not weigh him down.

Chapter Four

It was a week before Christmas and by this time Mark and Kelly had become very close. Elizabeth's day is brightened whenever Kelly finds time for a visit. One would never know where Kelly found time to sew for Elizabeth; she completed two jacket, skirts and blouses accessorized with handmade beadwork It's any wonder that Elizabeth is feeling better with every passing visit. If Kelly isn't at school or working she is with Mark and Elizabeth. The store renovations are almost complete and the plan to have shelves stocked and employees hired are on schedule for the middle of February. It's Friday afternoon about four thirty and Mark is waiting at the train station for Kelly to come home from Toronto. She was at a three day nursing seminar. Kelly exited the train and she wore her hair down and it had an unfamiliar curl in it. From where he was standing she was radiant. He didn't know yet that she had not slept well and she was very over worked; studied like she had never studies before. "Kelly we missed you around here. Are you able to spend some time with mom and me tomorrow?"

"I can for breakfast. I have a report to complete and an assignment to hand in before Christmas."

"Will you have to take time off work?"

"I guess so; grandma and grandpa can do without me for a few days I suppose. They pay me anyway, that's a benefit of being related to the boss. Oh am I ever tired and sore, I could sleep for a week."

"Ok then let's go out for a good meal and you are going for a spa treatment."

"Spa treatment?" I'll take a rein cheque please, I'm way to busy but I'll hold you to the dinner invite."

"Well then you will need to go home after we eat will you?"

"Yes."

"Well ok I'll drop in on you now and then over the next few days just to say hello and give you a break from your computer."

"You would be most welcome. I think I would really like some soup and a salad, maybe some frozen yogurt afterwards."

"I'm going to miss you, I had plans for us this week; you know Christmas activities."

"I'll be going to church with you and your mother on Sunday. Then I'm going to leave my computer alone."

"I would like to try this Italian restaurant; you should be able to get what you like here."

"There may be a long line in there."

"Well Miss Kelly, you are in quite a hurry to get home, I feel brushed off." Kelly yawned and didn't realize that he was kidding and she was embarrassed for her lack of concentration and apologized for it.

"You are tired aren't you? Tell you what, if it's busy in there I'll take you home but I really would just like to relax with you for a while."

"Then it's settled, we will relax together for a while."

"Tell me; why is your hair so curly today?"

I was up until four Am., couldn't sleep. I get that way when I over study. I drank some warm milk and had a shower and went to bed with wet hair. I was still so tired when I got up I didn't do anything but brush it."

"I think it looks real pretty."

"Do you like this? I will curl it for church and make it look neater though."

"Kelly you are a beautiful girl. The softness in your eyes calms me and your smile gives me thrills."

"How do you like the blush in my cheeks? It's natural right now." They held hands and entered the restaurant. They were immediately seated and decided to stay. They were seated at a quiet dimly lit booth. It was just the relaxation Kelly needed after her three day seminar. Mark started singing to her to show his appreciation for her company which she was enchanted with. It was a strange but very sweet thing for him to do in a restaurant. It was a quiet afternoon and he wanted to keep her attention. She was terribly distracted with the work she knew she had ahead of her and he knew this. He sang to her about the activities he would rather be doing with her then being away from her on this festive time of year. She fondly amused him and hummed along while swaying her head too.

"Kelly, how about going out later tonight for a walk just to look at the Christmas light displays around the neighborhood?"

"I can do that, I hope there is a light snowfall. Bring a camera ok."

"Ok will do. A nice walk will help you to sleep well tonight then you come over tomorrow for a nice breakfast to start your day of right."

"I will have you over to my apartment after I have finished my assignment and will cook a beautiful Chinese dinner for the two of us."

"Is your kitchen big enough, I remember you said that the apartment is very small."

"My kitchen is just the right size for two, all I need is a wok and I even have a kimono that I will wear for you. I love to cook Chinese."

"Beautiful! Will you wear your hair up with chop sticks? I am picturing you now and I am finding that irresistibly enchanting."

"I have one pair of wooden chop sticks so I will pick up some porcelain chop sticks somewhere."

"Kelly before I take you home will you go for a walk with me through the mall to look for chops sticks? I would love to see your hair put up with them."

"I have seen them in abalone or mother of pearl inlays; very intricate details and very expensive. I'm sure that we could find some cute plastic ones. Afterwards I really have to go home and get my work started."

"That's fine but I will only buy the ones that are suitable for your beautiful black hair."

Mark and Kelly had not been apart for as long as three day since they met and couldn't be without constant contact. They knew that this was more than a friendship. Love had blossomed in her absence. They both lead very busy lives but depended on daily interaction with each other for their individual happiness. They didn't find chop sticks for Kelly's hair but she didn't have much time and was getting particularly frantic about getting home. They would not see much of each other now until Sunday. It had been a part of Elizabeth's healing process to be able to attend church every Sunday with Mark and Kelly. More and more Elizabeth is able to smile; she sees her son's and her life in a better perspective now. She is away from the tragedy and the memories that would have lingered had they stayed in the west. She has a wonderful and hardworking son who was able to understand what was best for his mother. Elizabeth had made a friend in the wonderful sweet Kelly. If all she had in life was to be with Mark and Kelly, she would never be unhappy for the rest of her life. The Christmas program was scheduled for this Sunday service. The chapel was festive and cheerfully decorated with lights, wreathes flowers and Nativity scenes. The lights were dim as the choir sang hymns of Christ's birth. The three sat together as part of a larger than usual congregation and listened to speakers tell stories of the meaning and praises of Christmas. Kelly welcomed the special spirit she felt there that particular morning in church. She was free from the rigor of work or school. She smiled as she was with Mark, and gloried in the sweet hymns and the fellowship of well-wishers and the children's anticipation of the holiday. Elizabeth stayed for the entire service; she didn't want to leave nor was she tired. Mark was just like a child, he was thrilled to have Kelly's attention for the whole day and for his mother's willingness to stay in church for the whole morning. All headaches pertaining to his responsibilities disappeared for this Sabbath day and were replaced with the glory of the season. The warmth of family bond included his dear Kelly. Although the three had not wanted nor were planning a big commercial Christmas with all the glitter and noise, they did cherish this special morning together. They renewed their praise in the purpose for the season and held onto the tightening bond of strength, love and charity within a family circle in what could have been a very sad occasion.

The short ride home was peaceful but ok. They arrived back at Mark and Elizabeth's house and Mark helped his mother out of the car and into the den to her chair. She was happy to sit in the den by the fireplace while Mark and Kelly prepared some lunch. Mark didn't bother with any Christmas decorations or tree this year. They were just thankful for Kelly; she was their angel and the season was bearable now. Kelly was familiar with the kitchen now and as she scurried around, Mark surprised her with a green velvet pull string bag. "Mark, Is this something that I think it is? The chop sticks we couldn't find?"

"You are right. I didn't have anything to do yesterday since you were busy with your computer so I went shopping. I had to Google a location that sold them and drove thirty six km. to the nearest merchant for these and I think they are perfect. They will match with the divine feminism of your hair with its black silkiness."

"I don't believe this; the dark green sticks and mother of pearl inlay will match my kimono. How could you know this?"

"Kelly I just saw these in your hair, I didn't even look for a different pair. This is a serendipity situation."

"I have never put these in my hair, I'll have to practice."

"It can't be hard, let me try to do something with them." Mark stood behind her, pulled all her back and stroked it with his fingers and rolled it around his fist to pull it tight. He fastened the hair around the sticks from opposite side of the bun. A few locks of her hair fell out and to the side along his arm which pleasured him and the fragrance in her hair prompted him to go closer and he guided her to a mirror for her approval. She thought a couple pins may keep the sides from falling out of the bun but it was his wishes to have the hair fall just the way it did, his heart fluttered.

"I love playing with your hair but whether you wear it up or down it is entirely lovely. Let's plan on New Year's Eve for our Chinese dinner can we?"

"New Year's Eve, just the two of us, that is doable."

"Later I want the two of us in front of my fireplace so we can talk about us."

"We don't get too much time to spend alone do we?"

"Kelly I think you must know how I feel about you. I believe you feel the same for me by the way you look into my eyes. Every time our eyes meet, no matter the circumstance, the softness in your eyes is something I can't ignore."

Kelly was so taken in surprise by the emotion behind his words. She had wanted to feel this special closeness with him. "I'm happy Mark that you see the emotion in my eyes, they reflect these peaceful feelings within my heart. I can barely think of anything else." Kelly took Marks hands and held them to her face. A tear ran down both their faces and they whispered sincerely, I love you. They had not been this close before. The two brought their cheeks together and the delicate tears on their faces blended together and neither of them knew quite what to say or do next. With more tenderness than he thought possible he kissed her face and she closed her eyes. Love encircled them and Kelly knew that Mark was the eternal love of her life at that moment. In the background the timer for the microwave oven went off and the familiar aroma of hot buttery popcorn filled the kitchen. The chicken strips were braising in the oven that would top the Caesar salad. Mark forgot about the aromas in the kitchen; his focus was on the fragrance of Kelly's hair and he held her closer. "Do you want to put the popcorn in a bowl and I'll rip the lettuce for the salad?"

They reluctantly broke the embrace and moved closer to the counter to finish preparing lunch. The two of them, quite quiet then began doing what they came into the kitchen to do. With the salad made and dressed, garlic bread on the side and a bowl of popcorn, Mark and Kelly made up a tray and joined Elizabeth in the den. "Everything looks and smells nice."

"Glad you like it mom, Kelly why don't you turn on the television and I'll go back into the kitchen and bring in plates and cutlery and soft drinks. Mom we want to talk to you." By the tone of Marks voice and the romantic look in both their eyes, it was no surprise to Elizabeth what the purpose of the talk could be.

"Kelly it is no surprise to me, I couldn't be happier. We both love you"

"You know, when I was away for the seminar I could only text Mark, I couldn't stand it then. Here we are now not wanting to be apart and finding it painful when we have to be. Elizabeth, these feelings are nice but so unfamiliar to me."

"We are in Love Mother." Mark explained and his explanation put to rest any doubt of other reasons for their emotions. With that said Elizabeth rose from her chair, caressed Kelly and gave her approval.

It was a very touching moment for the three of them. They served there selves the lunch, chatted and watched TV for a couple hours. Elizabeth had not felt this good in months; however she knew she should rest before returning to the rest home. It' wouldn't be wise to return week. She may be preached at by the nurses. Mark cleared the lunch away and Kelly helped her to her bedroom.

"Mark I put a shawl around your mothers shoulders, fluffed her pillows, then when I came back from the bathroom with a glass of water she was sleeping like a baby."

"OK, let me check on her." He was worried that she over did it today. Elizabeth was already fast asleep; her color was good and breathing steady. She was fine, just tired.

"Mark she was so happy for us and had such a good time with our company, laughing along with us and reminiscing of your teen years. I enjoyed her. She loves you so much and wants for your happiness above her own. I have wanted it for you too. I cherish the day we met and I know that you are busy with the store and your mom but I will look for every opportunity to spend time with you.

"I didn't know how you would feel about being in a relationship with me. I know now that I have your heart as you have so beautifully and generously offered it to me Mark" Mark sat with Kelly on the love seat and reached to embrace her. They softly stared into each other's eyes as Mark stroked her cheek with his fingers. The soft glow of the flames from the fire place silhouetted their closeness as he kissed her on the forehead and gently whispered "I love you Kelly."

Chapter Five

Monday came and flew by for Mark without a visit from Kelly. Tuesday passed; still not even a text or email message. Kelly had not jogged or showered for that matter. She was barely eating and not sleeping well because she was busily working at the computer on her assignment. She needed to hand it in by four pm. Wednesday and she needed everything to be perfect. An A plus and two weeks holidays for Christmas would be her reward. Kelly worked hard and studied well, she put one hundred and ten percent of effort into her projects. This abundant effort showed in her work. She was one of the top nursing students and won the scholarship to go to Queens University. From time to time her focus would wonder and she thought of Mark and how well they get along in spite of how busy they both are. Kelly would graduate in the spring and was eager to go to work right away and she wondered if her new relationship would stand the test of time. She decided that worrying about it would only cause anxiety so with that conclusion she carried on with her work. She wore the chop sticks in her hair instead of a hair band to remind herself of a wonderful man that's waiting for her to finish up. It was just after nine pm when the phone rang; it was Mark calling, she almost let the phone ring for too long and picked up just before Mark hung up. "Sweet Kelly, are you ok?"

"Mark! I've lost track of time and I'm starving. Will you come over and feed me?" She ended that question with a sigh and a giggle.

"Kelly I was worried about that; give me ten minutes and I'll run over with some Chinese food."

"Thank you that sounds so terrific. My eyes are strained now that I am not looking at my work. Maybe we should slip out for a walk afterwards so I can get a breath of fresh air. I haven't been out in two days."

"Whatever you want, just take it easy, I'll be right over." They hung up their phones and Kelly decided that she had better have a quick shower and change her cloths. Mark called ahead to the Chinese restaurant to have it delivered and he hurried over and brought a comedy movie with him in case she decided that she was too tired to go out walking. Kelly was blow drying her hair when Mark arrived and she was fully dressed so was able to let him in. She didn't have to worry about tidying up because she was always neat and organized that way. Mark had only been in Kelly's apartment one other time to look at some picture of her family on the pc. He expected to find a cyclone of books and papers all over the place but not a chance. He was pleasantly surprised and glad that he had fallen in love with such a great lady. She stopped drying her hair to greet him and was presented with a multicolored poinsettia. He hid behind it at the door and she slid around playfully and kissed his cheek.

"You are very welcome my darling lady. I see your chopsticks sitting on the desk, have you been wearing them?"

"I had to practice putting them in my hair but with a bobby pin or two I can make them work. Let me finish drying my hair and I'll put them in for you."

"Sure go ahead: Mark put the flowers on the table and turned on the radio to listen to the top forty tunes. The dinner came to the door within minutes and Mark set in on the table and had everything nicely set for Kelly when she returned into the room and wearing her beautiful Kimono and her hair done up with the sticks. She also put on a little make up which she didn't need because she had natural color in her skin. She was beautiful and Mark turned his head slowly to see her and he smiled and gasped.

"For goodness sake." He was lost in this picture. "Please just stand there for a moment so I can take a picture of you with my phone. It's going on my wallpaper."

He then gently slipped his arm around her tiny waist and graciously escorted her to one of the stools. "Kelly I can see you sitting under an apple tree fully in bloom as to accent how lovey you are tonight. Allow me." He served Kelly and them himself after a most fitting prayer.

"Enjoy your food Kelly, you deserve it. It's not fit for a queen as it should be but if we can't spend a large quantity of time together we can do better with quality of time. Eating this with you makes it a quality dinner."

Kelly marveled at his creativity and said. "It was creativity that brought us together now love will do the rest."

Mark and Kelly were both skilled in using chopsticks and they even used some tiny china cups to drink their ginger ale with. "Everything is perfect for love but we need some Chinese lanterns for the atmosphere. I would turn the lights off and just see you through the glow of the lanterns, mm."

"I know where I can get some lanterns, thanks for the suggestions; I'll buy a few and string them up around the counter. I will have some for you the next time we are here together."

"Could we improvise with some Christmas lights? Do you have some Kelly?"

"Be right back, I have two strings of them in the closet by the bathroom in a white box. There are some thumb tacks in the end table drawer, will you get them? This is going to be neat Mark." They finished hanging the lights around the top of counter where they sat to eat and their soft glow with the lights off was a romantic improvise to their purpose.

"Kelly now this is really perfect. The colorful glow from the light is enhancing the shimmering silk of your kimono and the kimono is enhancing your beauty and the radiance in your eyes tonight. There is an orchestra playing in my heart and your beauty is the conductor."

"Mark, my word, Chinese food has never been more enjoyable."

"The flutist is playing the melody which is your name and the percussion instrument is playing the harmony and is blending perfectly in my dreams; whether corny sounding or not, it's a dream I can't wake up from." Kelly is melting with every word he speaks and she sighs unable to continue eating. She embraces Mark and they stand and begin dancing to the orchestra in their hearts. Tenderly he runs his fingers down the back of her silken kimono. It was comfortable on her skin as well as his touch. After a moment of silence Mark held the side of her face in his hands and led her to the deepness in his eyes where she saw eternal love and comfort. Mark gains a testimony of eternal blessings for him and Kelly but he couldn't bring himself to rush her because of her chaotic schedule. They just stood there embraced in the soft color of the lights for a few moments then continued eating. "Kelly I would like to take you for a walk, can you take the time?"

"Yes, I need some fresh air; how do I dress? I haven't been outside all day. I'll change quickly."

"It's cool but there is no wind and I thought it looked like it could snow if it isn't already." Kelly wore some black jeans, grey and mauve turtle neck sweater with matching hat and mitts. She put on walking boots and a mid-length coat since it was about ten thirty pm. and snowing lightly. They seemed to have the streets all to their selves as they walked through town and Mark asked her. "What have you planned for Christmas?"

"I have the same plans as every year, home in Stirling on Christmas eve for two weeks. I don't know if I should break my plans—it probably wouldn't go over very well."

"OH don't you dare break them; your family would never let me near you again if you did. I haven't made any plans at all for Mom; I'm lost with knowing how to handle it."

"Mark, I want both of you to come with me home for Christmas. Please say you will."

"I don't know what to say but I'll talk to mom about it. I know that she loves you so much and you are playing such a big part in her recovery."

"Mark what would you like to do?"

"I know that I don't want to be away from you for that long and I can't leave mom alone as grim as the holiday will be for her I couldn't do it." Mark became very quiet and stumbled over everything he tried to say from then on and tears filled his eyes. The season had left him with confusion and would really rather do without this happy season completely. He certainly wasn't feeling festive due to his loss but just the same, he didn't want to turn Kelly's happiness to the same level of confusion. He turned pale and was very choked up; felt like he had run into a brick wall. "Kelly let's sit in here for a while." They had just arrived at a down town diner.

"That sounds like a warm idea; we can sit and drink hot chocolate and chat." Mark was so upset at that point but he knew he had to deal with his feelings eventually. She was looking so forward to Christmas with her family and she had worked so hard all year. She deserved her holiday but she meant so much to Mark and Elizabeth.

"Would you like to sit at this table Mark?"

"It's fine. I hope you weren't too cold during our walk."

"It's all good. It's a perfect thing to do on a winter night; sitting in a little diner drinking hot cocoa and chatting with a close friend. Mark I don't want to be without you for Christmas but I can see you are having trouble with your feelings. I'll help you through these troubled times if you will allow me to."

"Dear Kelly you have done so much for me." Mark couldn't contain his pain. He paused for a long moment to regain his composure. "I wish my father could have known you. Known your pleasantness and your kindness you show to my mother. He loved her so much and I don't know why she hasn't died of a broken heart. He must be by her side still."

Kelly held his hand as he talked and cried. She could hardly bare his anguish. She only knew that she had to offer her hand and her heart to him in his time of sorrow. It was very important that she had his trust and she was compassionate.

"The bond of marriage is stronger than anyone knows. I am positive that your father is with her and that the angels are looking out for and protecting both your parents." With that said the tears shot out of his eyes and every comment that Kelly made of his sorrow was a victory for the Holy Spirit in that she was prompted to say the things that he needed to hear. The healing process had begun and Mark truly believed that God put Kelly in his path the afternoon in front of his store. Mark quietly praised God for this tender mercy. He knew that he had been given Kelly to enrich his and his mother's lives and he would now move forward in pure love. Mark did indeed love Kelly very much and the thought of being away from her whether for a day for her studies or for a Christmas holiday was unacceptable to him. Mark took Kelly's hands in his and told her, "Kelly, we have to make plans. We need to be together, I can't be apart from you."

"What kind of plans?"

"Kelly I love you dearly and I know you love me. Our love will make the perfect commitment and future with each other."

"Thank you Mark, nothing in my life has made me happier." Together they whispered "I love you." They didn't take their eyes off each other while they talked and drank cocoa. In thirty minutes Mark had made plans with Kelly for he and Elizabeth to join the Gerard's for Christmas. By what Kelly told Mark he was fondly looking forward to meeting her family and spend a real home spun Christmas with them. It was about midnight and Mark walked Kelly back home, they were tired and relieved to know that Christmas this year would indeed be a joyous occasion. Mark and his mother would meet Kelly in the morning for church and spend the day together because there was no working on the Sabbath day.

Kelly finally had a wonderful night's sleep and Mark picked her up for church at nine thirty. Kelly called home that morning to tell her parents that she would be bringing company for Christmas. She asked that they set two more places and the dining room table and prepare the guest wing. Mark also made arrangements with his mother and with the rest home for a four day leave. Mark was worried about his mother and that the ninety minute drive and meeting so many people might not be good for her. In reality it could be disastrous for her health being that she was still very mentally frail. In spite of Elizabeth's excitement about meeting Kelly's family, Mark rented a nice quiet motel for them in case of an emergency. The nearest hospital was only a half hour away so that was somewhat of a relief. Kelly's parent's home had a guest wing where Elizabeth could sit quietly and be away from the crowds of company and children. Kelly was the second in a family of six adopted girls. Her eldest sister Monique, who was twenty five, is a teacher and married with two small children. Monique taught kindergarten and her husband Brian was a police officer. Her next sister is Sharon who is nineteen and is in her second year of college where she is studying to be an addiction counselor and also volunteers at the John Howard Society and teaches Sunday school. Her three younger sisters have special needs. Although there is no sign of learning disability, her sixteen year old sister Carol, has juvenile diabetes which tends to pose as a restriction to doing what other sixteen year old girls participate in. She tends to get depressed but luckily has not drifted wayward because of that. The two youngest girls are identical twins, eleven years old with Downs Syndrome; Cindy and Sheila. Kelly's dad was in the Canadian Armed Forces so her mom was often alone to tend to the family's needs. Kelly's mother was a

Director of a Local Mental Health Department and did have her mother and her Aunt Barbara live with them to assist in providing a structured and nurturing home environment for the girls to grow up in. Kelly and her sisters were raised on 109 acres of rural property in a large century home with adjoining buildings that were added on through the years as need arose. The property was never used for farming but the girls all were involved in 4H clubs and raised small animals and had their own gardens. There they raised vegetables flowers and berries. There were many people involved in getting the six girls raised normally and pretty much without incident growing up. They were raised in the gospel and in girls clubs from ages five years and onward. Being raised with religious and military standards by parents with an eternal purpose in mind, the family thrives. The girls were always honored for their individuality; in fact one would imagine a household of strife, selfishness and disorganization. It was never the case. Where there was respect, love and encouragement for each girl to succeed in their own interests, there was learning, charity, love and above all, happiness. Although the parents both worked throughout the girl's childhood, it was work that kept the family on the path of togetherness and strengthened their commitment to one and other. It is no surprise that Kelly is the wonderful sweet lady she is. Anybody that would hire her would get a strong employee. She works for good grades and anyone who has her for a friend would never give her up. Certainly Elizabeth's health has greatly improved and Mark is attempting to deal with his feelings now that Kelly is very close to them. Kelly told them all about Christmas at home and they didn't dare miss any of it. Kelly has meant so much to them so far that they could not let her down or refuse her invitation.

“Here is some herbal tea and sandwiches’ I’ve made for you both. Mark maybe Elizabeth would like to wear her shawl and sit by the fireplace. I’ll set the side table up and we can join her.”

“Everything looks so nice when you make it Kelly thank you. Orange wedges and grapes make a garnish for the tray. Did you have a chance to call your parents?”

“Yes I called them before leaving for church this morning. They will prepare the guest wing; it will be quiet there and she will need the peace. The house will be full of people but she will love my aunt. My aunt Barb will tend to her and keep her comfortable. Elizabeth will love her.”

“Is she from your mother’s or father’s side of the family?”

“Barbara is my mother’s sister; never married or anything and my grandmother lives there too. She is my mother’s mom and lives in one of the adjoining houses. My Aunt likes to wait on people and she’ll be great to both of you. I don’t think you have any worries.”

“I believe you.”

“Barbara loves to talk and has a very easy and relaxing effect on people.” They all laughed.

“The whole world should have more people like your and Aunt Barbara, dear.”

"Oh yeah isn't that the truth, Aunt Barbara loves to talk and she is someone who you love to listen to. Personally I could listen to her talk for hours."

"I will remember to drink my herbal tea quickly in case I start listening to her so it doesn't get cold on me." They all chuckled again.

"Now there is my oldest sister Monique, she plays the piano while her husband Brian plays the guitar and sings Christmas hymns that they actually compose."

"I'll bring my guitar and play with them. This sounds great doesn't it Mom? Kelly I couldn't think of a nicer way to spend Christmas." They both looked lovingly at Kelly.

"Elizabeth I can help you get some things packed today after you take a nap. I have my papers to turn in on Wednesday morning and then I'm free for the holidays."

"I can't wait either Kelly. I have workers in the store until Wednesday and then I'm also free until at least Tuesday."

"Mark the two of you need some time alone. Thank you for lunch Kelly, I'm going to lie down." She hugged them both and told them not to get up that she could go upstairs herself.

"She is right Kelly; I missed you badly when you were in Toronto. If I had not been busy with the store I would have been with you." She laughed and assured him that they wouldn't be spending much time apart at her parent's house.

"You won't believe how much my mother decorates on Christmas Eve. She brings fresh evergreen and holy in the house and decorates it with lights and balls and little things we all of made throughout the years. It is a masterpiece; we all help and it stays up until after the New Years. The boughs are brought in fresh and by that time there is only a bit of cleanup. She loves to do this and has for years. People come over for New Years and talk about the decorations for months. Oh yes, my little sisters make gingerbread scenes and that is used for the table center piece." Mark commented on how pleased the little ones must be to be able to contribute like that.

"I am going to love every minute of this Christmas and spending the weekend there. Thank you so very much for this. We are blessed with such graciousness. It's very heartwarming."

"You are very welcome; certainly we are a family, well nearly." Mark looked very pleasantly surprised at Kelly due to her comment, he was very pleased. "It's good for the two families to get together to do Christmas isn't it?"

Mark nodded and hugged Kelly. "I am going to check on mom to see if she's comfortable and I think I need to take her some more shampoo and clean towels."

"Right, she said she needed them. I'll take the tray to the kitchen and start cleaning up. I'll meet you in the den to watch a movie." Mark found some clean towels and wash clothes in the hall closet and took them upstairs to his mother's bathroom and was able to scrape up some shampoo. He looked in on her and found her fast asleep. He left her CD. player playing soft gospel music. He returned to Kelly. "I love our Sundays together but do you know we never really go on dates."

"You are right about that, do you have something in mind? I haven't been around the city much; I have been busy with the store and mom."

"I know what that is like; the same thing is going on with me. I've only been here since May, I go to school and to work, I haven't had a social life at all until we met."

"Didn't you see any one in Stirling?"

"No not really. I went on a few group dates with my girlfriends to movies, concerts or house parties but the girls I hang around with don't date either."

"What? Are the guys in Stirling all rats or something?" They laugh uproariously together.

"Be careful we are going to wake Elizabeth. No they are not rats, just busy and most of them are preparing for missions so we prefer to keep high dating standards."

"Oh sure I played that way too. It's best to concentrate on serving a mission and leave dating for later. That's what I did. We'll have a couple days between the time you hand in your work and we leave for your parents' house so I'll think of something and we will have our date."

"Ok, for now let's see what we can find on the church website to watch. Surely there will be some Christmas musicals, I love watching those."

"I'll set up the computer and Kelly; maybe you can get us both a smoothie."

"I'll do that and be right with you, we'll spend the rest of the afternoon getting into the Christmas spirit and relaxing because tomorrow it's back to being overly busy." Kelly complained.

Chapter Six

Wednesday afternoon happened to find Kelly exhausted, she missed Mark and had not got her Christmas shopping done and they were leaving to go to her parents' house tomorrow morning. Her mind was so over worked from studying and working at the computer that she almost walked out into the street in front of a car. She would have been hit if a couple girls had not pulled her back. Their screams woke Kelly up and she was quite shaken by what had almost happened. The three young women stood at the curb for a moment talking to ensure that Kelly was in her right state of mind and was not attempting suicide. They offered to take a bus with her and even offered to pay her fare but she assured the girls that she would be more careful now and thanked them very much. Kelly thought of having Mark pick her but changed her mind in case it would worry him; he wouldn't let her out of his sight if he knew what had just happened. She decided to stop at a café to get a bite to eat and rest. She had forgot to eat breakfast being so busy and all and thought she might feel better and went to sit down for twenty minutes and eat. There was a little sandwich bar in the café and she headed right for it since she realized she had not ate since six pm. last night. She ordered a nice chicken rap and fruit cup. A nice glass of orange juice would pump up her blood sugar. She bought an herbal tea to drink on the way to the university. She entered the campus and it was relatively quiet being the end of the semester. She gladly and with no hesitation handed in her assignment confident that it was perfect. She received her coarse outline and supply list three weeks earlier so she picked up her books and went to town to buy the supplies that she needed. On the way out of school she met one of her fellow students, Patricia Lawrence and stopped to chat with her. Patricia looked quite ill and pale. Kelly thought it was possible that she had the flu. As she talked on with Patricia, she learned that a recent event found Patricia devastated and unable to hand in a finished assignment. Her whole years' work would be void. Patricia lets go to the campus diner and I'll get you something to eat and don't give me excuses of why you shouldn't."

"All right, ok Kelly, I am hungry" Patricia agreed. They didn't have far to walk to the diner and Kelly was horrified at what Patricia had to tell her of the past few days. Patricia usually wore make and had her short blond hair styled nicely. She was wearing modest cloths provided by St. Vincent DePaul. They sat at a booth and ordered some chili and garlic bread; Patricia took time to explain. "You will never be able to rap your head around what I'm going to tell you."

"Go on" Kelly urged.

"Do you know my dorm mates Linda Lee and Bonny Schuster?"

"I'm not sure; I think I know Linda Lee, she is teaching."

"Yeah, she's a Korean girl. Well those two have been busy making money using telephone scams. Somehow they scammed some little elderly lady into believing that they were family members and needed her to wire them money to get them out of some sort of trouble."

"No way! Linda is stable at least I always thought she was."

"Well it's all an act apparently. I came home feeling sick and the police came into the dorm room and busted them and arrested me too since I was there."

"Oh come on Patricia they can't arrest you because you were in the room with them."

"As sure as I am sitting I was arrested. I just got out of jail this morning." Patricia cried and rubbed her eyes under the stress and ran her hands through her uncombed hair.

"Patricia I'm sorry, try to calm down; its ok. When did this happen?"

"It happened on Sunday. An investigation of the camera footage at Western Union showed Bonny and Linda picking up twenty one hundred dollars last Friday morning. That evidence is all that saves me and they did testify that I was not involved. Unfortunately the justice system says I have to go to court to trial to sort this out unless my lawyer can get me exonerated."

"Sweetheart you are shaking like a leaf, please try to calm down and change the subject. Try to eat some more it will make you feel better."

"Ok" Patricia cradled her face in her hands and tried to breathe deeply and quit crying so she could continue talking. She ate some more chili and continued shaking but smiled at Kelly and claimed that it was better chili then she could ever make herself.

"It is good isn't it? I've never ate the chili here before."

Patricia was very appreciative for seeing a friendly face; the first is four days. It made the chili that much more enjoyable too. She dipped the garlic bread into the bowl and sopped up the remaining bit of chili that was left. The girls just sat quietly for a moment and let the warmth of the chili please their souls.

"Ok so I was in court this morning for the bail hearing and my name finally came up; I was released on my own recognizance on a thousand dollars unpaid unless I break the law. On the day of my arrest I was told that I would be released because I have no criminal record. No such luck. There was no authority to release me so I had to wait until this morning for a bail hearing."

"So were you held in a holding cell or—?"

"Oh no, I was put right into the detention center on the range as they call it. I had never been so petrified but thankfully the inmates had just been brought in from drug raids and were not really aggressive, just a little crazy is all."

"I'm so horrified for you; were Linda and Bonny there with you?"

"That was one of the hardest parts of being in jail, trying not to argue with the likes of those two. I wouldn't speak to them and they pretty much stuck to themselves and away from me. I can't get to my dorm room because it is now a crime scene. The police have taken my laptop along with everything else, cell phone and alike. Luckily for me I left my nap sack in a locker here and I had back up CDs in it of my assignment. I have to get it printed out but I have no money or I could do it in the library. I have no supplies, everything is in my room. I have to have it handed in by five pm."

"It's four pm" Kelly alerted her.

"Oh no, my whole year is void then, are you sure?"

"Great, by the way you are smarter than me I only finished mine this morning. I have an idea. Let's hurry over to the library and I'll call my boyfriend to bring some money over so you can get your folder together and handed in. We have an hour."

"I don't know how to thank you Kelly" Patricia shook as she cried.

"Come on no time for crying." Kelly encouraged her with kindness.

"I feel so awful. I was taken in and they wouldn't even let me get a coat. Someone grabbed some boots that weren't even mine and carted us off. The boots didn't fit and I had to walk around everywhere they took me in sock feet. When I left the court, some people were waiting for me from the good will with some winter clothes for me. That's why I'm wearing a linty woolen coat and plastic boots." Patricia washed her face and

Kelly lent her a comb and got her a tooth brush then called Mark.

"Mark is on his way, he'll meet us at the library as soon as he can. In the mean time you can get your pages printed and handed in. I'll wait for him while you are gone to pay for them. When will you be able to get back to your apartment?"

"I don't think I will be able to, not really sure. It's the end of the month, I have no money left and my parents are in England. They don't know yet what's happened."

"Mark and I will look after you and you will come to my parents with us in the morning. I insist. You've worked too hard to be pushed around like you have been these last few days and you need help now. We are going Christmas shopping later and we'll get you some cloths."

"I don't even Know Mark."

"Ok you don't need to know him; he's my boyfriend and he is a wonderful man. He will be devastated when I tell him what happened to you. Now we are going to help you. It will be fine you will get your work handed in and you will have a relaxing Christmas with us and a promising New Year." Kelly and Patricia arrived at the library and there were available computers. Most students had already left for their holidays which enabled them to get the work printed. "I guess you know what you are doing now, excuse me while I call my mom to tell her to expect another guest. I'll be at one of the cubicles when you need me."

"Sure I'll be busy here for a few minutes; you do what you need to do." Kelly called Mark to tell him where she was sitting and he assured her that he would be there in a couple minutes. She phoned her mom afterwards to tell her what had happened to her fellow student, the shocking and traumatic situation that nearly cost Patricia a whole year of hard work for her nursing degree. Kelly's mom said that she was to host one of the best Christmas's ever. There would be the whole family as well as others that they were reaching out to in charity. To Mary it made the season truly meaningful. Kelly's parents would need to set up an additional table but there was ample room for it in their spacious dining room. Kelly had not finished talking to her mom when Mark arrived. Patricia had just finished at the computer and so Mark introduced his self to her while Kelly continued to speak to her mother. He paid for the printouts and told Patricia that they would wait for her to return to the library. Kelly wanted her mom to say hello to Mark and she handed him the phone. They got acquainted over the phone and Mark concluded that she and Kelly were nothing alike. Although Mary was very nice to talk to, she was blunt a bit loud and excitable; in a very nice way. Kelly is not shy by any means; she is a combination of sweetness, intelligence and confidence. Kelly's mom rather surprised him, actually blew him off his seat with her humorous, controlling type of personality. "By the way your mother sounded on the phone, she has a lot going on there. I'm a little worried about mom; she isn't use to a lot of excitement."

"Don't worry, I know mom is very excitable but believe me, she and dad know her condition very well and that's why they have a nice guest room all ready for you and your mom. It's a very large home and it will be peaceful in the guest wing. My aunt Barbara will be a great help to your mom. Barbara will eat there with her if she needs to."

"Ok Kelly, I trust you and I suppose she will be fine. The fact that your mother is a director of a mental health clinic; she would surely know how to care for someone with mom's condition."

"My dad is also abrupt but he cares very much for you both and the tragedy in your lives and my relationship with you and Elizabeth. Be rest assured Mark, you will both feel welcome and comfortable."

"Will there be any chance of the two of us spending some time alone, I mean with such a crowd?"

"At some point I'm sure we will have some alone time, it will be a busy house I realize busier then you are used to but don't worry about anything, we're going to have some good times and dad will make a point of talking to you and getting to know you and Elizabeth."

"Do your parents question you about the amount of time taken from your school and work schedule spent with mom and I?"

"My time spent with you hasn't been a strain on anything. They know that I'm a hard worker and I don't give them anything to worry about. They taught my sisters and me many good characteristics so it's our job to make good choices."

I would say that so far, they have done very well with their family by what I see in you and here about your sisters." Mark concluded worrying about the trip to Kelly's home.

"OK Mark so no more worries. The store will be open till Midnight tonight so we need to go shopping after we leave here. Gosh I never should have waited until the last minute to shop but there is never any time in my schedule if I'm not spending time with you. I have made a list though and will promise to stick to shopping in the stores that have what I want."

"Where is Patricia going to go after she is done here?"

"I am going to take her back to my place; my landlord may have an extra cot she can use."

"I wonder how she is doing. I went by the stationary store on the way here for a minute and bought her some supplies to put the papers together with. I hope the stuff was suitable." Mark wondered.

"She probably was very grateful, she knows what she is doing and she didn't comment so I'm sure what you bought for her was used." Patricia returned and the color was back in her face.

"Hi Patricia, how are things going for you?"

"There were one hundred and nine pages in the entire assignment, it must have cost a fortune for you and I'll pay you back when I get in touch with my parents and have money wired to me. You are a life saver; both of you and I don't know how to thank you."

"We are glad to help you. This situation must be some kind of nightmare for you. I can't believe what those girls did, the very nerve; scamming money from an elderly women is just beyond belief for us." Mark said.

"I have a long fight ahead of me in clearing my name."

"You have spoken to a lawyer by now I presume?" Mark asked.

"Yes I was fortunate to find a lawyer who specializes in fraud. It was difficult though, most lawyers are already on holidays. I franticly dialed fifteen numbers on the police list and no one was available. I was worried that I would have to stay in jail until the New Year. Finally I dialed a number and a lawyer answered who happened to be Jewish and was of coarse free to represent me, hardworking and reliable."

Patricia specified. Both Kelly and Mark sympathized with her and offered her to stay at Kelly's apartment for as long as she needed to. They also offered to be character witnesses in court for her before they realized that that was only applicable for someone to be handed a lighter sentence. It was good intensions and a show of support to their friend. The three of them left the library together to take Patricia to Kelly's apartment. She was so relieved to have her work taken care of and to know she had a place to stay for the night that she collapsed in a chair in the hall outside the library and cried. She cried because her stress finally took its toll on her. Never has she needed anyone's support and help like she did now. The emotion she was feeling over the events that brought her to this level of stress was hitting her like a brick wall. It was all very different for her; a mess she certainly did not deserve. Mark didn't know what to say or do so he hoped Kelly could help Patricia in any way she could and he just sat quietly and waited. The two women sat together and talked until Patricia was able to regain her composure so that she could think about what she was going to do next. Since the hallway was not the most private and comfortable place to have a meltdown, Mark took her back to Kelly's apartment where she could relax, have a shower and rest while he and Kelly shopped. Mark bought her a long distance phone card so that she could phone her parents who were in England to talk. They made sure that Patricia was comfortable and ensured that she was able to reach her parents by phone. They told Patricia to just be comfortable and that they were going Christmas shopping. She would have some privacy for the next few hours. They left and went to the mall and after an hour, Kelly called home to check on Patricia but the line was busy so she knew that her friend was having a good conversation with her parents. Kelly bought gifts for him and Elizabeth and he bought gifts for her entire family. It had been days since they had time spent with each other and enjoyed their shopping spree. Kelly promised Patricia that she would shop for a few things for her since she had none of her clothes. Mark and Kelly had split up so that Mark could take some of the parcels to the car and Kelly called home again after three hours to find the phone still busy. She thought about the phone card and the possibility of the phone card lasting that long was unbelievable. She decided to start walking to the exit when she met Mark walking back into the mall still carrying the parcel's with a face red with anger. She had not known him to ever be angry "Mark! What's happened?"

"We're never going to get away! My car has been practically crushed in the parking lot by a snow plough. The driver at least stayed there and phoned the police to report the accident. I'll have to leave this stuff with you until I can deal with this mess and get a rental car; try to put it in a locker and sit somewhere in here to wait."

"Oh Mark ok. Just take a deep breath, oh actually I don't know what to say."

"Don't worry about me, do you mind waiting here for a while? You should probably get a couple of lockers to put this stuff into so you don't have to carry it around with you. We are stuck here for the next hour or so."

"It will be alright, I'll be fine. You go and do what you have to do" Kelly insisted. While she was looking for a locker her cell phone rang; it was Patricia calling.

"Hi are you ok?" Patricia was fine and felt much better because she had been able to talk to her parents. They grieved that they had left Patricia behind but her grandmother who lives in England wasn't well. Patricia could not leave at this time because the matter was in court. Her parent were to be gone for two months and were relieved that Kelly and Mark were there for her and they would send money for her to live on and to pay Mark back for helping to get her assignment printed up. Patricia asked Kelly to buy her a change of clothes since money was going to be sent to her account. She would then have a shower and try to get some much needed rest. Mark was busy attending to his accident and Kelly knew that Old Navy had two for one sale so she shopped there for her friend. She got everything Patricia needed and was happy with the great buys but was also beginning to get weary over the day's events. Kelly sat down and had a slice of pizza and salad and pop; it was now eight thirty and she didn't know what else to do except wait right there for Mark to come back into the mall to get her. She sat there a good long time in the food court, about an hour and a half because it was five after ten when Mark called her wanting to locate her. The car was towed away, the insurance company called and arrangements made for a rental car to be brought to them. Mark found her and she had some pizza and a drink waiting for him which he very much appreciated at that point. It had been a long evening. Kelly gave him an update on Patricia and he told her the situation surrounding the accident. There were four children running through the mall parking lot and ran in front of a snow plough. He swerved to miss them and hit three vehicles including Marks which took the worst beating. The driver was bumped up but is basically ok and gone to the hospital for x-rays and stitches in his leg. The parents of the kids were called and dealt with by police. The driver is not charged but it's up to the insurance companies to work out the damage. Mark was given a Toyota Tercell to drive and was grateful to have a vehicle to go away in. They had gifts to wrap and so did that at Marks house so they wouldn't disturb Patricia because it was passed one am., when Mark brought Kelly home. They had not been alone at Marks very often but they wanted to let Patricia rest since she did not sleep well in jail for the three days she had to spend there. They wrapped the gifts, had popcorn and hot chocolate and packed everything into the trunk of the car for the morning trip. Before Mark brought her home they sat together at the fireplace that Mark had just fixed a fire in. Kelly brought some more hot cocoa garnished with a candy cane. The two, very much in love with each other sat on the floor in front of the fire and Kelly suggested having a nice rug with big throw pillow there for their next winter evening by the fireplace. Mark agreed and was content to have time alone with Kelly in a romantic way. It was a rare occasion. All he needed in his heart was to watch the soft flicker of the flames glow against Kelly's porcelain skin. Kelly gave Mark a brush from her purse and sat in front of him so that he could brush her long black hair as she relaxed and hummed Silent Night. It was now Christmas Eve and the young couple sat quietly and gazed both into the fire and into each other eyes. They whispered many plans for future romantic evenings there and this would be the start of a tradition; that's wrapping gifts then relaxing by the fireplace exactly like they were doing on their first Christmas Eve. It was time to get Kelly home and before they left he got some thick blankets to put on the floor for Kelly to sleep on so they didn't have to wake Patricia try to find a cot. They arrived at the apartment at three fifteen; it was quiet and all lights but the Christmas lights were off and Patricia probably had not budged an inch all evening "Oh Mark the poor thing. She would probably sleep right through the weekend if she was left alone. I'm so glad I ran into her today and was able to help her."

"I think she will be ok. The two who were actually involved confessed that she was not so her matter may not even go to court and she may be released from any involvement in the scam."

I do hope so; it's just appalling and right in the Christmas season. It's because of situations like these that I refuse to stay in the dorm rooms. I work to keep an apartment, it's hard but it's the way it is."

"I am glad for you. I better get home now and I'll pick mom up at eleven in the morning then come to pick you up."

"Ok Mark, It has been quite a day! The two hugged each other before Mark left and Kelly made a comfy bed on the floor and fell right off to sleep after setting the clock radio for nine am. Mark went home, had a relaxing shower and set his clock for nine am. and he too fell fast asleep.

Chapter Seven

The night was crisp; just three nights passed since the winter solstice eclipse of the moon. The peace and stillness of the night was colored by the display of Christmas lights that adorned every house and building from neighborhood to neighborhood. If you could be out walking this night even as thousands of stars drew attention to peace and holiness, one would ponder of the love within each family that slept in anticipation for the big day ahead.

For most people the season is a time of charity, love, peace and goodwill. For those families that can be together to enjoy gift giving and a succulent turkey dinner can be blessed with the wealth of kinship. The beauty of the season adds to the meaning and brings memories of warmth and excitement to children. So much cheer and desire to make happy go into decorating and the joy of carolers with willing heart call out to all, Merry Christmas.

At the Gerard home the night surrounded the dimly lit house where the family slept. The outside doors were lit up as if the stars seem to have coordinated a design to suggest a make believe winter scene when one star had an idea and chose this house to have the other stars follow down from the sky. Where did the evergreen and holly come from that made the wreaths that decorated the doors and over the windows? Did the magic of the wilderness that night produce these artistically to make welcome the colors and symbols beheld? What people would see this display? Where would their thoughts wonder and what situation brought them to look upon this sight and enter into this home and what will they and who will they find inside of interest? The walls inside are connected by a ceiling of old and are trusted to hold the family, its bond and to keep perfect the unbroken circle. When daylight sees the events of the George and Mary Gerard's posterity, the walls within the home protect the members with strength as if memories are its cement. Maybe it's another world away from reality, who knows? It is a fact that in a ninety minute distance from the Gerard's home, there is a potentially broken world in Mark and Elizabeth's lives. The year brought them tragedy, grief, stress and complete bewilderment at how a life of commitment, hard work, success and stewardship could be erased in a blink of an eye. The Scott family, although small; Gordon, Elizabeth and Mark, were obligated in business, community and in each other as a family with one purpose. It was to build a life with respect and praise for everything that their God had provided for them. The family lived, loved and laughed together in some other perfect world but the death of Gordon brought them to a world of despair. Gordon and his brother's death was at first believed to be a murder As if the loss to the family wasn't tragic enough, people in their farming community were quick to turn their backs on the family. It was thought that their individual identities would fall prey to the prying eyes of the investigators. In fact, there were only a handful of true friends who lent support to the family in preparation of the funerals. One of their clergy members who Mark and Elizabeth trusted seemed to only give lip service because he too suggested that the accident was of suspicious nature. With their lives crumbled down around them, it was too much for Elizabeth to bear than she desperately slipped into a world all her own and she shut down. In her real world her trust in her friends and even her clergy had not the ability to sustain her in her time of sorrow so she made up this world for herself where no one could enter; where stillness and submission to bleakness and nothingness existed. Elizabeth did not hear or respond to anyone or anything around her. Nothing could penetrate the stillness that cocooned her. Mark in his twenty four years of age was very intimidated by the responsibility put on him. He was in shock because of the abandonment of his close community, even the families that he went to church with all his life quickly turned from him at his time of need. How could they? How this accident could be proposed as a murder with Mark as a suspect seemed ridiculous; it was clearly a tragic accident. Overzealous investigators looked at every corner of the business and personal lives of the Scott family and after six weeks called the tragedy accidental and closed the case. Gordon and his brother Geoff were buried and the business sold one month later. Mark had not the time or energy to morn for his father. His mother was taken to a rest home where Mark spent all the time he could spare just stroking his mother's hair or reading to her in an attempt to sooth and get her feeling again. Mark felt helpless but knew that they couldn't stay in their home town any longer so he being executor to his father's estate in the absence of his mother listed the property and moved his mother to Kingston in July and vowed never to look back.

Patricia woke up at about seven twenty am. and she was most grateful for a good night's sleep. She got up and went quickly about the apartment and found the clothes that Kelly had bought for her from the mall. She took her clothes with her to have a shower and change. Everything fit her and when she finished dressing she made some hot chocolate and notice that Kelly had her clock set for 9 am. She guessed that Kelly would sleep another half hour or so, so she went outside to have a breath of fresh air and check out the weather. While Patricia was outside Kelly woke up and saw that the couch was empty and blankets folded up and set to one end. Kelly fretted at the possibility that she left but had nowhere to go. As she looked around the apartment she found her old clothes and the bags with some of the new clothes in it. Her attention was soon directed to the hot chocolate on the stove and she poured herself a mug full. It was hot so Patricia couldn't have gone too far so she picked up her blankets while sipping away at her drink and waited for Patricia to come back in. Kelly dialed Mark to wish him good morning; he was getting ready to leave to pick up his mother for the weekend. He told her how relieved he was to have a car that is running well and is comfortable. Patricia walked in and greeted Kelly with a wave and she returned the greeting and indicated that she would be on the phone for just a moment. Mark needed to talk to Kelly about his mother; she was nervous about going away for four days and having to be around so many people for that length of time. Kelly hoped to be able to settle her anxiety, that her needs could be easily met at her parents' home. Mark told his mother that he trusts Kelly and would probably regret not going. So while the phone conversation was ending, Patricia removed her coat and boots and sat down to talk to Kelly. "Good morning, Kelly it was great to sleep here and so warm and comfortable and safe. I don't even remember lying down."

"Patricia you poor thing, you didn't even move a muscle all night. A good night sleep is what you really needed."

"Thank you Kelly, I really did need to sleep. In jail you sleep on a narrow plastic thing on a cement slab, I was on the top bunk and I was afraid to fall asleep in case I rolled off."

"You don't ever have to worry about that again; you are going to get yourself all depressed and upset talking about it like you did yesterday. I thought you were going to faint at the library."

"I almost did, if you had not been there to pull me over to the chair I would have. I am feeling better, it's surprising what a proper night's sleep and some friendly company will do for you."

"Good! You are going to have a very pleasant Christmas holiday at my parent home and that's an order. I see that the clothes fit you, they look nice Patricia. Did you find the make-up I bought for you I thought those shade would match your hair and eyes and I have some jewelry that you are welcome to use?"

"Do you wear make-up Kelly? You don't need it."

"I don't wear it much but I keep it on hand and wear some on Sunday."

"I would appreciate using your curling iron and some hair styling gel"

"You are welcome to it Hun, I have three different sizes I'll get them. Oh thanks for simmering some coco, I'm going to take a shower now and get ready. You make yourself at home and make some breakfast, you must be starving." Starving she must have been, Patricia is a wonderful cook. She prepared a breakfast to perfection for both of them; waffles, sausages and fruit cups on the side. The counter was nicely set to eat at and the meal would be thanks to Kelly for all of her help. She had not touched the make-up or curled her hair until breakfast was made.

"Patricia did you have food brought in? This is magnificent."

"I am a chef you know. I wanted to do this for you."

"Thank you so much, I wish Mark was here to eat. He brought this food in here for me."

"I would have thought so; I didn't think you eat like this all the time."

"Well this is beautiful and no I don't eat like this usually. I'm glad you made yourself at home though. I told you to and you needed this for comfort so let's eat Hun. Oh Patricia! These waffles, I've never tasted anything like this."

"There is pumpkin puree', ginger, nutmeg added. Do you like them like that?"

"They are heavenly; oh my crickets are they good!"

“Oh you’re what? Patricia laughed. The two enjoyed they’re breakfast and didn’t leave a crumb. They rolled over to the sink to clean up and they finished getting ready, Mark would be there soon.

It was going on ten am. and Mark excited yet anxious for his mother today, still wondering about her reaction to meeting Kelly’s family. His reluctance was soon forgotten by the love he felt for Kelly and the closeness that Kelly and his mother share. Elizabeth never pressed Mark about the idea of marriage but she dreamed of seeing Mark kneel at the alter with his beloved Kelly to be sealed for eternity. Elizabeth felt her faith returning with every thought of her son being together with Kelly. She desperately yearned to be a part of another family circle and to be void of her loneliness. It seemed like years that she had not been able to feel emotions or even taste food. She had not even been able to sleep on her own for quite some time but more and more she was beginning to see the light of day. Her broken heart was starting to heal through love of a devoted son and the new angel in their lives. She did not fear this day, she prepared herself and packed a bag to go away from the rest home for Christmas. The attendant gave her instructions and wished her a Merry Christmas and a wonderful time as she assisted in signing Elizabeth out. Elizabeth waited a few minutes in the lounge for Mark to arrive and she as well had been sitting by herself, there were six other patients waiting for their family members to pick them up too. Not a word was spoken by anyone; they all sat and just seemed to listened and watch for people to arrive. The lounge was a comfortable room with big puffy couches. There was a table with a bowl of fruit on it and paintings of flowers and streams that one of the attendants painted. The window looked out onto the part of the parking lot and the green houses were also in view. A receptionist was always at the desk in front of the security door. Elizabeth was concentrating on the bowl of fruit and she did not hear Mark come in. He walked in, thanked the receptionist for allowing him in then walked over to his mother. "Well you had better go and eat one of those apples before you forget that they are there." He chuckled with his mother. "Are you nervous mom?"

"I am somewhat nervous dear. I'm alright though now that you are here. I will be fine, no worries now. I am looking forward to meeting Kelly's Aunt Barbara, she sounds sweet; Kelly speaks so much about her in a comforting tone of voice." Mark knew right then that she was nervous because Elizabeth never speaks of the regimental way in which the household is run and all she had energy for was to sit and talk, drink herbal tea and sleep. Elizabeth knew that Mark had never met any of Kelly's family so He couldn't assure her that she shouldn't be anxious. Elizabeth was fifty four years old and was always able to keep her age a secret but this past year made it increasingly difficult because of the greying hair and darkened eyes. She didn't know it then but she was to be in the good hands of Barbara, Kelly and her sisters. He didn't want to scare Elizabeth so told her of his car getting smashed on the mall parking lot the night before and that was the reason that he was driving a new car. Mark assured her quite bluntly that he was uninjured or was not even involved and they would receive a new vehicle in a short time. He and

Kelly had a very chaotic day the previous day and it was a wonder that he didn't lose his own nerve about going away. He told his mother all about Patricia and the traumatic situation that she dealt with the past week. As shocked as Elizabeth was and how sorry she felt for the girl she was so very proud of Kelly and knew that quality of kindness in her was so terribly hard to find in people. She remembered then the desertion she experienced from her old friends in her home in Edmonton. How proud she was of her Kelly, that dear soul. She was so young, she shouldn't be interested in trying to heal the broken heart of a middle aged lady yet she did willingly and asked for no reward. Kelly simply feels in her heart the need to be charitable. How dear and darling she will always be to Elizabeth. Kelly then had the heart willing enough to extend her service to another lady in need of support. Mark and Elizabeth had some time to their selves in the car and talked this way about Kelly, Elizabeth didn't mind. Mark are you soon going to propose to Kelly? Would Christmas be too soon dear?" Her deliberate question excited Mark.

"Mom I have thought about it, in fact I can barely think of anything else. I suppose it would be best to have a chance to talk to her parents first."

"Well her father dear; isn't that the proper protocol?"

"Yes, but I do need to feel a sense of approval from both her parents before I get into a serious conversation with her father—oh I can't believe I'm doing this mom."

"I know it seems to be such an old fashioned tradition Mark, but every woman is daddies little girl and any daughter would appreciate the loving gesture, not only from her father but from her fiancé."

"I believe a proposal deserves family acceptance when family matters most. I don't want to pressure her though mom. We really haven't known each other for long and have not had a lot of time alone like dating and such; she experiences anxiety over having enough time to finish what she needs to."

Have you noticed that?"

"Yes dear I have. She does seem to be under a lot of pressure. She wants everything to be perfect and now she is in a relationship which is something very new to her."

"I have bought her a pearl ring just to let her know I want her to be mine. I am also giving her a pendant of three roses each one made of a different color of gold."

"Ok, Mark nice gifts. I hope you manage to get some time alone with Kelly." They arrived at the apartment and Mark went inside to get them and pack their bags into the car where ever he could find space. Kelly was acting just like a little girl wearing her Santa hat and Christmas tree earrings that the twins made for her last year. Her suitcase had decals of Santa and his sleigh with the reindeer ahead of it. She squealed with excitement and jumped onto Marks back and hung lightly to his strong broad shoulders and had a piggy back ride to the car. Elizabeth sat in the car laughing and snapping pictures of their Tom foolery with her cell phone. Poor Patricia was left jokingly to carry her bag.

"Aw just leave it for Mark and hitch a ride like I did." Mark plunked her right onto the roof of the car and walked over to where Patricia was and picked her up and through her over his shoulder to carry her to the car. A short snow ball fight broke out with Elizabeth tucked safely away and laughing hysterically. This little antic made light of everyone's anxiety. There was about a ninety minute drive after Elizabeth and Patricia had been introduced. There couldn't have been a more pleasant social time. The past few days' bad events seemed to have diminished from their minds and all the four of them wanted was to finally enjoy each other's company. Patricia was gratefully well rested and rode in the car among friends, trusted friends.

Mark and Kelly sat in the front seats and Elizabeth and Patricia sat in the back and she talked all about the suit that Kelly made for her for this occasion. Kelly spoke advising, "I'm more use to sewing and designing for children then adults, specifically my niece and nephew and for some family friend's children."

"Why wouldn't you find it easier to sew for an adult because of the larger scale of pattern?"

"It is a fact that there can be more details in children's patterns but the scale is still smaller and takes less time than making cloths for adults. I still find adult cloths a bit more of a challenge. I bought some knitting yesterday but I doubt that I'll have time to work on it." Elizabeth's heart melted just then when Kelly spoke of knitting.

"Do you look forward to knitting baby items Darling?" She put her hand over her mouth; what a pushy thing to ask of Kelly she immediately thought. "Oh what am I saying? I mean I know there's plenty of time—actually I don't know what I mean to imply, just curious I guess."

Patricia sat quietly and waited to hear how this conversation would unfold.

Kelly didn't know quite how to respond, she waited for Mark. "It's alright mother, everyone knows that Kelly is my true love" He took her hand in his. "I can see Kelly sitting by a window or a fireplace knitting a little baby blanket for our little darling we will have someday. I will imagine that the child will be the best dressed child in Canada with Kelly as his or her mother, and the best looking."

Kelly just quietly looked back at Elizabeth and smiled; she notice that there were tears in her eyes at that time. "Are you ok Elizabeth?"

"Yes dear, just wonderful. Just feeling sentimental and loving the idea of you being with my son and of all the wonderful things to come in the future for you."

"You have that right mom." He looked adoringly at Kelly and felt at ease at such talk of the future being in the open now. He thought that it was a good thing instead of having to talk to his mother candidly and with just her about his future plans. He was pleased with Kelly's positive response and could see she was serious and not just because it was such a festive day. He believed that more talk of the future would be taking up much more of their time now. Although he knew how

Kelly felt about him, she did not talk anymore about babies and did see in her eyes that she was a bit startled and surprised. They were all having a great time but Mark chose a different topic of conversation for the remainder of the drive to Stirling.

They reached the little town; comfort country it is actually referred to as. It's a charming little town with its own butter creamery and enchanting gift shops along the town's way. It is confettied with Victorian styled gingerbread type houses, very old world. Kelly directed Mark through town to the road to her parent's house and arrived on time to a scene right off of a Norman Rockwell painting. From around a hill at the side of the house, a team of Keidstale horses were pulling a sleigh full of neighborhood children and driven by George. Kelly waved from the car and the other three could do nothing but gasp at that breath taking sight. Was this real life or had they been transported back in time where there were no worries, only comfort and beauty? The three aw struck guests could hardly sit still in their seats. The morning's fresh snow glistened in the afternoon sun and truffles of snow nestles on the boughs of the evergreen trees as great gusts of breath bushelled from the nostrils of the great and gentle beasts. The horses, majestic were led by the drivers' reigns to gallop between the massive evergreen trees and the wind caught the glistening powdered snow to blow it over the horses as to form great robes of majesty. To those who beheld the sight noticed that the decorative metal pieces which adorned the sleigh caught the sun's beams and made unforgettable the perfect winter scene. "Oh lovely, I can't believe it. Kelly I've never seen such a picture of graciousness; truly heaven sent. Oh God is good, God is great. Mark I love it here already, I don't want to stay closed up in the guest wing away from this magnificent event."

"I know mom. Kelly this is why there is so much beauty in you in the person you are and the love for life you have and for everything in it. I see your world and I see you in it more clearly now, how wonderful for you."

"This is where I grew up; I have been here since I was adopted. My parents knew that they wanted a large property and they bought this after they were married and my parent made this home for their six daughters. The neighbors come from all over to use the horses and here they come now back to the house. George guided the horses up the driveway to greet his daughter and guests. The horses towered over the car and the three snapped pictures of them before coming from the car to meet Kelly's father. George was a military man, a very strong figure of a soldier very tall, slender with a very wide and large hand to extend in a welcoming handshake. His voice was striking and masculine, one that would hold the attention of a bewildering mind. One would comment on his presence of being stalwart yet friendly. He embraced his daughter with tenderness and his pride could not be hidden nor his fatherly love and protectiveness toward her. George graciously stood as a totem pole before his home and family and welcomed Mark, Elizabeth and Patricia to his home and offered them hospitality to which none else could hold a candle to. He offered his condolences on behalf of his family to the Scott's in reverence and respect for their loss. Such forwardness Kelly thought only for an instance may have caused Elizabeth to faint. She instead stood uprightly in receipt of such heart felt words, words that truly gave soleus to the mind. Mark was grateful for the strength that his mother glorified in and Kelly was reminded as she listened to this mighty man, this military officer and man of honor and obedience, speak words of true faith and kindness such as to enlighten Elizabeth's grieving heart. Kelly's brother in law took the horses to secure them and the children ran off to play with their sleighs and George helped Mark carry the gifts and bags into the house. Kelly's older sister was there at the door to greet her while carrying her year old daughter. "Oh please let me have her, she is so big now. Is she walking yet? Oh I can't believe how long her hair is, is she sleeping through the night for you?"

"Yes to all of the above questions. Look she remembers you; see how she's held her arms out to you."

"You dear little angel, I love you so much."

"And this is?"

"Oh Monique, this is Elizabeth Scott, Marks mom and Patricia Lawrence. She is a fellow nursing student."

"I'm please to meet you both and here comes Mark I presume, Marry Christmas and welcome to you all."

"I am pleased to meet you, Merry Christmas." Mark hugged Kelly's sister.

Kelly's mother entered the hall with Sister Barbara the twins and Carol, the sixteen year old, waved from the top of the stairs. She had just come from the shower and was only wearing a terry bath robe and pink slippers, hair soaking wet. “Hi Carol. Merry Christmas! Hurry and come down to visit with us.”

“I’ll be there soon, we are going to start decorating the evergreen branches but we are waiting for Sharron.”

“She’ll be here in about an hour; the highway 401 is plugged with traffic.” Her mother assured the rest. “She is on her way now.”

“Merry Christmas to all.” She kissed her daughter sweetly and took the hand of both Elizabeth and Patricia, welcomed them and advised that her home was there’s and that she was happy to make their Christmas’s brighter. Mary took their coats and guided them into the dining room where she had lunch waiting.

“Mary how did you prepare this feast, all this food in one morning? It’s a work of art.” Patricia graciously asked her.

“Don’t worry about that, just come in and sit down, everyone else will be in shortly.”

“I hear Dad, Mark and Brian coming in now with our bags. Mom come and meet Mark.” Kelly practically dragging Mary made their way into the hall where the men stood with the baggage and festively decorated parcels.

The Christmas tree which stood tall in the great room stood center of an abundant array of bags and colorful parcels already and the guests yet have to arrange their treasures before it. First, Mark had to be introduced to Kelly's mother and rest of the Gerard family and it was due time. Mark had been the buzz around the household since Kelly's first admission of her relationship with him. The anticipation of the other five ladies meeting him could only be described as the unwrapping of the biggest present under the tree and finding there what you've always dreamed of getting for Christmas. That is what caught Kelly's mother's eye; her beautiful raven haired daughter is coupled with a man so perfectly handsome and his tenderness toward her daughter was deserving of her approval. Mary was assured that her jewel had given her heart to Mark in devotion, unity and love. Mary was grateful and considered their union to be a blessing to the family; her eyes welled up with tears while her husband embraced her. She was nearly speechless and with much kindness George suggested that this young couple have made a wise choice in each other and the support of the family is with them now and with their future decisions. "Lets us all join together in the dining room for lunch. It will be an enjoyable time and then afterwards we meet in the great room to participate in our Christmas Eve traditions."

Mary and George sat at each end of the table with Patricia, Kelly and Mark, Elizabeth, Barbara, Grandma Diane on the right and Brian, Monique, baby Susan and son Ryan, Sheila and Cindy, Carol and Sharon on the left side. George blessed the food and gave thanks for his guests. The family and friends feasted on chili, biscuits, cheese, salads, rice and condiments. The chandelier was already decorated with holly, poinsettias and gold beads. The twins had adorned the table with their beloved gingerbread arrangements; so sweet. Each chair back was decorated with red, blue and green plaid ribbons with a gold rope and a blue and gold Christmas ornamental ball dangling from each rope. The room was decorated with flowers, silk colorful runner on the tables under ornaments depicting a Christmas winter wonderland. Sheila and Cindy sang little songs to which everyone clapped. Mary carefully read the origins of many of her ornaments in the room and George told stories of Christmas's past spent in that very dining room and that the aroma of evergreen will soon be throughout the corridors and all the way up the stairs and through the house. With that and the aroma of home baked sugar cookies which will be hung across the boughs, one will not ever want to be awoken for that wonderful dream. This is how Mary and her girls decorated every Christmas Eve for the past twenty years. Some years their friends came over to help and many hands made light work and lasting memories. Assembling all of it only took about three hours and another hour to hang the boughs along the ceilings. The work was well worth it, every year Elizabeth would be so excited to see the finished project; she would never tire of this project. Elizabeth was also excited to see the finished product, but after lunch and visiting with the family, Mary and Barbara showed her to the guest wing. There was also a room there for Mark and Patricia. Elizabeth needed her rest and although she was well acquainted with the family she needed to sleep and did for five hours. While she slept, George, Brian and Mark brought masses of evergreen into the great room to be arranged wired together and decorated. The decorations were set out in boxes, the same ones they used every year, and with homemade sugar cookies that were baked the previous day and patterned by the twins into snowflakes and such were being attached to strings. This was a beautiful day and Monique contributed candy cane and white lights to adorn the boughs as her special touch. George made the wire base to attach the greenery years ago and green floral tape is used to attach the greenery to the wire. George and Mary gave everyone a demonstration and everyone got to work with favorable results. Cindy and Sheila couldn't wait to attack the snowflakes and some didn't make it to the greenery so Kelly took them aside and showed them her make up case that was full of nail polish. Kelly got them to sort the light and dark bottles with glitter to separate piles and promised to paint their toe and fingernails later in the day as a reward for their work. Kelly loved her little sister as did the other girls; they were considered to be little blessings and the sisters protected and nurtured them under the watchful eye of their mother Mary and the education worker.

It was a lovely atmosphere there in the great room with the sunlight hitting the lead crystal pains at the very top of the windows lending colors and shapes of sunlight to cascade through the room and causing beams to dance off of anything that was shiny in the room. The aroma of evergreen, spice and apple cider filled the room and saturated the cloth in their clothes with a fantasy of fragrances. This originated from kinship and friendships and they bonded heart and hands to sing joyous Christmas carols and listen to storytelling. George began to tell a beautiful story of the first Christmas that he and his wife spent in their home there in Stirling. "Mary and I were married in the late part of spring on June fourth. I had just received orders and was being stationed in Africa for a compassion work mission. I was to be gone for two to four months and we had one week for a honeymoon and two weeks to settle into a home which was generous considering. We were offered an apartment in the back of a house and we were going to except it until we noticed this property on a shopping day while driving through Stirling. The house wasn't the size it is today and we saw it was listed and we were in Heaven, remember Mary?"

"Yes, we were in love and that's all that mattered, that and having this house for our very own. I foretold that this is where we are going to raise our six children. I don't know why I said that, I just did and it came from my heart."

"With that the decision was made and we drove to a pay phone to get an appointment with the real-estate to view the property within two days. I drained our bank account, signed the deal, it was ours."

"I had Marry move in with my parents while I was away; I didn't return until the middle of November, Mary had procession of the house and had it cleaned, painted and floors and carpets laid. She moved in the wedding gifts so that it wouldn't look baron when I returned to Canada and saw it for the first time. She planted bulbs in a flower garden. I was so in love with Mary and watching her prepare our home was all I cared about, nothing else in the world mattered to me. Christmas was getting very close and we had spent just about every penny we earned on the renovations. We didn't yet have furniture or money for gifts."

"Oh it was the weirdest feeling then to not have a bunch of gifts to put under a big ole tree but the reason we didn't was more important than the gifts so George went out to the woods and brought in this sort of little Charlie Brown tree and we taped out wedding pictures to it. I used his boutonniere he wore on our wedding day for the tree topper. I had some left over lace from my wedding dress to use for garland. We shut off all the lights, lit some candles, put five logs in the fireplace and lie down to eat crackers and marmalade and drank warm cider just like we are drinking today. That was our very first Christmas eve here in our own home, this very house." Mary ended,

"That day was one of the best memories for Just my Mary and me." There girls gathered around them to embrace their parents and all the memories of all the Christmas's since then. Kelly suggested that the girls share their favorite memories of Christmas to add to the momentum of what has started in storytelling. The three older girls began to talk all at once of the fond memories they have and George examined that situation as a natural occurrence in the household and suggested that they start from oldest and going down the line from there. "Ok dad," So Monique began her story.

"Mine is the first Christmas that I remember here. I was three or four years old, not sure which; but I was in the living room with Mom and Grandma Gerard, we didn't have the great room at that time so the tree went in the corner there beside the front window. When I saw dad trying to maneuver a tree into the front door of the hall and into the living room that was there at the time, I squealed and asked why daddy was bringing a tree into our house. I remember this, like it must have been the first that I was old enough to recognize. I just couldn't stop being so excited about actually having a tree in the house." There were many ooo's and awe's with the understanding that the world would be just opening up to a child of that age.

"I guess I was asleep for the first three years of my life anyway dad brought out the box of Christmas lights, I remember that they were the old fashioned kind of big colored bulbs. I couldn't take my eyes off the lights and how beautiful the glow was against the tree. That is one of my favorite times in this house, the realization of the tradition of the Christmas tree." Lovingly Mary thanked her daughter for the story.

"I never knew that dear. How it warms me and makes me realize that there are a lot of fond memories held within these walls. Kelly gave her mother a hug then began her story.

"I am not sure if I can remember a favorite Christmas so I will just follow Monique and begin with the first Christmas that I remember. I was about three or four and we went to a church bazaar and Nativity play. Someone was selling a handmade gold spray painted cardboard Nativity scene. It was decorated with macaroni and colored beads on the roof and cotton balls on the base for snow. I thought it was the most beautiful thing I had ever laid eyes on."

"Do you remember that it use to sit by the tree every year until you were about thirteen?" Mom asked.

"Yes Mom, it was only then that I realized it wasn't really made of gold. Where is that any way?"

"I think I've seen in in the attack, it's in a hat box." Sharon said. "I think I know right where it is, I'll go and get it for you now."

"Sharon wait till later, I'll take Mark with us and we can explore all the neat junk up there." They laughed.

"After the bazaar we ate at the banquet and watched the play in the cultural hall. There I learned about the baby Jesus and the Wise Men and the meaning of gift giving and that we do special things on occasions at church. That night I spent hours in my room just looking at and touching my golden Nativity scene. I fell asleep beside it on the floor. Well Sharon, it's your turn."

"I won't tell about the first Christmas I remember because I was injured and taken to the hospital. Do you two remember that?"

Kelly and Monique both agreed that they did remember and remembered the details of the accident. The three girls and some cousins were building tents with chairs and blankets. Sharron ran through the tents and stepped on a wooden block, fell and hit her head on a wooden table and bounce to hit again on some steps. The result was a head injury and sprained neck."

"I think therefore my favorite Christmas was the year we had the 4-H club in and had a party. We put up the garland early that year for all the guests we invited so they could see and experience the grandeur of it. The entire members helped to make the cookie snowflakes and we learned how to make corn husk angels and decorated the garland with those. Mom dressed up as Mrs. Santa Clause and read us the story of the kids in the orphanage. Before the party, each girl made another present that we drew names for. I was given a silk scarf that was hand dyed and some maple flavored candy canes. I made Delores Marsh hand painted stationary. The true meaning of Christmas has always been prevalent to me by living in the family I do and for the sisterhood of the 4_H club."

Carol decided that her favorite Christmas happened eleven years ago when her twin sisters came to live with them. "I was five years old and it was just one week before Christmas when Mom and Dad came home with Sheila and Cindy. Patricia wondered first if they had it planned to bring them home just before Christmas or is that when they were legally released.

"Yes, we heard from the adoption agency that fifty six year old women had just delivered the twins and was unwilling to take them let alone raise twin disabled children and we agreed to adopt them that they wouldn't have to be raised by government institutions. The girls were four weeks old when they were determined healthy enough to go to a family. Go on with your story Carol."

"To me they were just new babies, I didn't know of their disability. I loved to watch grandma knit those little red and white Christmas dresses for them and she helped me sew the little red velvets hats with white fir to wear with the dresses. Mom took the ensembles to bring them home in and when they came home I sat by the fireplace and was the first to have my picture taken with the new babies wearing the little hats I made for them. I still have that picture hanging in my room." Carol has always been a loving mother influence to her little sisters. She taught them about sorting and they have a love of scrapbooking and doing crafts and such from greeting cards and coloring. Coloring is just what the twins were doing with Aunt Barbara when Carol finished telling her story.

Aunt Barbara brought the girls into the great room where everyone was decorating the garland and George invited the girls to share their favorite Christmas story. Cindy told, "I like this Christmas and making sugar cookies and I made a card for Mark and one for Patricia." Cindy colored herself and Sheila with Mark on a card and added a little star and a verse that said "I like you." She made one a like for Patricia. Sheila colored each Mark, Patricia and Elizabeth Christmas trees. The three recipients took the girls in hand and dearly thanked them and talked to them while Mary snapped pictures of that Kodak moment. Kelly stood close by her mom with a hand on her mom's arm and her elbow across her back watched the camera screen of the five people in the picture.

"Oh this is just the sweetest picture; Mom I'm going to take the chip to the printer and print it off on eight by ten papers immediately. I'll make you all a copy and one for Sheila and Cindy. Come on girls come see, you come with me to get a picture." Away they ran with Kelly into the kitchen to the printer. Kelly showed Sheila how to turn on the power and showed Cindy how to put the chip into the printer. Kelly found the photo on the screen and said, "There you are girls with your friends; I'll push the print button and you watch the bottom of the printer for the photos to come out."

The girls watched with excitement and sat on the floor arm in arm and watched the picture come from the printer. Kelly explained how the printer worked when they were astonished to see there selves so quickly in photos made by the printer. "Our gingerbread men and lady cookies are cooled now. We want to put them on the tree now, can we?"

Kelly walked over to the counter to where the cookies cooled and with encouraging words, told the girls that this year's cookies took first prize of all other years. Sheila added that they have red ribbons to string them up on the tree with. "Did you make that idea Sheila?"

"We both did and we both cut our own ribbons." Said Sheila.

"This is a very great idea girls. When we get the dolls all strung with the ribbon, we can ask everyone to help us hang them on the tree."

Cindy just laughed so sweetly and asked, "Can we put our picture on the table with our gingerbread scene?"

"Cindy!" Kelly beamed, "That's another A plus idea. We need to make a frame and we will surprise the rest but first let's hang the ornaments and go tell the rest to come." More pictures were taken of the twins by the tree and Sharon found a plastic free standing frame that the girls could put their photos in so that people sitting on both side of the table could see. The girls decorated their frame with Christmas stickers and taped curly stickers on to the corners. The picture was placed among the gingerbread ornaments on the center of the table and another cherished memory had been recorded within the walls of this cherished home. The girls joined the other in talking about the years events and decorating the Christmas garland. They played Patti cakes with their little niece and nephew or built things with Lego blocks while watching Frosty the Snowman on DVD. The household was at its busiest now; latters were placed and poles with hooked ends were raising the festive garlands at the very tops of the eleven foot walls where permanent hooks would hold the treasured greenery. The hooks adjoining the garland were like the smiles that connected the family in the beauty of the tradition that Christmas Eve in 2010.

After the cleanup was done the Gerard's and their guests sat in the living room and talked while the children played in the middle of the room. That could have been another scene from a Norman Rockwell painting. Three of Mary's spa partners came over and Elizabeth had awakened and joined the festivities. Mark and Kelly sat arm in arm and seemed to be more in love since spending time in Kelly's home. Everything about the house and everything they did called out LOVE ONE AND OTHER. Mary had planned a special surprise for the women and asked the men to retreat either to the den or the barn, it was their choice. In the den they could watch or listen to a big screen TV and surround sound or admire George's military items. There was enough in there to keep the men busy for the next six hours or so. Mary's friends from church, Lillian, Bonny and Christine came over to show the women how to make spa salts and fizzy bath balls and to give manicure and pedicures. There would be facials for who ever wanted one and foot rubs. Grandma and Aunt Barbara prepared little fancy sandwiches and low calorie cookies with hot ginger herbal tea and hot cocoa to drink. The three women set up a table for each center. Bonny first demonstrated how to make fizzy balls but they would need to dry overnight and would be ready in the morning to slip into someone's Christmas stalking. Lillian then set the women up at her table and gave manicures, soaked their cuticles and prepared them to be pushed down and nails filed. Fragrant Epson salt scrubs were massaged into their hands before the nails were painted. Mary's invitation to the ladies for a spa day was a provision that made Kelly feel like mother's little girl again. She had such a great time but she was beginning to wonder what Mark was doing during the spa session. She left the others and went upstairs to change her clothes and in the meantime, Mark came around the corner of the hall looking for his beauty. Kelly caught Marks eye just then walking down the stairs wearing a pepper grey cashmere sweater and a black and grey dog tooth skirt and navy leather pumps. She accessorized her curls with a pearl brett and a silver broach in the shape of a tiny K and encrusted with pearls. She saw her Mark glancing adoringly up at her so then she playfully slid down the bannister into his arms. Kelly lie there in his strong arms for a long moment; there eyes fixed on each other and their love radiated from them. Her perfect beauty was before the front door window where outside icicles were hanging but could not shine as brightly as her face did even with the sun shining on them.

He recorded that vision in his mind. The loveliness of the women he embraced left him speechless. His eyes remembered every curl in her accolades of black hair that adorned her face that told a story of escalating romance where their hearts beat in unison. Marks apprehension for proposing to this lady broke and with the beating of his heart; a heart that could no longer stand in stillness and want, caused him to yearn to be her husband. “Kelly, I need to keep you close to me.”

“I feel your heart beating beside mine dearest Mark.”

“Where can I carry you so we talk? I don’t want to put you down. I’m not trying to act inappropriately; I just can’t put you down.”

“There is a landing upstairs with a sofa there; it would be all right to go there.” Before she could finish talking, he was half way up the stairs with her. The evening had cast its mellow shadow by now and the twinkling lights on the garland had followed each and every step they took on the staircase lent to the light in Kelly’s dark brown eyes but was not nearly as meaningful. Mark reached the darkened landing where there was a brown sued couch that he sat Kelly down on his lap. Their eyes had not broken the gaze and they sat embraced; her hair rested on his shoulders as her face sweetly rested against his.

They closed their eyes in anticipation that they would kiss but his lips pressed ever so passionately against her temple. Tears warmly fell from her eyes and she was in love; she loved being in love, a new feeling and it was young yet vigorously molded her thoughts. Mark cherished her and this special quiet moment they had to spend alone together.

While the women were still playing like grown up little girls, Mark looked for a chance to talk to George about he and Kelly. "We have only known each other about six weeks and already my mother loves her as a daughter. She has been a blessing to my mother. They immediately became friends and Kelly has been non-judgmental to my mother's condition and to our recent afflictions. I had a girlfriend who turned tail and ran after the accident and investigation took place."

"She was self-absorbed then." George sympathized.

"Oh yes, she saw that she wasn't going to have an easy time and life then was not going to be what dreams were made of. Anyway I needed her support and she was nowhere to be found. Kelly is different, she didn't even know my mom and yet she served her herbal tea, drew baths for her and was just so courteous. I have been drawn to her for her kindness to my mom, her beauty and sweet spirit. I don't think she has a mean or lazy bone in her body. Already I love her to no end George, I want to marry her."

"Thank you Mark, everything you said about my daughter was worth hearing and for a father it means a great deal. You approached me with the intensions you have with my daughter. I remember my dating years, they seem like time wasted and I didn't marry until I was twenty nine years old. I experienced one empty relationship after and other. Then I met Mary. The name Mary means special spirit; to me it means love of mine. After a four month courtship, I knew that this was not a fly by night relationship.

We were married two months later."

"I understand that, I was told by my father that I would definitely know when the lady I am going to marry would walk into my life. Kelly has walked into my life when I most needed her and I believe that she loves me very much."

"Are you going to propose to her here?"

"I only have a little pearl ring, sort of a steady friendship ring I guess. I didn't expect to do it this soon. I didn't want to rush her you see and would have waited until the end of the semester but I don't feel that I can wait. I don't want to wait but I have to do what's best for Kelly."

"You already have Mark. I'm truly impressed with your consideration of my daughter and I am relaxed with you here. I can see that you are putting her feelings and comfort first and I'm very glad of that. You will find the right time." Those words "you'll find the right time" circled through Marks mind and through to his heart and he remembered sitting with Kelly there on the couch, playing with her curls and talking about the day's events. The time they had spent together then had to be short, he didn't propose to her on the upstairs landing. He knew it was too early for her and they were still a bit nervous with each other, perhaps because they know enough to not let their feelings of passion carry them away as it could; he was not going to be reclus with her. Their quiet times together led them to conversation mostly Kelly telling him about some of her favorite memories in that house and the years it took her parents to build what they had. She talked about everything in that home that had meaning and held memories for the members of the family. Mark did divulge to Kelly that he is hoping to build that kind of foundation and future in his new home for he and his mother and Kelly. With that Kelly smiled in willingness and told him, "I Love you Mark, I'm truly in love with you." The home was beginning to hold memories for him and her words had not left his heart. He decided to make his first memory that very moment and gave Kelly her Christmas present, the pearl band to as a promise of his devotion and love for her and asked her to be promised to him. He professed his deep love for his cherished Kelly and the two in love and overwhelmed in affection were carried away with the moment, caressed and their lips accidently brushed ever so lightly together but with passion which concluded in a loving embrace. They softly cried, they didn't speak, they couldn't, and their hearts did the talking from that moment on until they left the landing to join the others.

Everyone was gathering for supper and they would be remised if they didn't join. It was about six thirty pm. and Mary had caterers brought in for the event and an event it was. The silver service, blue willow dinner dishes and soup and salad bowls, silver wear and corn flower crystal glass were antiques. The place settings were decorated ever so carefully with blue silver and brown plaid napkins and proudly displayed, the twins gingerbread ornaments traditionally adorned the center of the table arranged and garnished with red carnations, holly and berries and silver candles.

A separate buffet held a succulent roasted turkey, hot dishes of mashed potatoes and yams, mixed vegetables seeping with butter, steaming rolls and cheese platters. There were the anticipated deserts; they were a splendid work of art, a tapestry before the guests of flavors both sweet and savory waited on the cart in the hallway out of eye sight. Mark and Kelly joined Elizabeth and Patricia at the table. Mark hugged his mom and with concerned for her asked, "How are you feeling mom? I'm sorry I disappeared there for a while"

"Patricia and I have been enjoying Kelly's little sisters' thank you"

"I videotaped your mother playing with the girls and your mom was teaching them and the little kids how to sing Twelve Days of Christmas. Monique brought out some curly ribbons and your mom and the girls decorated gifts with them." George added.

"Thank you Kelly for this wonderful weekend and I'm feeling just fine and I'm hungry."

"Monique, will you let the baby sit with me? I can help her eat."

"Sure she can sit with you. Do you recognize the ribbon in her hair? It is the one you made and sent with the hand knitted sweater."

"Yes and it fits her. I got the pattern from my grandmother along with about thirty other books. I've been through every one of the books and have made choices of what I want to knit." Elizabeth beams when Kelly talks, she loves to listen to every word she says especially when she talks about her crafts. Mark sat beside her with his arm resting on the back of her chair and watching Kelly pay sweet attention to her little niece. "I can see you love to have any chance you can get to be with the baby." Monique commented.

"I haven't been home this time since June because I met the Childress's and found out that they are my maternal grandparents when I applied for the job there."

"I never asked how you found them, so that's the story is it."

"It was during my interview, we just candidly talked. I told them where I was from and that my father was in the Canadian Armed Forces. Grandpa recalled that the people that adopted their granddaughter were a military couple somewhere in south eastern Ontario. I knew my mother's first name, that's all I knew of her and together we researched the adoption papers and well, it's a small word."

Monique continued the conversation by telling Kelly when she met her maternal parents. "I asked mom if she would help me find my mother and she did and my mother was willing to meet me. I was seventeen. She got pregnant at an early age, just fourteen and a half. She herself lived most of her life in foster care; hers was a very tragic story. Anyway I keep in contact with her by email because she lives in Manooth." Elizabeth, Mark and Patricia were intrigued with the stories told by the two sisters that brought them together with this family. George was preparing to welcome all to their festivities and to offer a blessing on the dinner. He stood at the head of the table as tradition would have it and Mary at the other end of it. He stood and the chatting quieted and he spoke. "Here we are all together finally and you look beautiful to Mary and me and through this year you have all made us proud because of your personal accomplishments. Most importantly you have helped one and other with growth and faith in God in your participation within the folds of our family circle. We welcome our guests with open arms and we trust that everyone has been acquainted with each other. Mary and I have had our meal catered to lessen the work load so that we can enjoy your company. I ask that he bow our heads together and give humble thanks for our food and may there be an abundance of love and charity and gratefulness for the many blessing given to us by our Heavenly Father. Let us pray."

As in many families, members catch up on news and the same was the event this day. Since Mark and Kelly arrived, no one had taken the leap to ask what their future plans were. Mark was still very apprehensive in talking about marriage. It saddened Mark a little because he knew that they were still very busy and he had large responsibilities. He loved her so very much and dreamed of their wedding day, whenever it was going to occur. Kelly announced, “Mark and I enjoy whatever time we can spend together, even if just for a half an hour. I’m always thinking of him and creative ways to get a chance to be together. Mark and I care very much for each other and are now promised to each other, this beautiful pearl ring confirms it. Everyone was thrilled and with the ice broken, Elizabeth sat quietly, tears in her eyes and her hands folded at the table. She sat in gentle realization of the token of their commitment. They weren’t going anywhere separately from here on. Kelly walked around the table to show everyone while desert was being served and the dinner dishes being cleared away.

“I love pearls and I don’t know how he would have guessed to buy me them and this is the most beautiful ring that I could imagine him giving me.” Kelly told everyone.

Mark said, “I chose pearls because they represent purity and softness.” Mark stood up and joined Kelly to display to the family their promise. Everyone knew that Kelly wouldn’t be alone and she and her partner loved to express their want of support at this time; yet he was taking his commitment to her one step at a time.

Chapter Eight

Christmas morning came very early, seven ten am. to be exact. The twins and Carol were the first ones up and everyone else just had to join and the whole family except for Elizabeth and Patricia were sitting by the Christmas tree waiting for George and Mary to sort through the packages to find that very package that belonged to one whose name was upon the tag. It was time for Mark to open one of the gifts from Kelly. It was in a box very tastefully wrapped with a large chiffon brown ribbon. He opened it carefully because his beautiful Kelly had wrapped it and inside the tissue paper was a hand knitted hat, scarf and matching gloves. "For Pete's sake Kelly, where do you find the time to do things like this?"

"Some nights I knit myself to sleep; it's very relaxing you know. It doesn't take very long to knit simple pieces and I knit very quickly."

"I love these, thank you; here is yours."

"Are you giving me another present? What is it?"

"Open it Kelly to see." She tore through the tissue paper inside the box and took out a great leather purse. "Look inside of it, there's more."

"Ok, well in this pocket I have found concert tickets; in here, Oh! It's a hundred dollar bill. This is getting good!" Kelly exclaimed.

"There's more."

"Ok, here is a coupon for a visit to the spa and one to Chapters Book store. These are really thoughtful gifts, I can use all of these and it will look like we are going to have our date to a concert finally. Mark, thank you very much." Just as everyone was finishing opening up their gifts, the doorbell rang. Kelly asked who was expected on Christmas morning.

George commented that it must be a surprise and he went out to the hall to answer the door. No one knew of any surprise or guest coming and they all just conversed among themselves wondering who was stopping by. George came into the room with the Childress's; they were passing by on the way to Port Hope to visit family. Port hope was about a ninety minute drive from Stirling. They wanted to surprise Kelly and meet all the Gerard's. They had met George and Mary but none of the others. Kelly was so excited to be able to show them her pearl band that her beloved Mark gave to her. Although Bob's first meeting with Mark was very abrupt, it was all water under the bridge and they now appreciated the happiness between Mark and Kelly. Kelly was delighted to see her grandparents and leaped from the floor to greet them and wanted to be the first to introduce them to her family. Grandma and grandpa I love you for coming to see us Christmas morning, what a surprise."

"Thank you dear, we love you too. We are on the way to see Cecil and Marie" Grandma told her.

"Cecil is still recovering from his pi-pass surgery and I want to be there with my brother in case this is his last Christmas." Bob added.

"We were going to miss you for Boxing Day, we totally understand though so we decided to pop in here and we brought you all gifts from the bakery." Grandma whispered into Kelly's ear with her sneaky little voice she uses, "We brought you some of our private stash Kelly."

"What, pumpkin pancakes?"

"We just brought the mix dear, a whole bucket full for you all to enjoy while you are here."

"Thank you dear grandma; mom you have to try these pumpkin pancakes, you can make them in the waffle maker too and they are heavenly."

Mom gratefully commented, "This is a wonderful thing you have done Mrs. Childress, it will be a real treat to lay out your candies and pastries later for desert." Mary kissed her on the cheek.

The room was filled with chatter and the noise of the children playing with their new toys. There was Christmas music playing in the background and Elizabeth and Patricia finally decided to join the rest. Patricia helped Elizabeth get ready to come down from the guest wing. She did her hair and make-up and they sang Christmas carols hoping to relax Elizabeth. She had a rough night; too much excitement the day before. She didn't tell Mark but she thought she would have to leave at one point and Patricia was with her the whole night to keep watch over her. Patricia promised that she wouldn't speak of it to prevent from worrying everyone. The Childress's brought Kelly a gift; it was a set of exquisite colored glass animal figurines. They had got them in Niagara Falls at a glass blowing shop and actually watched as some of them were being made. "Mark look at the glass figurines; what a very personal and thoughtful gift."

"They are an amazing keep sake gift, a family heirloom perhaps."

There lay six figurines tastefully wrapped in individual tissue papers tied with ribbon and placed in a colored wooden box. Kelly did not bring their gifts because they planned to visit her grandparents when they returned to Kingston. Grandma and grandpa, you're not going to believe this but Mark gave me this beautiful pearl band last night before dinner and I got to walk around the table to show every one, now I am thrilled to show you."

"Kelly, very good. It's perfect. How did he know you love pearls" Grandma warmly congratulated her. "Mark thank you dear for being so good to our girl here."

"Kelly makes my dreams come true. The perfect little pearls inlayed in the band represent security to me."

Grandma inquired what he meant by that.

"The pearls represent hopes, dreams, plans, love and the circle represents eternity; a plan for commitment and joy."

"I think that is marvelous, Kelly did you here that?"

"Yes I did, I guess he didn't have time to tell me that, I've just been captivated all weekend with him grandma and still he thinks of these romantic ways of describing our future. Mark and Kelly stood arm in arm before the people in the room as the newest addition to the family of love. Monique, Kelly, Sharon, Carol, Sheila and Cindy were the center of George and Mary's universe. Kelly was the second of their daughters to seek and find maternal family members of their pasts. Four years before, Monique inquired about her parent's whereabouts to ensure that there would be no chance of heredity health problems that she would pass on to her children. She found her birth records and her mother was Italian and her father was native Indian. In one year she found all that she needed to know and fortunately, there were no worries of congenital health problems.

She did discover though that her mother was in a prison. Her father is a lovely man and is married but has no children due to infertility problems his wife faces. Monique's contact with her father and his wife was a bitter sweet story for George and Mary; they now share their daughter with another set of parents. Their names are Chad and Maureen Brant. From the very beginning the Brant's did not want awkwardness to hinder their relationships between the two families so they keep in touch with Monique mainly by email and cards. They gave Monique their best wishes for a healthy family and are thrilled to know that Monique's daughter looks like the Brant family. Monique joined Kelly in telling their stories of being reunited with family members.

Sharron and Carol have no desire to seek and find their maternal family members although George and Mary never discouraged it even though it secretly worries them that they could eventually lose their girls. Most assuredly though their children love their mother and father more then they realize and they acknowledge the Gerard's as being their parents in all ways. Indeed Kelly's meeting was only by accident and it's not likely something that would happen to all the girls.

There were eighteen people to set around the breakfast table. Pastries, eggs, sausages, French toast, and juices spread across the table and filled the room with the most splendid aromas welcoming all in and perhaps seep outdoors through any possible way to allure anyone passing by to come in feast upon a Christmas morning meal and to fellowship. After and opulent morning, the Childress's had to be on their way and most of the family went outside to play in the snow. Kelly and Mark and Elizabeth went to the barn to brush the horses. Patricia played with the twins and their new snow toys. Mark was hoping the interaction with the horses would be therapeutic for his mother. Maybe if the horses would let Elizabeth brush them or take a carrot or apple from them, it would help to relax her and she may enjoy being away from her room. "There is just something about a horse' personality; shy and cautious yet sweet and willing to make happy" Elizabeth acknowledged.

"There you go Elizabeth, you are not afraid of them being giants either are you? They love to be brushed if you think you would like to do that."

"Just brush his chest there mom a bit, that won't be so hard for you to reach and only if you are not scared, he will sense it."

"These horses are beautiful, giant and gentle animals." Elizabeth was lost for words at the breath taking majesty of the Keidstale horses. The smile wouldn't leave her face as Mark escorted her back to the house and chatted candidly about the experience. He had left Kelly at the barn but told her that he would return. She had not seen the horses in months and wanted dearly to spend some time with them. Patricia joined her there while Mark was gone and Kelly welcomed her company so that she could show off her horses.

"I hope you are not afraid."

"Nope, they are giants though aren't they?"

"Yes they are but they are very tame. There are brushes with long handle in the corner to reach their shoulders and backs if you are strong enough and want to try to brush them."

"Oh I don't know Kelly, I think I would rather use a latter or maybe I'll just watch you."

"So how are you feeling?"

"Well I talked to my mom and dad in England, just got off the phone with them and they are going to send me enough money to stay in a motel because I don't know when I'll be able to get into the dorm room if I will at all. The police have still got it closed off and could be in there for another month. They have contacted lawyers and have found one with good experience and have made an appointment for me for a consultation on January fourth."

"That is really good news, they sound like they are on with the program."

"They are devastated really. You should here my mom, my gosh, she hasn't slept since I told her what happened and I'm worried about her. They are going to come home in a month hopefully as long as grandma will be comfortable with care givers. My dad has a temper and I wouldn't want him getting his hands on those two, they are better off in jail."

"Patricia if there is anything I can do to help you, you call me and I mean it. You are staying here with us until Tuesday right?"

"That would be nice thank you, but how about going shopping with me on Monday at the Boxing Day sales stores. I need some more cloths."

"You don't have to twist my arm Hun." Kelly laughed. "I got a bunch of gift cards from Mom and Aunt Barbara; I might as well make good use of them at the sales."

"Kelly Marley is stomping."

"She's just happy, keep brushing."

"The whole barn's shaking" The two women laughed just as Mark walked in to finish having some time alone with Kelly and the horses.

"Here Mark." Patricia passed him her brush. "You take over for me and help Kelly pamper the horses."

"How are you doing dear?"

"I'm feeling good Mark, just talked to my parents and they're doing all they can to help me from England. I just came in to tell Kelly."

"I'm glad for you Patricia that you have your parents support, everything is going to be fine just don't worry and take care of yourself." He hugged Patricia and she assured both of her good friends of her confidence for a happy ending to her ordeal. Then she left Mark and Kelly alone together.

Mark began to brush Marley as Kelly brushed Timber in the stall beside him. The horses were quiet and still while they listened to Mark and Kelly talk as if they were waiting patiently to here certain secrets being passed. "Let's give them a bowl of pellets, that's a reward for being co-operative."

"Are you kidding, there are pellets for horses?"

"Yeah sure; pellets are like candy to them, watch." Kelly bought over two very large metal bowls and dipped them into the barrels holding the treats; filled herself a bowl and one for Mark to feed the animals. "Here you go, jiggle the bowls and watch how exited they get."

Marley stomped and Timber nodded and snorted to hear the clanking of their treats. Mark and Kelly held the bowl way up to their mouths and they began chomping away at the treats like kids in a candy store, they even licked the bowls when they finished showing their approval and pleasure. Mark saw his love in a new light and wondered at what other surprises were in store for him as he got to fall in love with her over and over again. Kelly rubbed Marley gigantic nose and scratched her under her mouth much to Marley's pleasure given the snorts and whinny's she displayed.

"Will you whinny if I scratch your chin my love?" He wrapped his arm around her from behind and kissed the side of her head. There was music quietly playing in the barn and Kelly turned around to face Mark and they began dancing right there in the barn with those majestic beast as their enchanted audience. She laughed as he dipped her and picked her up in his arms and spun around with her three or four times before sitting with her on a bench.

"I wish I didn't have to leave this place Kelly, it's like paradise and then you are here with me in this seemingly make believe world. This place and everything about you is like a dream or a scene off a Christmas card."

"You just have to visit here in June; there will be flowers everywhere and the blossoms fall into the ponds and streams and the lawns are peppered with little violets and buttercups. There are swans that visit our ponds and the rabbits here are as thick as mosquitos. My sister's and I and our 4-H club planted flower gardens and perennials all over the property. The pool area is surrounded with fragrant lilies and sweet pea."

"Kelly, I'll see it in a dream that I won't want to wake up from and you are in it. I don't want Tuesday to roll around and pull me away from here and back into reality. You and I should stay here and walk hand and hand in this bliss."

"I'll be there Mark but really we'll take our memories of this special weekend with us when we go to Kingston and our minds can go back here any time we need to."

"We will need to, I have four or five more weeks of work to get the store open and I was thinking of asking Patricia if she would want to work there."

"She will probably be so busy with trying to finish school with these charges legging over her head and it may take months to get into court to get her matter dealt with."

"What about you my darling girl?"

"Well my good man, I'm only next door and I don't really know hardware even though I grew up here in rural Stirling. I could work in accounts receivable and be there to rub your shoulders after dealing with an irate costumer."

"The job is yours dearest." Mark said in hopeful jest. They put away the horse brushes and held hands as they walked out of the barn. The two in love walked through the snow around the property chatting about their schedules, both work and school and made plans that they had to make including some time for date nights. They promised each other to have more alone time then they have had in the past few weeks. They are still very cautious in the matter of their moral standards, the respect for one and others virtue is a top priority yet there is no rushing Kelly which is a decision Mark holds to. He wanted to have their relationship progress gradually so that there would be no pressure put on Kelly. In this he believed that a deeper love would evolve for them.

Chapter Nine

Tuesday morning came too quickly for Mark and Kelly. They and Patricia loaded up the car to take Elizabeth back home to Kingston. The family said their pleasantries and their goodbyes. Elizabeth was enlightened and rejuvenated by the good hospitality offered by the Gerard family. No one in their right mind could not have a festive and meaningful Christmas in that home, Mary handed Elizabeth a beautiful bouquet of flowers to take home for her room. It was received and such a lovey gesture. Patricia, grateful for all that Kelly had done for her, had tears in her eyes as she hugged the twin's goodbye. They took quite a liking to Patricia and she promised to keep the special card that they made for her. Patricia knew how it was with the little girls and about their special needs being that she was studying nursing. Although Patricia had a happy Christmas after all, she got a phone message that worried and confused her that she was to reply to by Thursday. She decided to keep it too herself and didn't tell Mark and Kelly until later when they got home. The three tried to make it a quiet restful ride home for Elizabeth. It was a ninety minute ride home and Elizabeth was due back at the rest home and they arrived there at about two thirty pm. Mark got her admitted and comfortable in time for afternoon tea. Some of the residents like to partake of a card game or watch some TV. before having a nap at about four pm. Elizabeth requested that a vase be brought to room for the flowers and had several photos that were already framed for her to place around her room from the lovely Christmas festivities. Mark left her with all her gracious memories to talk to the nurses about her health and then rejoined Kelly and Patricia for the short jaunt back to his house. It was still midafternoon and the three of them relaxed in the living room, unpacked their treasures and snacked on pretzels and potato chips. Patricia decided to talk to Mark and Kelly about the suspicious phone message she had received. "I have received a phone message from a lawyer representing Linda and she is looking for my help to get her bailed out of jail on Thursday morning."

Kelly is shocked and almost explodes. "She dared to ask you to bail her out?"

"Whoa, Kelly calm down dear, let's just listen here and help Patricia decide what to do about this situation." Kelly was acquainted with Linda and was absolutely shocked at her involvement in the scam.

"Linda is really a good friend and has asked if my parents would put up bail but there is no way in the world that I would dare ask it of them since I got caught up in her mess."

Kelly commented to Patricia. "I can't understand why oh why Linda would get involved in a scam and through away everything?"

"Linda's parents separated two years ago, which was six months after her parents passed away tragically in a car accident as they were hit by a drunk driver. Her mother went into a weird state of mind, took off with the inheritance and is divorcing her father."

"What?"

"Yeah, very tragic happening have befallen her family in recent months and have left Linda clinging to the end of her rope; she desperately needs money so she and Bonny arranged the scam. Linda regrets the crime and knows she has done it and that she will not be able to salvage her college career."

With concern, Kelly asked, "What does she expect you to do since you have your own problems now because of her that you need to sort out? You know that this is uncalled for and there are agencies available to those in her situation. She knew what she was doing." Kelly scorned about Linda for trying to reach out to Patricia of all people for help and expecting to get it.

"This was her first offence; she had no criminal record before this, not even so much as a speeding ticket. I am surprised too that she would consider asking me and my parents for help but there is nothing that I can do for her."

Mark was starting to realize the situation for what it was and he asked, "How much is the court asking to bail her out?"

"The lawyer didn't say; I don't think that will be determined until the day of the hearing, but I can see it being five or ten thousand dollars. I guess I'll just call the lawyer to tell him that I won't help her."

"I wonder if there is a chance for her to get a conviction that will be something other than jail time since it is her first offence." Mark commented.

"I don't know how the system works. It's too bad; she made the wrong choice here."

"Yes but people do strange things out of desperation and it sounds like her world had crumbled down around her." Mark said.

Unbelieving of his sympathy for Linda Kelly inquired, "Are you thinking of posting bail for her? You don't know her or what you are getting into."

"In hearing that she is very sorry for scamming that woman and that she is normally of good character, I may look into it. I think everyone is entitled to make a mistake in life and she has no support from her family. Maybe at least her character and conscience can be salvaged with the right encouragement."

"Mark, please, you can't be serious."

"This could be dangerous; a tricky responsibility on your part Mark." Patricia added.

"I hear of her bad misfortune, losing her grandparents tragically and being deserted by her parents and I feel nothing but sympathy for her plight. That could have been me if I didn't have my faith. Do you still have the lawyer's number; I could call him and leave a message with my phone number."

"Yes I saved the message; I'll retrieve it and give you the number. You don't have to do this because you want to be of charitable nature. She could have gotten assistance the honest way and she has chosen this path." Patricia commented.

"I know, more and more I'm starting to believe that you are both right but I'll just call the lawyer and leave him a message to return my call and I'll go from there." Mark did indeed call the lawyer and stated that he me be willing to post bail for Linda and would he call back with the details. Kelly was fit to be tied but just sat quietly and shrugged her shoulders at Mark. Questions lingered in her mind; did she know what she was getting into? Did she love Mark enough and know him well enough to carry on with the relationship? Would she be so very upset if she ended the relationship? Kelly was very unsure of everything now.

"Kelly I know you think that this is the wrong thing and dangerous for me to do. I know that we are already busy and there is mom to look after but I just have this very strong feeling Kelly that I should help this girl. I feel very sorry for her problems and I feel also that she is very sorry for what she has done, why else would she have called Patricia? I believe that she should have made the better choice but there was no one there for her except Bonny. Let's look into Kelly. I don't think that we will be sorry but I know that we will be blessed."

Thursday morning turned out to be a very mild and rainy day. Mark climbed out of the shower at seven fifteen am. and the news was on the TV. in his room. The hall light reflected on the TV. Screen and it exposed the steam billowing from the bathroom when Mark opened the door. In two hours he was to be in the court room for Linda's bail hearing. Mark had never experienced such a situation and he had no idea what to expect of it. He spoke briefly to Linda's lawyer the day before and was only directed to be in court at nine am.; bail would be accepted and there would be some papers to sign. As long as Linda did not break the law again he would be reimbursed the amount of bail he would pay. Patricia was comfortable in her hotel room until she could make other living arrangement or be able to return to her dorm room. Kelly planned to attend court with Mark for Moral support. She had never experienced anything like it either and was nervous for Mark. While he was dressing the phone rang; it was Kelly.

"Good morning Mark, I didn't wake you did I?"

"No Hun, I was just going to make some breakfast. I'm almost finished getting ready and I'm wondering if the lawyer missed telling me anything of importance. I am hoping she keeps straight and I don't lose my money. The lawyer said it would be up to the judge the amount of bail to be paid in her case."

"You know Mark; you don't have to go through with this just because you have already agreed to do it."

"I know Hun. I have prayed about it and I'm inspired to go ahead and help this girl because she has no one, I'm just nervous. You don't have to go but it would be good if you did because you know her and it will make the situation less awkward for us all."

"I can see that you really feel bad for her because she has no one. I'll go with you for support."

"I'll be there at eight thirty to pick you up Hun."

"Ok Mark, I'll see then. I love you."

"I love you Kelly." Mark went to the kitchen to pop some frozen waffles into the toaster and took a couple cups of yogurt from the fridge and made a cup of herbal tea. From the table he glanced at the pictures of he and Kelly that were stuck to the fridge. He was taken back to their Christmas holiday; Kelly promised that the photos would bring loving memories and the house was certainly quiet and lonely especially since it was raining which emphasized the pitiful silence. Kelly's abundant beauty carried him back to the bottom of the staircase after she playfully slid down the bannister into his arms. The cascading locks of her hair flouncing and brushing across his shoulders, her smile and the sweetness of her vanilla breath is the aroma he remembered and he closed his eyes to imagined being with her. Mark would have carried on with that thought but the sound of the toaster popping distracted him and stopped his romantic thoughts of his lovely Kelly.

Kelly was nervous that morning and she couldn't go out for a jog to release her tension. Yoga helped her relax a little after she was done talking to Mark on the phone. Kelly truly wished that Mark would ring her and say that she was right and he had changed his mind about posting bail. She climbed into the tub for a soothing hot soak and got ready anyway. The doorbell rang at eight forty; it was Mark there to pick her up to go to court. The court house was about a ten minute drive down town. Mark parked the car across the road and put enough change in the meter to cover two hours parking. They nervously walked across the road sharing an umbrella and kept their eyes straight ahead as they made their way through crowds who stood in front of the court house smoking cigarettes and pacing. “Mark that just gave me the most sickening feeling.”

“Oh I’m sorry, you don’t have to stay. You can take the car and go back home if you feel this uncomfortable. I mean, I don’t want you fainting or anything.”

“I don’t want to faint either but I don’t want you to stay here alone either. I’ll be alright; this isn’t exactly a cozy day at the spa is it? I’ll survive, I think.”

Mark and Kelly found the waiting room and looked for someone to tell them where to find Craig Solmes, Linda’s lawyer. They found the list that stated the names of the people with bail hearings and found Linda’s name. A duty counsel lawyer walked through the room and Mark was able to learn that Mr. Solmes would be right with him and to wait in interview room “c”.

“This place is a dank and grey looking place isn’t Kelly?”

“If it were not for scattered police officers walking in and out of here, I would think that this wouldn’t be a safe place and I would be right out of here.”

“I know, I think the people waiting here are also posting bail, some of them may even be bondsmen. At least we are sitting in here and away from the restlessness of the waiting room.” Just then a short man with red hair, and wearing glasses and a brown suit walked into room "c" and Mark stood up to greet him and shake his hand. Hello Craig Solmes, I'm Mark Scott and this is Kelly Gerard and acquaintance of Linda's."

"Pleased to meet you both thank you for attending today on Linda's behalf. This would have been her final hearing and without your willingness to post bail today, she would remain in jail until a court date would be scheduled."

Mark requested further information from the lawyer as he had never been in this position before. "Where is Linda right now?"

"She is downstairs in what they call the bull pit with the other prisoners."

"Do you know yet how much the bail will be?"

"That is up to the judge but I would think it will be about five to seven thousand. You must pay the court upon release; there will be papers for you to sign agreeing to be her surety. You will be responsible for her and she must not leave your home and if she dose—"

"Whoa! Whoa! Right there man."

Kelly gasped in disbelief. "What is this?"

"She has to stay at my house with me?"

The lawyer finally decided that he needed to clarify the conditions they are bound by when posting bail. "As surety you agree to be responsible for her at all times and she must live with you until a court date is scheduled. If she breaks her conditions, you must phone the police and you will lose your money. I'll give you a few moments to decide if this responsibility will be too much of a challenge."

"I only agreed to post bail, I didn't know she had to live with me, I can't—Oh my word—what am I—Kelly you will have to,—Oh no!"

"I'll give you both a couple minutes to talk. Court won't go in for another forty minutes."

Solmes left them startled and nearly unable to speak. "Mark what have we done?"

"I don't know; nothing yet. I can't have a woman other than family staying at my house with me. The elders would flip and I would risk being unordained."

"I don't really want her staying with me either."

"Oh no way is that happening. He clearly stated that she must remain in my home; I thought she would—Oh I don't know what I thought. I guess Solmes thought that I do this all the time and I know the procedure."

"You don't have to do this, we can leave right now, you know you don't have to feel guilty either Mark. No one told you about all this other stuff, let's just leave."

"Kelly, first let's pray about this. We'll leave it Gods hands." And so they did, Mark got down on one knee and they bowed their heads in humble prayer then sat quietly and waited for an answer as they held hands.

Amazingly after they had sat quietly for a few moments Mark received his inspiration. "Kelly I have a plan dear. I feel very strongly that we should go ahead, I'll post bail, she will stay at my house with you and I will stay at your apartment just for a few days and I will have a better solution very soon. You will be safe I promise you that. Will you agree to this dear?"

"Mark if you strongly feel that this is the answer, then yes of coarse I'll do it. Please tell me though; what do you think a better solution will be?"

"I am not sure yet, please trust me and trust in the Lord, he wouldn't steer us in the wrong direction. For now let's just take this one step at a time. We'll deal with this business first, I am so inspired Kelly."

"I'll do this but I am still very nervous I have to tell you."

"That's alright; you have the right to be nervous. Believe me though, she is regretting her mistakes and means us no harm. Linda is reaching out to us; we cannot turn our backs now." Mark and Kelly embraced as to comfort one another and to seal their decision most assuredly. Soon after Mr. Solmes entered the room and asked if Mark had made his decision, if so they needed to enter court room "a" and they should enter quietly as court will commence shortly. The lawyer then disappeared as if into thin air and Mark and Kelly were left alone to find their way to the court room to quietly have a seat and wait nervously for Linda's hearing. The benches were dark and grimy and the walls were grey and resembled bitter grey skies. The bench where the judge would sit seemed to be a thrown; all in all, it was a cold and hollow experience for them both. They sat holding hands and glanced repeatedly at each other because in the court room there was to be quiet. After about ten minutes of that, the judge entered the court room and everyone was asked to stand until the judge sat down. They later commented that it felt like they were on trial because of the seriousness of the atmosphere. Lawyers discussed the scheduled business at hand and decided who would be served first. It was not Linda's time and Mark and Kelly sat through seven hearings, some were not eligible for bail because of they had been charged with violent crimes. Finally Linda entered the room in handcuffs and was directed to the prisoner's block where she sat down. Kelly's heart pounded with nervousness at seeing a once respected student and acquaintance. She was wearing her civilian clothes that she wore at the time of her arrest. Linda looked around the room, she knew that Kelly and Mark were there for her and she caught a glimpse of Kelly. The court room had cleared considerably since the time for hearings was coming to a close. Kelly turned her head away in disgust. The lawyer took the stand for the fourth coming hearing of his schedule before the judge and Crown attorney. He stated Linda's charges, and the judge asked her to say her name. "Linda Lee" and "Yes your honor" is all she said as the judge read her the conditions of her release and bail order. The judge continued on and asked Mark to step forward and was asked if he understood his responsibility to court in agreeing to be Linda's surety, He answered yes and the judge set the bail at a staggering ten thousand dollars. Mark felt his face turn white and Kelly's jaw dropped to the floor. Linda was even shocked and was in disbelief but very relieved to have the bailiff unlock her cuffs while Mark and Kelly were escorted to the interview room to sign release papers and to endorse the cheque for ten thousand dollars. It was in that room that Linda would be left to Mark's supervision. Kelly remained very quiet while Mark and Linda discussed the arrangements that he and Linda made earlier and gave her the responsibilities that were expected of her for their assistance in her legal matters. Linda was relieved and grateful for their charity although Kelly was reluctant to believe it. After about twenty minutes of finalizing the agreement, the three left the court house together and it had stopped raining by that time and snow was melting. That tender blessing had broken the awkwardness of the day's events. Mark wondered if Linda was hungry as he was beginning to feel that way and lunch time had passed by hours ago. He decided to take the girls to a nearby diner for a bite and this would give everyone a chance to relax with each other. Kelly had been very quiet until Mark made the suggestion for a lunch break. She walked along side of Mark holding onto his hand while Linda humbly accepted the invitation and buttoned her coat as walked down the street to the Cozy Sinclair Avenue diner. They walked pass the car and luckily the meter maid had not reached the meter for it had expired. Mark added another two hours' worth of change and continued on walking to the diner and chatting among there selves. The three were seated, Mark and Kelly sat in a booth and Linda sat across from them in an arm chair. Linda suddenly felt alone and bewildered as she watched the loving couple across from her. She sat quietly and her eyes welled up with tears. Neither Mark nor Kelly noticed her emotions at that time because the server brought the menu and the two entered into small talk with her. Linda excused herself for a moment and got up from the table and went to the rest room. It was there that Linda could not contain her emotions; seeing the two of them together was not easy for her in her present state of affairs. She stood at the sink at tried to compose herself. She stood and looked into the mirror, partly in sorrowful shame but relieved that she had been released from custody. She grieved for her school work that was now null and void and for the family she knew to have once been close and looked out for each other in life. It all appeared to be gone, she had nothing now but these two people who were in a sense forced to care for her well-being. Once she had partially composed her feelings, she stood simply staring at the floor and Kelly walked in. "Linda I was concerned that some- thing happened to you. Forgive me for barging in on you; are you alright?"

"I'm fine now; I just suddenly had to be alone for a while. I guess I should go to the table and order something to eat."

"Yes come ahead and order whatever you like. It was a long morning wasn't it, we are hungry so you must be too."

"I'm not too hungry, I haven't had too much of an appetite you see but I would like a coffee."

"Well listen Linda just take your time, relax and have something light to eat, maybe some soup. You should eat three squares, especially in time of stress."

"Are you being my mom too or is that the nursing student coming out of you?" Linda was still half crying but managed to chuckle.

"Ok pull yourself together, it doesn't matter who is doing the talking, it's the truth, now let's go and order some food and don't worry about the bill." The two women joined Mark and there was juice and menu waiting for them at the table. Linda took Kelly's advice and did order soup and a turkey sandwich. Then they chatted. Mark had to explain the living arrangements to Linda and the reason for it.

"Linda you will live in my house but since I am an elder in the church I cannot have a women living with me. Kelly will stay in my house with you and I will stay in her apartment until I can think of a better arrangement."

"I know that this situation has made it difficult for all of us and I'm sorry for it." Linda replied.

"It's ok, I was inspired that I should help you and I also did it for personal reasons. It will work out for you, I know it will and I don't think there will be a problem with you obeying the conditions of your bail."

"Oh no, you don't have to worry; I'm regretting every minute of being involved in the scam. It's all a blur to me right now but I can't believe I let myself be manipulated. I was just so desperate for money. What other living arrangements could you come up with?"

"Mark, are you thinking of bringing your mom home permanently?" Linda inquired.

"No, she is getting better with every passing day and a big part of her recovery has occurred since you came into our lives but she isn't ready for full release. I have got some other ideas that I'm working on and I'll run them by you later Kelly."

"Is there a chance that you will be able to get into your dorm room to get your clothes?" Mark asked Linda.

"I don't know." She stammered almost unable to breathe while trying to answer him. Linda was obviously traumatized by the experience. Now it felt to her like everything was gone and she buried her face into her hands and cried uncontrollably.

"Oh Linda I'm—" Mark couldn't finish and Kelly helped her to her feet and walked with her into the ladies room where she could help her get composed.

"Linda I'm sorry, Mark didn't mean to upset you, and he is a very caring man and wants you to feel better; he just wants to do everything right. Don't worry about it, he will inquire and in the meantime, I'll find you some clothes to wear, ok?" Linda really felt sick and the horror in her facial expression told Kelly everything about her feelings. She knew then that this person had really come out of a desperate situation and thanked God that Mark was inspired to step forward and take charge the way he did. Kelly realized that she must not be afraid to be a friend to Linda and a help mate to Mark in this matter. It was the charitable thing to do for Linda and for God. From that moment forward Kelly was not skeptical about helping her.

"Linda, maybe we'll just get you back to Marks house and get you settled in so you can rest, you need it right now."

"Ok thank you." Was all Linda could stand up to say.

By the time the girls got back to Mark he was waiting quietly and had the server pack up their food to take home and then they all left the diner. They arrived at Marks house; he let the girls out of the car and told them he had to go to the hardware store for a little while. He told them to make there selves comfortable and go ahead and eat their take-out food without waiting for him. That was only an excuse. He was really going to the jewelry store to pick out a diamond engagement ring to give to Kelly as soon as he could. Yes that was his plan. He wanted Kelly's hand in marriage and now it was to be for absolute sure. He couldn't hold it off any longer. First thing was to buy a ring and the next was to call her father; announce his intensions and ask for his daughters hand in marriage, then to the florist for a dozen long stem red roses gift boxed and tied with a golden ribbon. He was so excited that he forgot the reason that he had to speed up his intensions and it seemed like it took forever to get to the jewelry store. It was the very store where he bought her Christmas present, the pearl band. The jeweler remembered Mark and questioned if the ring was to her liking. "Kelly is wearing the ring now and pearls are her birth stone as well as her favorite jewel but a diamond for my love is what brings me here today. There are recent events that have led up to my speedy decision for a proposal of marriage and I need to marry Kelly as soon as possible."

"Oh how lovely when is the baby due?"

"OH heavens no baby, that is not the reason for my proposal." Mark was shocked but after thinking about what he just said he could imagine how one would be led to think that a baby is on the way. "I didn't want to push Kelly and we are both very busy, too busy to plan a wedding but everything is leading into it all of a sudden so it has to be. I love her so very much, rather we are in love with each other and working on a strong marriage with Kelly is the best opportunity for both of us. Now if I may see that ring in the shape of a flower and the heart shaped diamond; I will get on with my decision and proposal to my lovely Kelly."

"Yes sir, these are marvelous choices, this heart shaped diamond is a total two karat weight and the brilliance is third on the scale of clarity in platinum setting selling for $6,689.00 and is guaranteed for life. The flower is matched with its own band as a bridal set in yellow eighteen karat gold, total weight is 2.6 karat weight and selling for $7,228.00 for the set; again with exquisite clarity and quality. Both are lovely choices and I'll give you a moment to decide if you wish."

"That's very good, thank you but I'm in favor of the flower set. It's what I think suits Kelly the most between the two. I thank you and please wrap this set up, I'll take it today."

"Congratulations, if there are any questions about the rings or concerns, please come in and talk to us. I'll gift wrap it immediately and I wish you and your Kelly the very best,"

"Thank you." Mark responded quietly with relief then as nervousness took over he imagined in his mind how he was going to speak to her father. Everything had moved so quickly the past couple days but he never recounted the reasons for his quick decision. All of his heart was in the right place and would make Kelly his bride as soon as possible. After a few moments the jeweler handed him the intricately wrapped box, he thanked her with Visa and left to go sit in his car and pray that he could reach George Gerard before searching for the nearest florist. He could hardly wait to get home to his Kelly and arrange the perfect proposal of marriage. Mark was grateful that George answered his cell phone. He had given Mark his number guessing that he would need it in the very near future.

"George, its Mark calling."

"I know it is and I can only guess for sure the nature of this call."

"Oh really?" Mark laughed nervously.

"Yes Mark." George answered graciously. "I guess we need to talk about your intensions with my daughter except I didn't expect the call to come so soon after our last conversation."

Mark explained the situation with the court conditions and he and Linda having to live under the same roof alone. "Kelly has been wonderful throughout this whole ordeal; understanding and supportive when she had every opportunity and right to turn away and she didn't. She truly understood and made herself flexible when it really wasn't fair to her. None of this was fair to her and we truly are in love with each other, and can't bear to be away from each other any longer anyway."

"I know that in my heart and I wish you success in your proposal and I give you my daughter's hand in marriage Mark." Those words rung out to Mark like a song of the heart, pure sincere and beautiful and most of all, true.

"Thank you George with all my heart I thank you. Now one more thing, it's now Thursday and we need to be married as soon as possible like early next week. I guess the earliest would be Tuesday and I can make the call to the temple myself if you could arrange to prepare Kelly with the Temple ready classes, we would be well under way to be getting married." There was a pause, still and quiet as if Mark had fallen into and eternal black whole.

"So soon Mark?"

"Yes, I know it's awfully short notice but if she agrees George which I believe she will—all in all I know that the present situation has led us to this choice, I am so inspired that it's the right choice for us both." Mark stammered.

"Wow! Let her mother and I know what you two are doing as soon as you can. Please!"

"George I don't think you have to worry about that, Kelly will be on the phone to you in the same breathe it took her to say yes."

"Ok—well—I'll talk to Mary now and wait for your phone call. Good afternoon Mark."

"Oh boy, that took him back a bit" Mark mumbled to himself. He sat and closed his eyes and laid back his head on the seat rest in hopes that Mary would be less taken back by the urgency of his proposal. As he sat silent to catch his breath, he wondered what just happened that day. Christmas just got over and he and Kelly just nicely got over the first awkwardness of their relationship by meeting her family and by giving Kelly the promise ring. Now he wanted to offer her an eternal marriage. There was no turning back, which was only a momentary fear, of course not. He was to propose to his lovely Kelly whom he felt had been missing from his life for a long time. With a ring as a betrothal, Kelly's father's blessing and now to purchase a dozen red roses, Mark was prepared. There was a flower store in site, he parked the car and entered Greenley's Florist in loving hopes of finding red roses as fresh and beautiful as his own flower waiting at home who unaware of the blessing to be porn upon her. Mark beckoned the florist to pick the most perfect roses for they were to offer his heart. On the card he wrote this.

To my dearest Kelly

Today I offer you my heart.

Except these roses and remember

This day of our engagement

For Eternity

Love, your Mark

He closed his eyes and sighed at the thought of Kelly reading this card. He knew that it wasn't perfect timing but their connection and bond was. He felt no apprehension nor did he believe that she would. They had a lot of planning and work to do in a short period of time and decided he better not stand there any longer. Mark returned to his car and before going to meet his bride to be with his gifts of engagement, he decided to call her first. "Hi Kelly, are you able to get Linda settled in and comfortable?"

"She is understandably uneasy, mostly I think because she feels she is imposing. She did eat her soup and is having a cup of hot chocolate right now and watching TV in the den."

"Ok I hope she will be able to relax soon. I have to talk to you alone; I'm coming home right now if you could meet me in the sun room."

"Sure Hun, I'll be there. How far away are you?"

"I'll be there in probably ten minutes."

"Ok I'll see you when you get here." They each hung up both smiling at the anticipation of seeing one and other again. She told Linda she would be in the sunroom for a while with Mark and she sat and waited listening to some songs of the season and glancing through an "O" magazine. It had been less than ten minutes when Mark popped his head in the door with the boxes at his side and closed the door behind him so that he could have this special time alone with his love. What he saw when he entered the room was Kelly with her legs crossed, her black hair laying over one shoulder, her petit frame enhancing the beauty of the yellow wicker high back chair she sat in. Her eyes were fixed on him alone and her smile left the whole room in a certain glory as to admit that her love had entered in. Mark couldn't have asked for a finer moment to bend down on one knew before her and place his love in her hands.

"Kelly my dearest Kelly, I've brought you these flowers and oh—I can hardly speak, I'm sorry. They are the most red and lovely flowers in the world at this moment because they are for you. Open the box please so I can see if they match your beauty."

"Mark you are giving me red roses? I know it's been a hectic day but you really didn't have to buy roses for me but I'm glad you did." Tears welled up in her eyes as if she knew what was coming next. She spent no time opening the box and tenderly picking them out of the box and laying them across her lap. "They are Mark, the most beautiful roses I have ever laid my eyes on. Thank you so much, I love you so very much darling." And she rested her head on his shoulder when he gently caressed her face. She shyly sat back as if to wonder if there was something to come next. Then beginning to wipe her tears away while clutching her bouquet, Mark asked her to open the next gift.

Trembling she whispered, "Mark I love you and I can't believe this is happening." She untied the beautiful gold ribbon and lifted the top off of the box and found within another box, purple satin safely tucked in velvet inlay. Mark and Kelly held hands as she slowly opened the second box and she shuttered with love and excitement. Their hearts pounded in unison, nearly pounded from their chests and her tear filled eyes strained to see what glistened there in the tiny box. Kelly took the diamond ring from the box and Mark took it, placed it on her ring finger and asked her to marry him.

Yes Mark, Oh dear yes, I'll marry you and be your wife for eternity, please yes."

"I love you so dearly Kelly."

"I love you Mark, thank you so very much. The ring is more than I could ever dream of having. You are more to me and your love is a dream come true for me and the roses, the roses are fantastic." They embraced and both released their emotions in gentle sobs and sighs holding each other and the gentleness of the moment cradled them as they were bestowed with the tender grace of love. The two sat for the longest moment admiring the ring on her finger and Mark requested that they marry early next week and arrange to attend the temple ready classes on the weekend. They would buy the marriage license on Monday and phone the temple right away to set the date hopefully for Tuesday.

"This is such whirlwind decision; I hope I can pull it off. I know I still have another two weeks off from school and I suppose we could plan a small reception for the weekend at my parents' house."

"We would like a week for a honey moon. How would you like to go to Lake Louise?"

"Would we stay at an inn or a cabin?"

"I thought we would stay in our very own cabin."

"That would be even greater, oh my, pinch me so I know I'm not sleeping, please."

"You are not dreaming my love and either am I?"

"I have to call my parents Kelly reported."

"They already know, I phoned your father directly after buying your ring and he told your mother."

"I'm a little nervous now but I appreciate that you considered that Mark, It was a beautiful gesture. Thank you. I'm going to call home and get started on our wedding plans."

"Ok dear I'm right here with you and anything you need is yours." She dialed her parents number and texted a picture of her diamond ring to her mother's cell phone.

"Mother hello. Where are dad and grandma and the girls? I have news, the greatest news you could ever wish to hear from me."

Her mother told her, "George already told me about it and to get ready for a whirlwind. I want Mark and you home this evening so get packed up right away. The pastor has already been notified and the temple booked for Tuesday at six pm. You can buy the marriage license in Stirling and George and President Cassidy will teach you the Temple ready classes. We must be at the temple by one pm to participate in the preparatory steps to being sealed in the temple. Your father and I will take care of all the other arrangements too."

"Mother, talk about whirlwind. You have been doing a lot of fancy dancing in what has been less than an hour."

"Yes dear I know, you certainly surprised us, so surprise, I don't mess around. We should be at the temple earlier than one pm. so we can get you a dress and all the other necessary apparel needed. Major Bonder is going to be your photographer and Childress's already have the cake in the oven. Monique is making the flowers and I have some dresses on the way for us to pick out for your sisters, they will be here about eight pm. tonight so you see, you need to get here as soon as you can dear."

"Mother, I can't get a word in edgewise. I know you are never lost for words but how have you done all this in one hour?"

"Kelly never mind, just get off the phone and both of you high tail it home. The caterers will be here at nine pm to go over the menu with us. There will be a light reception at the chapel after pictures are taken. I'm just sorry we couldn't book a sealing room for earlier in the day so pictures will have to be taken indoors. Hurry dear get on your way. I love you dear we all do; we'll see you when you get here."

"Mark I'm just stunned."

"I know Kelly; you are a certain shade of pale right now. I could hear everything your mother was rambling on about. I guess we just need to bring ourselves and get married."

"I am so stunned at mother, if she could just snap her fingers to get us there at this moment she would do it."

"Well listen you just relax here for a few minutes and I'll go and tell Linda what's happening and when you are ready I'll take you to your apartment to pack some things and we'll go."

"Oh I'll go with you, it isn't going to do mother any good if I am sitting and staring into wonderland."

"Ok my dear, I believe she is in the den."

Chapter Ten

"Hi Linda how are you feeling right now?" Kelly asked with womanly concern.

"Oh I don't know what to think or where to start to redeem myself or how to fix this mess I am in. I know that my whole future is uncertain now. I can't think, my thoughts are muddled together and I feel like hiding but I can't run anywhere." Linda looked up at the two of them and saw that they were both beaming brightly. She noticed the diamond on Kelly's finger and couldn't recall if it had been there earlier in the day. Linda felt even a deeper imposition on this household and she moaned. "Oh excuse me, I don't mean to darken you're your day or rain on your parade or—."

"Hey Linda you have no need to feel unwelcomed or desperate, take this slowly and try to calm down, we are here to help you."

"Yes she is right Linda. This is not an imposition or a hand out, please try not to be afraid to except help from us. Help is what you need at this time and we will help you with whatever problem you are having."

"Well I guess I'm thankful but like I said my thoughts are muddled right now, anyway it looks like you two have some good news."

"We have come to discuss some spur of the moment decisions we have made with you." Kelly continued. "Will you come with us to Stirling to my parents' home?

We are getting married Tuesday and that's the other arrangement that Mark had in mind at the diner. It was only a matter of a little bit of time and it was inevitable that we would marry, we are speeding things up as a convenience to our situation we are faced with here."

"You want me to go away with you after what I've just been through? I barely know you Kelly and I've never met Mark. Can it be arranged that I just stay here alone until you get back? I don't feel like going anywhere, I can't get to my dorm to get cloths and I have nothing."

Kelly and Mark didn't think of her reservations about being juggled around so soon after being released from jail or her state of mind. Kelly felt remorse for Linda and she wanted some time alone to talk. "Mark will you call Mom and Dad and tell them we'll be there in a while, Linda and I are going to talk."

"You've got it Kelly take your time." Kelly sat down with Linda and Mark kissed her on top of the head and she reached out for his hand and held it to her cheek before he walked away. Linda was still looking forlorn and off to the side as Kelly began to speak, she quietly listened and responded when she felt it was necessary.

"Kelly we are here for you, I know it's hard right now for you to realize it right now but when you get a better grip on yourself I know that your feelings will lighten up."

"It was kind of you to help; really I want you to know I appreciate it. The place I never thought I would be is in trouble."

"Don't worry about showing us gratitude but you are most welcome. I'm praying that your consequences will not be as severe as you are probably thinking they will be. I would like you to except our understanding—."

"Have both of you ever been arrested and been in jail? Have either of you lost loved ones closed to you and do either of you know abandonment? I can't just rise to your joyous occasion Kelly, please just ask the court if I can stay here alone for a few days. I won't steel anything from you; I just want to be alone."

"Oh dear Linda, I have to tell you about the tragic death of Marks father and uncle and the devastation it's caused for Mark and his mother. They left Alberta mainly because the community turned their backs on them during a murder investigation. The main reason he stepped forward to pay your bail was because he could have been in your shoes. He understands only too well what tragedy and abandonment can do to a soul. Now about me, I am one of six adopted children in one family. I have had a good and loving upbringing but I have my story to tell too. You see, we are reaching out to you in your time of need. There is plenty of room in my parents' home; you don't have to be surrounded by people. Marks mom will be in the guest wing too there are four rooms and you will be comfortable in there. Elizabeth is quiet and won't bother you. There are plenty of clothes there and you are about the size of my sister Carol and we can get you anything else you need before we leave."

"Well I suppose if you put it all out like that I guess I can go with you and make the best of it."

"As far as anyone else in the family knows you are a guest of ours, you never know Linda you may find some relaxation that you need and your mind will be more at ease so that you can think of how better to cope."

"I could use a long hot soak, is there a tub in Marks house?"

"Is there? There's only a shell shaped jaquozi, the shelf is stocked with bubble bath and I'll get you some warm towels and a bath robe. Come to think of it, Elizabeth is quite tiny and there will probably be something of hers that you can wear for now. You take your time and I'll light some candles in there for you."

"Well sounds nice, candles and warm towels. Are you sure you won't leave me here for the weekend?" The two laughed and Kelly was relieved that she had been able to reach Linda and bring her out of that grey fog. She met up with Mark again while she was in Elizabeth's room picking out some cloths for Linda to wear.

"Your Mom wants us there by eight pm. Is that possible Kelly?"

"Oh sure, that gives us lots of time and Linda will be fine."

"Sure she will Kelly, you work your magic with people; you did with Patricia and mom and with me. You never stop amazing me and I love you so thoroughly. You are an angel, my angel. You bless the lives of all who know you and I can just imagine how our children are going to look at you."

"If they look at me with as much love in their hearts as you do I'm the one who is blessed."

"Kelly the future is ours, no more me myself and I, it's you and I together. My wife."

"My husband. Us."

"The two of us." Their eyes were fixed to one and others gaze and the eternal purpose engulfed them in an unbreakable bond of love sent from Heaven. Mark held her in his loving arms which were always open to her and he cared to fold the length of them around her tiny frame. He stroked her hair so that it fell to her back then brought it back to rest on her shoulder the way it was. Once he had his eyes focused on her beauty, she held his attention in the longest of gazes especially when they were alone like they were. The softness of her almond shaped brown eyes which were framed with fern like lashes, her satin skin shone through billowing accolades of porcelain strands of soft gleaming hair. He loved her with a fierceness that privately took all of his strength for control because it was her trust in him that he would not jeopardize. He would not find himself looking at his dear Kelly as a temptation because her angelic beauty was matched with her loyalty to her covenants with the Lord.

"Kelly I am going to pack for myself while we wait for Linda."

"Sure I'll make us a sandwich with hopes that she'll be done within a half hour and we'll be on our way."

Mark made arrangements with his mother to be picked up at the rest home on Monday morning. The three of them arrived at Kelly's parent's house at about seven fifteen pm and as promised; Linda was introduced as a good friend from school. George and Mary knew the situation and promised that Linda would have no need to feel uncomfortable and wish them all three of them the best in whatever they had to do in Linda's matter. As was foretold, Mary had taken control of the wedding arrangements and the wedding cake was already baked at Childress's bakery and was cooling off so it could be decorated in the morning. The girls had the great room set up with tables and were preparing and sorting flowers and ribbons and tewl. Monique makes wonderful bridal flower arrangements for all of her friends as well as for her sisters. When Kelly entered the room Monique was busy designing the bridal basket. The little girls, Cindy and Sheila were playing with some colored tewl and lacey gloves to pretend with besides given a little job to do by folding all the table utensils in napkins. The florist just left with their work order, the caterer was on the way and the dresses arrived at seven fifty pm. Several racks of designer dresses fit for a princess were for Mary's girls to marvel at. Aunt Barbara and grandma had little pinwheel sandwiches and pastries with tea all prepared as snacks for everyone. Linda actually began to relax during all the fun and girl talk and soon realized that one doesn't get away with feeling miserable in the Gerard home with its atmosphere, busy and hospitable in the most delightful way. People who visited there were made to feel like royalty. Linda with her problems and trauma was no exception. She ate so much and soon fell asleep in a big arm chair in spite of all that was happening there in the next room. A wedding was being arranged in the great room and it beheld quite an enchanting picture to the neighbors and friends who showed up to bring gifts and well wishes for Kelly and Mark. The evening had turned into a bridal shower for Kelly and she couldn't imagine how in such a short time, fifty six women could get together, go shopping and wrap gifts to bring her. Mary was running around like some kind of robot; signing work orders, paying them, greeting guests and visiting with guests but loved every minute of the occasion. This was her time to shine in her daughter's eyes and oh how she loved being mother to those six girls of hers. It was such an impromptu evening that extra food had to be ordered in. Some of the women brought food but Stirling had the best pizza parlor in Ontario and chicken wings and pizza were on the menu. There were seven punch bowls being continually filled. People brought their children and the twins had enough company to hold a pajama party and little tents and air mattresses were being setup in the loft. The children invented their own little tea party and entertained as kings and queens so only royalty were invited. This evening in the Gerard household was of course like another scene from a Norman Rockwell painting and by one am. Friday morning; all the guests had either left or found a corner somewhere and snuggled into a sleeping bag. There were no dishes to do, just a lot of paper plates and plastic cutlery to through away which simplified the tidying up for those in charge and the garbage bags taken to the garage and floors swept. Mary and George then got the family together in the living room to discuss the plans and designated jobs for everyone to do the next day.

They hugged all of their children and bid them a very good night's sleep. Soon the house was blessed with peace and sweet dreams and outside the snow fell gently and blanketed the ground while the outside lights caused the fresh snow to glisten under their glow. The stillness of the night was broken only by the soft glow through the foggy barn window and inside Marley and Timber stirred. That night five inches of snow would replenish what the mildness and the two day rain took from the earth. Soon enough it was seven am. and Mary, Aunt Barbara and grandma met in the kitchen to start the morning biscuits and bacon and pancakes, to put on a large pot of hot chocolate for the eager guests. The three women worked like a well-oiled engine in the kitchen and it wasn't until the stack of pancakes were made and set in the warming oven that there was a peep made from either of them; just gentle humming. "Mary, that young guest of Kelly's is a quiet one" Noted Grandma.

"Yes isn't she strange though? She hardly spoke a word all evening but ate like she hasn't seen food for days." Replied Aunt Barbara.

"I don't exactly know what her story is, just that she is a friend to Kelly and they are helping her with some sort of private situation. I think she will be either staying with them or taking over Kelly's apartment. Anyway whatever they are doing for her is the reason they brought her here for the weekend and we are hoping she will feel welcomed and able to lighten up socially."

"Mary you must be exhausted, you go back to bed for a couple hours and we will cover your tracks." Grandma urged.

Marry laughed out loud. "You have to be kidding; President Cassidy will be here at noon until four in the afternoon to assist George in Kelly's temple prep class and the Childress's will be here today."

"Will they be decorating the cake here?"

"Yes Barbara I believe so. They need to match the color of the icing with the flowers and have the cake ready to transport in pieces to the chapel."

"Barbara will you prepare a cheese platter and perhaps cut up some apples to put alongside of the pancakes. I'll check on the little ones, nine kids stayed here last night and what wonderful little kids they are; all of them."

"Mary it just seems funny to me, this girl shows up and all of sudden Mark and Kelly are getting married." Grandma commented mischievously.

"This house hasn't seen this much action since we held the district 4-H club meeting five years ago."

Mary was really trying to get Aunt Barbara and grandma side tracked and off the subject of Linda's presence. "I remember Grandma; how could we forget one hundred and eighty eleven to fourteen year old girls in one yard. My goodness I still wake up hearing giggling." Mary boasted.

"Now be careful with the knife will you, cut up the apples not your fingers Barbara. I'll go now and check on everyone to see who is up, we have to get the day started." Monique and Carol were already in the great room working on the flowers and Linda sat with them watching their nimble fingers put beautiful flowers in wonderful arrangements.

"Good morning girls; Linda how are you?"

"I'm doing ok Mary; I haven't slept so well in days. You have a wonderful home here; I am pleasantly impressed on how well you have pulled together these wedding plans. I don't know how to make flowers but can you think of anything I can help you with?"

"You can come to the dining room and have your breakfast; come on girls and eat. You come back here when you're finished with breakfast. Has anyone else stirred upstairs?"

"I'll go up and check Mary." Linda offered.

"Good tell everyone to get up, the day's half over." Eventually everyone had sauntered to the dining room for a scrumptious breakfast and to enjoy what morning had to offer; the pancakes, the fireplace with its roaring fire and windows which framed the basic blue sky against the pure softness of the snow; the smell of the hot syrup and the chocolate waffling through the corridors for the wonderful company and the joyous spirit that brought the family together round the table that morning. George returned home at ten thirty am. and brought Major Bonder who was an experience photographer and was available to volunteer to take the wedding pictures on such a short notice. He came to meet Mark and show him and Kelly some of his sample photos to choose from. As military men go, they are usually large, strong and clean cut of course, he was dressed in his uniform handsome and authoritative which made Linda stand up and take notice, it curled her hair. Kelly noticed her reaction as soon as she laid eyes on Ted Bonder. Linda was so smitten she stood right up next to Mary and Barbara as they flipped flat jacks for George and Ted. Linda served Ted herself and forgot all about George. Ted was a single man and welcomed the attention.

"Look at Linda go! She's feeling better" Kelly laughed impressed by the sight.

"My goodness he is a giant beside her but he seems to be enjoying her advances" Mark and Kelly were astonished.

"Can you believe that, Mark she's stroking his hair!"

"You better go get her" Mark is now laughing out loud at the sudden change in Linda and her boldness. Instead, Mark walked over and began talking to Ted about his cameras because the last thing Kelly and Mark needed was their photographer being stolen away for the weekend by Linda. Apparently she had asked him if his buzz cut was as bristly as it looked and Ted invited her to find out for herself. It was a perfectly innocent gesture but Linda had been so withdrawn and unwilling to lighten up until Ted Bonder walked into the house. There were obvious sparks between them but there would be no chance of them disappearing together.

"It looks like Linda is able to relax and have a good weekend after all." Mark was glad for that and was very surprised at her forwardness.

"Ted is not that much older than her, I think he is in his early thirties, they look funny together though. He is standing about six feet four inches and she is all of five feet two inches."

"Do you see how he is flirting with her? He is putty in her hands." Mark jokingly scoffed about his seeming authoritative presence.

"So let love take its course; it's the perfect time for it with all this love in the air. The courts can't stop Linda from falling in love."

"Kelly let's get some poses picked out before he carried her off onto cloud nine." After a brief introduction, Ted, Mary, Kelly and Mark and Monique looked at photo samples.

"I have seventy poses for you to choose from and feel free to make your own suggestions." Ted offered.

"I'm thinking of starting off at home here using a back drop and soft lighting." Mary suggested.

"As you can see the Christmas tree is still standing so we'll need some done by the tree later tonight. I can't wait to see the wedding pictures though, we are having red carnations and holly and berries in the bouquets' so we'll have to have a few pictures taken out doors for contrast with the snow and the red and green in the flowers."

"Mary it will be a long drive to the temple, will there be enough time to take pictures that morning?"

"George is having us flown that morning to Brampton and it will only take about thirty minutes to get there."

"It is amazing how you can make so many arrangements in such a short time; can you pull a rabbit out of your hat?"

"Well Mark like I said yesterday, you two didn't give us a lot of warning so that's what all the fancy dancing is about around here."

"Thank you Mary, with all my heart I thank you. You won't be disappointed in me as a son in law. I'm going to make it up to you for all the rushing around you have done for making our wedding day possible."

"Mom I know that it's going to be the perfect fairy tale wedding that I have always dreamed of."

"That surprises me dear; you never seemed to show any interest in relationships even when I was planning Monique's wedding you just seemed board with it all."

"Mother Kelly was usually too busy with the 4-H club, school and her crafts to care much about weddings." Monique remembered. "I did have fun, I just had so much else to do but I'm learning to show enthusiasm in the interest of others."

"Mary Kelly is one of God's favorite daughters. She is a natural in the nurturing of other's needs. She simply needed the opportunity placed before her to prove her abilities."

"It is because of her enthusiasm that she has learned to do all that she dose and she perfects her skill in everything she dose. I agree with you, yes she is one of God's favorite daughters because she uses her talents to help others; she is an exemplary young women to all who know her. Kelly my dear girl, you are going to be the best nurse in Canada once you graduate this spring and start working."

"Mother thank you. I can't believe that four years has passed and I will have a registered nurse degree."

"You must be so proud of such a great accomplishment dear, you know that your father and I are proud of you dear and you have been such a help to Elizabeth."

"Kelly has been the angel sent to us. We suspect Mother will be released from the home within weeks now. She actually gets restless when she has to go back; it used to be a relief for her. She used to feel more secure in the home then being out in public. Kelly has helped to change all those feelings around for her and I'm so grateful to Kelly for it. I love her incredibly; I never knew what love was before this, I'm sure of what it is now."

"All this talk about me is embarrassing but keep it going all day if you both wish to." Kelly blushed.

"What time will the dress be here mom?"

"I'm not sure, Monique what time did Marie say she would have the dresses here?"

"It won't be today. They originally wanted to have them here on Sunday but I told her that wouldn't be possible. Marie will be here first thing Monday morning. The seamstresses will be working on the alterations non-stop until Monday's delivery; that's cutting it close but I realize the whole arrangement is going to be a task and a half and if we pull this thing off we should go into the wedding planning business."

They all laughed but what a great idea. They entered into the living room for refreshments. Ted and Linda also joined them and much to Kelly's surprise she learned that they already know each other. Ted and Linda have mutual friends and have attended several of the same parties. They were not close by any means but seemed to be hitting it off quite famously. He did not know yet of her pending difficulties with the law. Mark and Linda were only happy to see her enjoying herself and relaxing even if it was just for the weekend and decided that he didn't need to know unless she wanted to tell him. Aunt Barbara and Grandmas performed their usual magic with lunch. They served lots of herbal tea, punch, mini quiche and stuffed mushrooms, peppers and salad with sandwiches; for desert, a bounty of fresh fruit and cheese. George was soon expected home shortly with President Cassidy to begin the first session of Kelly's temple ready classes. Every other plan was under control and it was time to socialize. Ted and Linda chatted about their mutual acquaintances and how their paths never managed to cross so they could never get well acquainted at the parties they attended.

"Linda I've had a nice time chatting with you and I have some spare time here and there; I would like to spend some time with you now that we have a chance to so after the wedding is over I would like to make a date with you. I have always regretted that the opportunity never seemed to arise."

"Yes sure. I don't know where you find the time for socializing what with your responsibility to the forces but I would enjoy some time spent with you."

"Do you have a flexible schedule? I'm afraid I don't, I have to just take the free time when I can get it."

"Um, well don't worry about my schedule; here is my cell number. Call me Ted when you find it convenient." Ted was quite taken with Linda's fun personality and pretty appearance. The interest she had in him fueled his interest in her. Ted didn't even bother to ask personal questions for example about, what she did for a living or what association she had with Kelly and Mark. He just liked her because she was fun and pretty. She was a breath of fresh air and she gave him relief from the regimental responsibilities of his rank in the forces. As a civilian he was a teddy bear type, someone Linda could goof around with. Linda came back down to earth after he left though and her good feelings hit rock bottom as she remembered her troubles and imagined that Ted would drop her like a hot potato as soon as he learned of what she had done. She became very quiet again and left to go to her room and stayed there for the rest of the day. George and President Cassidy arrived early just in time to eat before the teaching began. There was some socializing and reminiscing of the memories he had of

Kelly and watching her grow up with her sisters in the church. They were happy memories and the Gerard girls were taught and guided by diligent and loving considerate and wise parents. The girls had been such wonderful examples to the other young people. It made President Cassidy's job a pleasure associating with the young people of the church. Here he was teaching another of the Gerard Girls her classes preparatory to being sealed in the Holy Temple.

The company present began the meeting with a prayer and Mark offered it. They read scriptures pertaining to the sacred ordinance that Kelly would soon participate in. The Holy Spirit touched her heart form the beauty in all that she was learning and her parents gloried in her countenance. After the first four hour session her testimony of the precious truths of the eternal commitment was strong and their decision to be sealed was full of purpose for her. Her love for Mark was abounding in joy and her heart was full. Because of her faith and righteousness she was richly deserving of the feelings in her heart. She and Mark couldn't take their eyes off of one and other as they held hands; their fingers locked together and they were one in their celestial understanding. The family was all together for a late supper; it was Friday night and New Year's Eve. There was no wind and the snow fell lightly and Mark thought how wonderful it would be to take Kelly for a sleigh ride, just the two of them. He could wrap up with her in a thick fir blanket and listen to nothing but the clomping and swish of Marley and Timber's gigantic hooves through the winter's frost. He was interrupted by a suggestion from his precious love to go outside for a sleigh ride. Of course they would have synchronicity of thoughts. He pulled her to his loving embrace and met her eyes with the brilliance of his deep brown eyes; with fierceness of love is his soul he picked her up and breathed her name and professed his love once again to her. She had read his thoughts then the two in love entered the icy night and the majesty of the wooded path guided by the gentle beasts. They floated it seemed on the magic of their feelings and the warmth of their love was far greater than the comfort that the fir blanket was able to provide. With the protection of the two horses they just quietly with their faces caressed their glances meeting from time to time, enjoyed the gentle night in love.

Saturday morning opened the sea blue sky and the brightness of it fell upon the window and enticed the occupants to wake up. President Cassidy was scheduled to return for the second session of Kelly's lesson and brunch at eleven am. It was only seven thirty am. but the family retired early to bed the night before to compensate for the prior late night. Kelly was up and dressed in a new pair of black jeans she received for Christmas and a mauve satin blouse, also a gift. She could smell something very wonderful in the hall ways coming up from the kitchen and decided to share what lingered with Linda and she checked on her. If Linda was willing to get up and eat it would be the first chance that anyone had seen or heard from her since Ted left yesterday afternoon. Kelly hoped that she was only catching up on her sleep or carried away in a good book. Kelly reached the guest wing where Linda room was and knocked three times, called out and there was no answer. "Oh my goodness, she's left, Linda are you in there?" She fretted. Kelly opened the door, it was unlocked, and she walked in and was relieved to see Linda in her bed.

"Linda I knocked and called out, didn't you hear me?"

"I heard you." Linda had not slept and had cried for hours. She didn't look well at all. Her hair wet and tussled and darkness around her eyes left Linda looking very pale and weak.

"I'm going to take you to see a doctor Linda, there should be a clinic somewhere open."

"I don't need a doctor I need that that mess never happened. My life is ruined Kelly, I'm done for."

"Come on Hun, up you go on your feet, you are not well. You were so relaxed yesterday and now you are bottomed out and this is not normal; you need to get some help."

"I'm not taking any tranquilizers so don't go there."

"Did I say anything about taking a pill?"

"You need to realize Kelly; I'm done for. I have nothing, no money, and no family. They have all gone nuts since my grandparents died. The whole family is in turmoil and all I have is you and Mark and you are forced to help me. Look at this, you and Mark have to get married and go to all the trouble to see that I don't break the law and lose Marks ten thousand dollars.

Don't get me wrong it was nice of him to do this for me but I'm done for, there really is no hope for me now. He might as well go to court and get out of the deal."

"Oh Linda please—." Kelly pauses not knowing how to respond. She took Linda by the hand and asked her. "Linda I'll be right back, will you be all right for a few minutes?"

"Yeah." She dried her eyes and laid her head back on the pillow.

Kelly went to look for Mark who had been looking for Kelly. They met each other on the landing. "Mark please I need you to come with me to talk to Kelly. She is very much caught up in her dilemma and she's torn right to pieces. And wants you to tell the court the whole thing is off."

"Ok—Oh no! Do you think she is going to be ok?"

"She won't talk to a doctor; I suggested that already because she does not look well."

"Hi Linda." Mark and Kelly entered the guest room and Kelly lie there as if it's a bed of nails.

Linda did not sit up, only rolled over and Mark was stunned by her appearance and deeply saddened knowing her plight and seeing her looking so unwell. "Linda I know only too well the feelings of abandonment as a result of the investigation into my father and uncles deaths. I also know how to pull through devastation to land back on my feet. I had to and you have to. Your future and your wellbeing depend on it. Yes your future, you still have one you know. The worst of it is over and you have friends in Kelly and me. We are going to help you have a future. It may not be the one you planned on but it will be bright and I'm telling you to count on it."

"I feel bad about what I said to Kelly about you two being forced to look after me; I'm sorry. I just don't see how anything good is going to come from this mess I'm in. I may have to go back to jail for up to five years."

"Linda I prayed in earnest before I agreed to the court to bail you out. I was strongly prompted to see that you are cared for and that you will learn from this mistake you've made. I don't deny such strong promptings so believe me; your consequences will not be as severe as you are afraid that they will be. Please trust in me and Kelly and we will get you through this. You have my word."

With that promise Mark and Kelly both hugged Linda and tears shot from her eyes as Linda held onto them for her future life and for relief of her troubles. Linda submitted in thanks giving to them and vowed that she will learn to stand uprightly with Mark and Kelly by her side to lean on. She called them her team.

"Linda you can stay with us at our house for as long as you need to. I will give you a job; I am owner of a hardware store which I will have ready to open in February. It will be a start for you."

"Oh that's interesting; a hardware store?"

"Yes downtown. I'll be back to work getting the store prepared in about a week and you can start work then if you feel up to it and I'll begin paying you immediately."

"Hey Linda who knows, maybe Ted will be interested in asking you out." Kelly commented. "You looked like a couple of flirting teenagers; I just had to laugh at you playing with his buzz cut. I was busy with the sample book but I did notice." Linda smiled excitedly.

"I have met him at parties but I didn't really get to know him until yesterday. He is fabulous in his uniform is he not?"

"Well I wouldn't know." Kelly said stupidly. "I have known Ted for about five years. He is a major by rank and a joker by character."

I know that Kelly for true, I fell for him over his charm and sense of humor. I am hoping to see him again and turn this bummer weekend around."

"Ok girl I am going to put a lot of hard work into getting you two together this weekend that's every spare moment I have. It's going to be great."

"Well I am going to leave you two girls alone to your match making talk, I smell something tremendous waffling up the stairs. Excuse me." Mark left Linda's room to go and investigate the kitchen.

"Now are you going to be ok Linda?" Kelly brushed the hair out of Linda's eyes.

"I will definitely get up out of bed and get a shower and, oh do you think someone here has a change of clothes to fit me?"

"Yes you look like Carols same size. I'll go and ask her for some clothes for you to wear today. I'll lay them on the chair of you, ok?" Kelly left Linda's room so she could get ready to go down stairs and join everyone else for breakfast. The day began with a family breakfast and the bishop made his appointment to teach Kelly her temple discussions. After four hours the discussions were finished and a lovely luncheon was on hand. When the bishop left and well wishes were given everyone returned to the great room to put the finishing touches on the flowers. Mark and Kelly and even George and Mary danced around the room to the wedding music chosen for playing at the reception. The Childress's arrived with the cake and the fondant and decorations all ready to ensemble and to be flown to the chapel at the temple grounds on Monday night. There was a list of to dos to be made.

Gifts were arriving by currier or by visits and before anyone knew it evening fell upon them again. It was just two and a half days until Mark and Kelly's wedding day. The Gerard household was a bash with nuptial excitement and family memories were being made within the house.

Sunday morning arrived and so did the wind. It was a bitter cold day; one that made you wish you could stay curled up in bed or logged cozily in front of a fireplace wrapped up in a warm blanket with a loved one.

Even Marley and Timber protested George noticed when he opened the door to the barn to feed them and offer some warm bales of hay for their stalls. The barn was heated with a forced air wood burning furnace but the wind seemed to penetrate through the wood and steel walls of their stalls. George treated the beloved animals to an extra bowl of pellets and a bag each of apples and carrots as trues for such a cold day. Inside the house the family and guests emerged from their slumbers to get ready for church which started a ten am. When church would dismiss Mark and Kelly planned to go back to Kingston to pick up Elizabeth. Guests were arriving at different times during the day and taking up logging in nearby bread and breakfast establishments. George and Mary were both away from their jobs on eight day leaves. The girl's dresses had to be delivered to the house at four pm. as would the tuxedos. Bags were packed for Monday's plane ride to Pearson airport in Toronto so that the wedding party could occupy their hotel rooms nearest to the temple. The women's church auxiliary were taking care of the decorations for the reception and the dance. George and Mary anticipated an attendance of two hundred and twenty three guests; all those on just five days' notice. Everyone in the household was so busy that no one had time to house clean so a maid service was hired to come in the morning which was a very unusual occurrence. The floors were scattered with Christmas tree needles and the waist baskets were beginning to overflow. The house was overall very untidy with everyone being home and so many guests had passed through. Mary would come home to a nice clean house which pleased her so she could relax and enjoy her second daughter's wedding. She would have liked to have someone in to clean while they were in church but it wouldn't be appropriate to have someone working on Sunday. Six cars pulled away from the house together so they could meet together again at church. After three hours of church Mark Kelly and Linda left for Kingston to pick up Elizabeth. Mark and Kelly were very much looking forward to seeing her again and having her watch them take their vows. Mark was still driving the rental car but the insurance company was in touch with him and a settlement had been quickly made and the insurance payment would be in Marks hand by Thursday so he could replace the car without further delay. Linda had been reluctant to go to church with the family; she was not of their faith and she felt ashamed even though Mark had tried to reassure her that weekend. Linda had been given some clothes to wear and she had still not heard whether she could enter her dorm room to get her belongings, nor was she sure she even wanted to return. None of the parishioners knew her or of her situation, they were just simply happy to have a visitor in church to try to convert. Every member a missionary! She didn't mind the attention too much but was grateful when they got to the car to go back to Kingston.

They thought they might stop by the university to inquire about entering the dorm room to get some of Linda's belongings and to see if the police were finished investigating there. It was a seventy minute drive and when they arrived they found the lock had been change and the dorm manager was on holidays. Linda took for granted that she had been moved out. There would be no way of finding her things until the first of the week. Linda felt that she had taken one step up and two backwards. Her mood plummeted again as she hung her head and became very quiet as she sat in the back seat of the car. When they pulled up to the rest home Linda again pleaded to Mark and Kelly to let her stay behind at Marks house. "I promise and you can trust me, I won't go anywhere or cause trouble for you and your mother may feel uncomfortable with me anyway."

"Linda if you don't mind, this is all very new to us and I don't know you very well. Tomorrow you don't have to join us and you don't have to go to the wedding; you can stay in your motel room where you will be nice and quiet. We will get you anything you need until you can get your things next week."

"Ok, I'm very sorry to have worried you. I wish to stay here in Kingston though; I don't particularly feel like being around people."

"We understand Linda." Kelly added.

"I'll be back here in about ten minutes, I'll see if mom is ready to go."

"Sure Babe."

Mark entered the home and signed in and when he reached his mother's room he was surprised to see her suitcase already outside the door. She was inside and arranging the lovely bouquet of flowers that Mary gave to her when she stayed there for Christmas. "Mom how are you? You look wonderful standing beside the flowers like that, you have your hair all done nicely and the white pant suit looks smashing on you."

"Thank you darling, someone was in from the church last night and did my hair for me. Do you notice the streaks? They are gentle ones never the less they are there and add some brightness. Then she trimmed and set it for me. I nearly slept sitting straight upwards as to not tussle the curls."

"Oh don't you worry about your curls, there are lots of girls at the Gerard's who can look after them for you. Put a hat on though it's windy and the curls will be straightened out in two seconds."

"Is Kelly in the car with you?"

"Yes she is with Linda. Linda is pretty down right now though. She can't get into her room until next week and she would rather stay home by herself."

"You can't let her do that can you? Oh I guess it would be aloud but it's probably best that she comes with you, just in case the court raises the roof. Are there going to be corsages for the mothers?"

"Um, I think you'll have to clear that up with Kelly; are you supposed to have one for the wedding?"

"Yes dear and the groom and groomsmen will wear a boutonniere. I guess you don't pay attention to kinds of details do you Mark?"

"No."

"Well I'm ready, let's be on our way to Stirling. I almost forgot; I have this little violet plant for Linda. I planted it in September and it is starting to blossom. I hope it helps her to feel a little better."

"That's nice of you mom thank you. It's a good idea you know because she was really worried that you would be uncomfortable with her being with us. This plant will be a nice little ice breaker."

"Ok, bless her heart. I knew my little violet would be a meaningful gift for someone." Elizabeth carried the plant to the car and Mark assisted in carrying his mother's baggage. When they got to the car, Kelly stepped out and hugged Elizabeth and introduced her to Linda then sat in the back seat with her so Elizabeth would have the front seat.

"I'm happy to meet you Linda, please except this flower as a little gift, I've been growing them in my rom since September and I would like to have this one."

"You would? How very kind of you. Purple is my favorite color. Thank you very much, you have a wonderful green thumb and it's amazing that you have been able to grow a mature plant in four months."

"Elizabeth has six more in a variety of colors growing in her room. It's all done with the right plant food and the way they are watered that makes them grow so nicely."

As they drove back to Stirling Linda found herself in a much better mood. When they arrived at the Gerard's the house was full of people. Family, guests and the company that brought the dresses and the bishop was also there one last time with some more counsel. Dinner was almost on the table and the quick rush wedding was folding together and they were making the plans for the flight to Toronto to the hotel rooms for the next morning. George and Mark had decided between the two of them that it would be better to present the new car to Kelly tonight since it would be such a busy time in the morning. It was kept in one of the garages; a beautiful red mustang with brown details and a convertible roof was adorned with a wide white ribbon and bow, and enormous wedding card and a box of red roses. What a dream ride and a fairy tale wedding gift. She and Mark would slip away on a silver lining of a cloud in love in that vehicle. Its presentation awaited the moonlight and the chance for Mark to escape with Kelly from the hustle and bustle and business going on that evening. He didn't know of any other way that he was going to arrange to get Kelly to go out to the garage with him but to tell her he had a gift hidden in there for her. Instead he asked her to take a walk with him to get away from the noise in the house. Kelly hurried at the chance to be alone with him and so they went. Mark was full of pride to be marrying such a lovely lady, radiant, smart and loving with a smile that made the brightness of the moon seem dull. He walked with her and guided her to the garage her car was in. "Your father has a lot of garages, that's a big deal. Does he have them all full? What's in this one? I see there's a light on in there."

"Well there shouldn't be a light on; we better go inside to see if everything is ok in there then shut the light off."

"The door is probably open so we won't have to go in the house to get a garage opener." Marks heart was pounding into his throat as they approached the door to open and hoping that there was nothing amiss. Kelly was struck with the surprise to see the classic ride and the name on the enormous card was her own.

"WHAT!" She walked around and around again holding onto Marks hand and trying to breathe, she was speechless as Marked handed her the keys tied to the ribbon on the box containing red roses.

"Are you kidding Mark; this is mine?"

"It's your my sweet lady." Tears streamed down her face; she had been overwhelmed with stress in the last few days and now she had just kind of lost control of her emotions. Mark held her in his arms, her back to him and looking at her new car with his arms wrapped around her and her head rested on his shoulder. She didn't want him to let go of her.

"Kelly just imagine the two of us driving off in this car on our honeymoon and pulling up to a secluded cabin in the woods." He picked her up in his strong arms and held on to her with her arms around his neck and there it was again; there eyes meeting and locking in romantic love. Her long silken dark hair hung loosely over his shoulder and she rested her lips on his chin and gently on his neck. He simply held her and gently rocked. He closed his eyes and allowed her gentleness to remind him that Kelly would be his wife in two days and he opened the driver's door of her new mustang and put her in it.

"Wow is this how I'm going to get into my new car every time because I can handle this just fine thank you."

"Any time you want anything for you. I'll open the garage door so we can take it for a drive so buckle up."

"Hey Mark let's take off and elope tonight. We can keep it quiet and still make it back for the wedding on Tuesday."

Mark was shocked at her but happy with her suggestion' still the same he ran his fingers through her hair and gave her a very passionate look that nearly melted her in the seat and she drove off and out of the garage into town for an hour's drive. They stopped off at a neighbor lady house who is famous for her doughnuts and got some to take back home as a fun gesture to celebrate Kelly's new car and their upcoming marriage. The twins were still up but ready for bed and were permitted to share a cherry stick and warm glass of milk. Linda, Carol, Mark and Kelly relaxed in the great room by the fire and shared a plate of doughnuts and a few stories of weddings that they have attended in the past. Carol commented on what seemed to be a spark of interest between Linda and Ted. Ted would be a responsible husband being that he is in the Canadian Armed Forces, He would be good for Linda."

"It would seem to be so Carol; I didn't know he was a Major or in the military, we know each other through mutual friends and have met casually before and I always thought he had a very strong personality, without a hair out of place. I was always impressed with him but we were always paired up with dates at occasions we attended and never met personally until he came here to visit. He is a nice man and I am sort of hoping that we sit together and maybe dance at the reception."

"Hey girl we'll arrange that; you'll be strategically placed beside Ted. I can't wait for the reception to see how this all works out." Carol was excited with her plans.

Mark and Kelly looked at Carol and laughed. "We are going to give you a little cupid to wear on your blouse at the wedding and you can watch out for all the potential romances that could have a chance of blooming on our day. You are officially assigned to that job because we will only have eyes for each other."

Carol didn't know about Linda's problems and Linda just went along with Carol's teenaged excitement and interest in match making. Linda was hoping to look for any interest that Ted might have in her but she knew that because of his rank and her criminal record, it is likely that a relationship would not be possible. This was her first time and would probably never break the law again and it caused Linda's reluctance to show any more interest in a relationship with Ted. "So Linda what did you choose to wear to the wedding? I saw your interest in the little purple "A" line. I liked the flouncy little flowered chiffon number you tried on too." Asked Kelly.

"I'm wearing the purple "A" line. It's more suitable for a winter wedding and its form fitting, I'm wearing black velvet pumps and Mellissa lent me a black stole."

"OOO, that's sounds flattering and well I think I'm going to turn in now so if you will all excuse me, come on Carol you better go too."

"Yeah you are right, I'm going to pick out the shade of nail polish to take with me tomorrow and matching jewelry. I want to look sensational in my bride's maids dress."

"Remember the colors in the flowers."

"Oh yes the flowers, thanks Kelly."

"Good night girls. I'll check in on Mom, she's probably asleep by now. I love you Kelly, I'll see you in the morning."

"Goodnight Mark. I want to hurry and go to sleep so I can dream about you . . ."

It was Monday morning and it seemed like everyone had been packed for days because everything was so well organized. The house was now empty and several vans had left the property and were being driven carrying family and guests and luggage to a small nearby airport where five charted planes awaited to fly the occupants to the airport in Toronto. By car it would be a two and a half hour drive but from the time they left home to the time they were expected to arrive at the Marriot Inn would only be ninety minutes. Luckily the hotel room reservations were one of the first arrangements that Mary made directly after the phone call that Kelly made to announce her engagement. All the rooms were booked without incident; it was just after New

Year's and business had quieted down somewhat. By one thirty in the afternoon some church members from the Toronto branch had volunteered their services to transport the Gerard party and the wedding accessories to the chapel to get prepared for the reception. People had already arrived and were decorating the cultural hall and set up the tables and such. What a wonderful blessing it was for Mark and Kelly to have so many people they didn't even know to help them prepare for their day. It was such a whirl wind decision but one that was necessary for their present situation. It would have definitely been their future plans anyway. They had a great love and knew that their relationship was unshakable. The Childress's got right to work resembling the cake amongst a tewl wrapped table with ensembles of flowers draped at the corners of the tables. A festive winter scene was a work in progress and lights meshed in silvery blue satin adorned a circle of love for which the people dance under. A gazebo which was attached to a little wooden bridge for the wedding party to enter in the room was decorated with holly, evergreen and white snowflakes. A bride and groom snow people welcomed those that entered the gazebo. The table center pieces were made up of snowflake electric globes with little winter scenes inside them laid on silvery blue table cloths. The cultural hall was on the way to looking like a winter wonderland. Lovely, Kelly and her mother commented. Kelly wept as her mother held her, she was so grateful for the beauty and the work that everyone there had done to make her day wonderful. Kelly was astonished at how wonderful her mother really was that she could put this wedding together in just days. It was a work of art. During the tender mother-daughter moment, ten young men and women dressed in costumes entered the hall carrying instruments and amplifiers. They began setting them up to play a sample of music for Kelly and Mark. Kelly squealed and jumped up and down like a teenager at the excitement of having a live band play at her party. Five would play the instruments and the other five would sing. They began with a copula medley which Mark and Kelly enthusiastically danced to while the attendants busily finished the preparations. The dresses were hung with care in the bride's room and awaited to be worn the next day. The flowers were left in a room in the chapel for the opportunity to be held during picture taking. There are to be no flowers carried into the temple ceremony; photos would be taken outdoors or in the cultural hall after the ceremony. A room was set up at the chapel for poses. The weather forecast reported a sunny but cold day, no precipitation at all for Tuesday which was a dream come true, with the good weather in place all the preparations were completed. All that was needed was for Tuesday to roll around on the calendar. Everybody met at a restaurant to eat at about six pm. and returned to the hotel to visit and get rested up for the big day; if possible.

January fifth 2011; the morning was bright and the span between the time that Kelly woke up and the hour that she would kneel at the alter across from her beloved Mark was hallowed and blessed. Mary, Elizabeth and Kelly had been together since six am. to prepare her for the sacred walk through the temple for ceremonies necessary prior to the temple sealing. Mark, Mary, George, Elizabeth, Aunt Barbara, Grandma and Brian and Melissa were to be in the temple at 9 am. Kelly and her mother would meet the temple matron to be escorted to the bride's room to be dressed appropriately to prepare to Meet her bride groom. The rest of the Gerard girls including Linda were beginning to stir. They also had a busy morning planned what with meeting for breakfast then with the hair and make-up stylists. Mary booked four artists to be at the hotel. When all the girls were awake there was a buzzing between rooms and the feathers were flying. Women were running with towels wrapped over their heads and crumb coated terry bath robes as they munched on breakfast bagels and fresh fruit and smoothies. The little girls played with nail polish and bobby pins making glamour girl faces in the mirrors. Cindy got into some hair spray and accidently sprayed it into her eyes. That delayed Mary's appointment as she attended to her daughter's burning eyes. Some eye wash and a cold cloth enabled Cindy to see strait again. An aspirin subdued the stinging and her Panda Paula comforted her while she went back to bed for a little nap. Sheila stayed quiet after the commotion and watched some TV. in bed. Mary and Kelly had to meet George and Mark at the temple to participate in the preparatory ceremonies. Later in the morning Kelly was ready to meet Mark at the altar. Her immediate family and Marks' mother surrounded them as they took their sacred vows and participated in the living ordinance of the eternal sealing. What is sealed in the temple is eternally sealed in Heaven. Marked had married his Kelly; his angel was now his wife. His best friend was his eternal partner and help mate. She is not his inferior nor is her superior; they are partners in life and for eternity. Ted and Linda, Carol and the twins met Mark and Kelly and their family members as they exited the temple to pose for a few photos. Luckily it was a mild day and the air never looked more clear and bright to Kelly; the world looked different to her, her heart was purified. Holiness surrounded the couple; she was radiant in her long flowing white dress and Mark, a handsome saint in his all white suit and tie. His countenance was glorified when he looked at his Kelly and they kissed. Before the ceremony they never kissed. They saved that part of their love until he could call Kelly his wife and she could call him husband. Mark and Kelly Scott joined their guests at the chapel for a lunch and more wedding pictures and festivities. Ted was thrilled that Linda was along as a guest and she showed interest in helping him pose the wedding party. She was showing every bit of interest in his flirtatiousness. Kelly was unsure if she should smile for the camera or drop her jaw wide open every time Linda stood extremely close to Ted. Mark and Kelly were having a wild time watching the sparks fly between Ted and Linda. Ted worked for forty minutes taking picture when he told everyone to have a fifteen minute break to socialize when he reached into his camera case and found a folded piece of paper that Linda had dropped in there with her cell phone number and email address on.

"Ok Linda, I see I got through to you."

"I happen to know that Mary has placed us sitting together at the table for dinner."

"Well there you go! That's what I'm talking about! Mary and George have been good friends for a long time. Hey stand beside that plant there by the pillar;

the shade of the leaves will look really great beside the Jewell tone of your purple dress. Cross your right hand over your left shoulder, tilt your head back and then to the right, there the shadow is nice."

"Is this for your own personal scrap book?" Linda smiles hopefully at him which caused her to be even more photogenic. Ted snapped dozens of pictures of her.

"This is my new hobby you know; I'm taking you everywhere with me from now on."

"I'll go along with you; do I get many new dresses?"

"One with every color of the rainbow."

"Purses and shoes too please."

"I'm picturing you with corn rows in your hair and a camouflage uniform."

Linda laughed so hard. "I'm getting out of here. You are a cook or something."

"Well it was the only other thing I could think of at the spur of the moment. I was actually picturing you with corn rows and a camouflage bikini but I didn't think I knew you well enough yet."

"I can compromise and ask you to imagine that I am wearing a camouflage bikini"

"Awe yes, if you only knew how hard my heart is beating right now; Linda lets go to lobby and talk. We have about twenty minutes free time while Mark and Kelly are greeting their guests."

Linda couldn't stop smiling while she walked along the hall with Ted to the lobby to sit on a comfy couth that there were two of there. At the same time she began to feel anxiety because they were acting on their attraction to one and other and she feared that it would be over once Ted learned of her pending charges. She wanted to grasp every moment she could have with Ted anyway. The truth she realized may squelch her hopes of having a relationship with him. Before Ted sat down with Linda he pulled one of the flowers from an arrangement set on a table and handed it to her. He thought she was so divine sitting there with the purple in her form fitting dress how it blended in beautifully with the colors in the couch while holding her rose colored daphnia. Her short satin black hair framed her petit face and her eyes, so black and lovely; his desire was to stare into to those eyes that were so expressive. He couldn't snap the perfect picture of them because each picture he took of her was better than the last. Her eyes expressed approval for the sight of that man beside her, that handsome figure of a man in his dark grey suit, beige shirt and burgundy tie. There was an extreme difference in height between Linda and Ted but they did not look awkward beside one and other; they were instead quite suited to one and other in appearance as they left the lobby to join the other guests for a time. It was predicted that they would be inseparable and indeed they enjoyed each other's company for the remainder of the day. There was no obligation for Linda to admit her situation and criminal record to Ted at this occasion. They mingled with the guests as Linda held onto his arm. Ted happily accepted the gesture as he introduced Linda as his date for the evening and the two mingled together with the others delighting in each other's company. They were inseparable and grew closer and more intimate as day progressed.

The twins posed with the family for a photo session and they were lively in their coral taffeta mid-calf dresses. Their cheeks were rosy and their eye shadow was dusty melon, and of course their nails were painted nicely. Flowers adorned their sunny blond hair and the white patented leather shoes were accessorized with little velvet bows incrusted with pearls. Sheila and Cindy smiled proudly as they stood with their parents holding hands and clutching their little white velvet purses. Mary got it all together in a sequenced periwinkle dress jacket and taffeta gown. The bride and groom, most gracious; both in white stood arm and arm at the middle of the Gerard family. Her flowers cascaded at the front of them and after the picture was taken, he kissed her appropriately to show her his fondness of her that very moment when he stood with his eternal partner and his new family. Kelly's five other sisters stood around her and Elizabeth stood on Mark's other side proudly and well, when she looked at her new daughter in law, her heart swelled with love. Elizabeth was most grateful for Kelly and wouldn't have any further desire to retreat to her room in case of missing one second of her son's and daughter in law's wedding day. When that session of picture taking was done, George escorted his wife and Elizabeth to the hall and was seated for the wedding dinner. They followed the bride and groom and led the Gerard girls to the brides table. The master of ceremonies began the festivities with introductions and blessing for the newlyweds and a blessing on the dinner. Caterers and servers delivered a grand meal directly to the guests. Two hundred and fifty four guests enjoyed beef Wellington, Yorkshire pudding and Waldorf salad, Greek salad and, creatively prepared vegetable dishes and a seemingly endless variety of bred rolls and cheese. As toasts go and they did go on and on, the first toast was to honor Mary for magically arranging out of five days, this marvelous wedding day for her daughter. It was a day that one would imagine that months of preparation had been gone into it. George's brother Barry stood in as Best Man since Mark had not a chance to meet many people since he and his Mother arrived in Ontario in July. Barry was the next person in line to give a speech. He began to talk about the day that George and Mary brought her home to her big sister Monique, who was five and a half and recalled that she collected all of her dollies to give to her new baby sister. Monique looked at Kelly with the mature adoration and right then and there she knew that Kelly was a part of a family and would know her place in it. She belonged to a family that worked together to create a family circle. As the family circle carried on, it grows and never breaks. "Today we welcome Mark Scott into that family circle. Mark, you have chosen to be a part of Kelly's life and today you gain the support her family members and of the Lord. Be at peace and God be with you both."

Monique, Kelly's oldest sister and maid of honor gave a very heartfelt, beautiful yet comedic testimony of her observation of Kelly's position in the family which caused everyone there in the hall to simultaneously sigh and say AW! Wasn't that lovely. The cake cutting ceremony was picturesque as tiny candle lights surrounded the bride and groom standing by the cake admiring the bride and groom that preciously adorned the heart shaped tear. Kelly's grandmother Childress stood nearby to advise Kelly of the best technique to cut the cake to feed all of the guests. They were photographed easing the floral and mother of pearl knife into the bottom tear of the cake which started the party. All the guests whistled and cheered. Aunt Meredith entered the room and let loose a multitude of white and pink balloons. Thus the bride and groom were invited to be the first to enter the dance floor for their first dance as husband and wife. Hundreds of tiny white lights and glittering bubbles in the air enchanted many of the couples and they joined Mark and Kelly for the first waltz. No couple was as beautiful as the bride and groom. Kelly at five feet ten inches wore a mermaid style pure white dress with a silk pleated skirt, silk and lace half jacket with velvet cuffs and pearl buttons on the cuffs and velvet lapel. Her hair was pulled back tightly in a single bun and one thick tail held by multiple velvet bands and her bangs swept across her forehead. As pearls are her favorite Jewell, she wore a pearl and diamond studded tiara. The gems were a Gerard family heirloom and it was with a matching choker. The light from the Jewells matched her striking brown eyes and her eyes were all about admiring her handsome groom who towered her slender figure by six inches. The dashing Mark swept his bride off her feet in his white tux and tails and pearls buttons adorned his shirt; which were visible since he wore a bow tie. The universe evolved around them and they were one in the universe; so beautiful and their blessings were sure.

Mark and Kelly had made arrangements with the court and Linda would be under George and Mary's supervision for four days so that they could go on a honeymoon to Lake Louise. They left the reception at seven pm. and made the forty minute drive to the airport to catch their plane. Finally they could be alone in love and matrimony. Nobody that met them knew that they had just been married but they were led up a path as if the stars had aligned in perfect harmony for them and everyone treated them as a king and queen. Their every need was met with pleasure and the red carpet seemed to be rolled out just for them all the way to their cabin on Lake Louise. The picturesque scenery that surrounded their honeymoon abode was unlike any beauty they had ever laid their eyes and hearts on before. Mark and Kelly arrived at their own cabin at five am Wednesday morning. Their guide helped them take their luggage just to the door and presented them with the key and information about the site as well as flyers advertising local attractions as if they were going to be needed. Mark tipped the guide then he disappeared as quickly as he could. "Kelly I'm going to hold to custom and carry you over the threshold."

"Can you manage to unlock our door?"

"Well you know, I'm love struck but I know enough to unlock the door first. Come here my darling wife, I love you."

"I love you, let's go inside, I can't wait to go in and warm up. I hope there's a fireplace."

"Kelly welcome to your honeymoon, it's perfect. The curtains are closed, there's a fireplace and a fire already burning."

"They have left flowers on the table and biscuits and cheese; Mark this room is wonderful."

"I'll bring in the luggage and shut the door. Will you light some candles? Are you hungry?"

"I'm not really but this food looks so lovely to relax with; I'll fix us a plate and meet you at the fireplace. Mark these cheese platters are beautiful, I'm going to have some baby bell, some garlic and herb cheese and some grapes and orange wedges."

I'll have the same and if there is any bananas and Swiss cheese, I'll have some of those. So the luggage is all in and this food is great; you've set the plates deliciously Kelly. I'm glad to have these nice thick pillows here, come and sit close me."

"Ok just let me get a quilt off the bed."

"Ok so are you nestled nicely?"

"I'm nestled nicely and comfortably and it's warm in here now."

"The grapes are sweet Kelly, taste this one, this one in my lips."

"Mmmmmm."

There were many pillows around there by the fireplace and it was still dark outside. The only light in the cabin was thrown by the fireplace and the few scented candles around on some of the tables. The fragrances that lingered in the cabin, the candles, pine, fresh bread and fruit added to the comfortable atmosphere in which Mark and Kelly reached for each other in romance and tenderness. When finally the sun glowed through the dainty fabric of the curtains they had fallen fast asleep in each other's embrace and their dreams were at one in fantasia. They woke up about one in the afternoon and Mark put more wood in the fireplace because they did not want to leave their spot in their private universe. Mark brushed her long hair while the peace in the room caresses them both. He massaged her skin with a gentle fragrant lotion of her choice until she was again wrapped in the arms of his love. Neither hungered nor thirsted for hours more.

Linda was comfortable is Stirling at the Gerard home. George and Mary had gone back to work but Aunt Barbara and grandma were there for her supervision. Linda sat in room most of the time since they came home from the wedding. She had received Teds email address and had numerous emails from him. Ted and Linda had made plans to keep in touch with each other. Elizabeth also stayed back from Kingston and had the guest room next to Linda and Elizabeth was concerned to the point of anxiety over Linda's contact with Ted. Linda happened to tell Elizabeth of her fondness for Ted even though she knew it would likely have to end due to his rank and her criminal actions of the recent days.

"Linda you need to tell Ted for Pete's sake. It's disgraceful you know, you are trying to carry on and escape with him."

"So in so many words you think I'm dreaming, thinking a relationship would be possible?"

"Listen dear, I know that you are regretting your involvement in the scam and will probably never do it again; but with his rank come security issues will block and forbid him from associating with a person charge with fraud."

"Mark and Kelly encouraged our introduction and Mark is giving me a job which will help to minimize the conviction."

"I know Linda, I know you are going to do a wonderful thing in cleaning up, but the fact is you have a record now and will unless you can be pardoned. If he falls in love with you, it will be a terrible thing because he will have to break it off and that will be hard on you. Linda thinks about this, it may be a mistake. I wish you all the best and I pray that you will make the right choice in this matter. I'm weary already, I have to lie down. I'll see you at dinner Linda."

"Holy smokes that was cold." Linda whispered to herself as she fell back onto her bed resting her arms over her head. She wondered why she was so alone in the world; why did this happen? How could she have thrown everything away for a few thousand dollars? How was Linda going to make right all that was wrong in her life? How is she going to make the right choice and confess to Ted what she has done wrong? She began to cry and cried herself to sleep for a couple of hours until Cindy and Sheila burst into her room. "Oh girls you scared the life out of me. You are like a pair of monkeys jumping on my bed like that. You could have broken it."

"You have been here a long time." Chanted Cindy

"Do you want to stay in our house so you can show us how to put make-up on and play with us?" Sheila asked gleefully.

"Oh yes of course, didn't you know that?"

"Yeah, you are nice lady."

"We love you Linda, come for dinner at five thirty, that's what aunt Barbara said."

"Thank you girls."

The girls jumped off the bed, they were wearing their dress up clothes and hats and skipped out of the room. Linda just lie back and began to cry again wondering how she would face everyone especially Elizabeth after what she said earlier. Linda thought; she just didn't care about what happened in court. I've ruined everything; I just want to climb under a rock like a worm or something. A mass of blackness fell over Linda. Mark and Kelly would not be back until Saturday and by that time she would be depressed. The only way she found that she would recover would be to go to sleep and wake up to find that it was all just a night mare. If she could only wake herself up and walk down the street to her dorm room, her father and mother wouldn't be divorced and would be waiting there for her with an order of Chinese takeout and a tray full of apple blossoms. Linda was only twenty one years old, her life had just begun and so quickly, it was over and it was going to get worse even still. She needed to scream and throw something but all she could manage to do was to open her mouth and scream a quiet cry. The tears jet from her eyes until they stung. She certainly wasn't going to meet the rest for dinner to have to look them all in the face and pretend to be just a guest of Kelly and Mark's. She couldn't call Kelly on her honeymoon even though she suggested doing just that if it was necessary. Linda's heart ached as she remembered the hour of desertion when her mother turned on her husband and family when she received word of her inheritance. There was never a perfect world in which her family lived but no one ever expected that her mother would turn so selfishly over money then take it and run from her own family. Linda lies on bed and tried to see through tear strained eyes and turned her head toward the voice behind her door. It was Ted. Oh why Ted this very moment? Why? Linda fretted. "Linda excuse me for the intrusion. Elizabeth thought that you may not join the family for dinner so I asked if it would be appropriate to check in on you. I'm glad I did because I supposed I would find you upset."

"Elizabeth? Elizabeth has spoken to you? What right has she?" Linda was choked up as she questioned.

"Honey, calm down. Here is some water to drink, it's cold. Just sit back and we will talk a bit once you've calmed down some."

"You probably shouldn't be here you know."

"If I weren't, you may be alone in the world."

"What, what do you know? Did Elizabeth actually tell you about some things?"

"No. She simply told me that you may not be coming down stairs for dinner and that she thought you were depressed. Linda I know what has happened to you. George told me the day I was here with the photo samples. He noticed our fondness for flirting with one and other; we work closely together every day. I know about the trouble you have gotten yourself in and the tragedy in your life in recent months."

Linda, now stunned couldn't imagine where this conversation was leading to. "I'm so very sorry for the devastation in your life and I regret that I didn't get to know you before you made your choices."

"Oh so what are you doing here now then? Why have you been so friendly regardless of knowing about my arrest?"

"Do you forget that I already knew you Linda? I have always had my eye on you but the appropriate opportunity never came for us to get together. I think you are a great gal Linda; beautiful, intelligent and wow, are you ever a great dancer. You have literally enchanted me and I can barely get any work done throughout the day or think of anything else, I find myself imagining you in a camouflage bikini half the time."

"I don't believe it."

"Believe it Linda. I had a hard time trying to believe George when he told me about your troubles; my heart went out to you Linda I promise."

"Wait, can you do that? I mean you could get into trouble having any association with me, isn't that true?"

"Because of my rank, just let the forces try to tell me who I can be friends with. No Linda I won't be in trouble. You were in a hardship situation, everybody know someone like you. I know that you regret your participation in the scam and you have some really good people willing to help you. Don't give up even though it seems that everything is lost at this moment. I'm urging you to stay strong in this matter, be co-operative with the court and most of all don't give up, don't give up."

"Help me please Ted; you'll stay with me won't you?" Linda reached out to Ted as if she had found a new beginning and didn't want to let it go since it could leave her at any second. She cried and gratefully thanked him for his support.

"Do you have a lawyer and a court date?"

"Yes I have a lawyer and there has already been a court date but it has been remanded until after Mark and Kelly come back from their trip and my lawyer is also busy. I have an appointment with him on January twenty first."

"Ok. Linda I'm not a criminal lawyer but I know that there is support out there for people in your situation.

I'm not talking about repeat offenders; I'm talking about hardship cases. You could get a pardon and be ordered into some kind of rehabilitation. It would be a more suitable option then going to jail. You are then able to rebuild your life and gain further needed support to keep you on the right track."

"Is this all reality? I've never heard of such a system."

"Well you've never had to deal with the system before. I've researched your option already and I know that there's help for you and it's not the end of your life. I am going to walk with you through your ordeal if you have no objections."

"Oh Ted how could I refuse? Please yes, stay with me. If all you say is true I promise you that I will do my best to deal with all that will be put on my shoulders and I promise to lean on you and those who are willing to be there for my benefit. I won't let you down."

"Good girl, that's what I wanted to here. You must be hungry; you don't have to go down to dinner with everyone else. I'll get take out Chinese food and we'll eat here in your room. How does that sound?"

"Ok Ted, hurry back will you." While Ted was gone Linda let out a sigh of relief into her pillow and just sat there like that. She was still in disbelief when only ten minutes had passed from when Ted left to buy food; he walked in with two large trays of food from down stairs.

"Oh I see that there was left overs."

"Oh yes, this is Greek food at its best. I couldn't pass this up so help yourself. I don't know what you would like so I just brought bowls of everything and a couple plates to use. There's more, I'll be right back and I'll bring drinks."

"Oh sure this looks way better then take out. Please thank Mary for this for me." Ted was back in a jiffy and Linda had a table all set up for the two of them to enjoy their delicious Greek meal. Ted brought another tray of fruit, cakes and drinks and a small bouquet of roses adorned the tray; he picked them out of the table canter piece.

"Did you steel some more flowers out of someone's arrangement or did you quickly run out to the flower store?"

"Oh no worries now; there were lots of flowers on the table and we're all good friends. I thought you would like these small flowers and there was room for these ones on the tray. Mary lent me the little porcelain vase for the tray."

"Well thank you Ted, it's a very colorful tray. The fruit match the colors in the plates. Mary is such a romantic isn't she? She has such beautiful things here. Did Mary cook this food?"

"I don't know; I presume so, assisted by Barbara and grandma."

"Well this is just splendid."

"I think it sounds like you are feeling better."

"I am and I'm very glad for all you do for me Ted. So much has changed in my life and I'm utterly lost for words right now."

"Well good then you can eat something' here try some of this. It's really good food, all of it. Then how about going for a drive into town? We can take a walk around the mall or something."

"A walk in the mall sounds good, it's too bitterly cold outside."

Ted was very sensitive to Linda's hardship knowing that she is a really good person and she just slipped, not realizing really what harm she was doing being involved in the scam. He knew that she was living a nightmare and it was something that made sense to do at the time. She did what she did out of desperation and knew that all was not lost in her situation, just bogged down. He was determined to make matters right if not; he would make them less detrimental for her. In their past meetings the situations never made it appropriate for the two to get together and Ted was always left wondering "What if?" Linda always took his attention away from whoever he was with. She had put a special charm on him it seemed. Ted wanted to make ample use of this opportunity he had been given through the surprise meeting at the Gerard house. "Well Ted it is a delightful invitation but I'm really not supposed to leave this house. The court gave Mark special permission to allow me to stay under George and Mary's supervision."

"Oh how pleasant a thought it was to have gone for a walk with you. I did forget; I got carried away

In being in your company and I wanted to enjoy some exercise after eating all of splendid food."

"I don't particularly feel like joining the others; if you just want to sit up here we can—."

"I have an idea, would you like to take a horse and buggy ride, there are plenty of blankets for the buggy and I know the property well."

"Oh gosh; this is great vegetable moussaka. I buy this in the grocery store from the frozen section and its rubbish compared to this that Mary cooked."

"Well Linda come for a horse and buggy ride."

"No thank you, maybe tomorrow when it warms up if it does."

"I am broken hearted. I was looking forward to admiring your beauty in the moon light and watching the crisp night pinken your olive cheeks."

"My goodness Ted, what is this, a romance novel?" The two laughed and Ted tried again to show Linda his interest in encouraging her to not stay shut up in the splendid but lonely room. Her present situation began to worry his heart and he grieved for Linda. It had been his plan that evening to sweep her off her feet, out of her dark mood and into the clearness of day, his day yet the bitterness of her looming trials halted all efforts and triggered a bewildering silence between the two. For the very first time ever within the walls of the Gerard house existed a certain darkness and dread which was charged to Linda's room only. Ted was now privy to the loneliness and grief felt by Linda and he had a better understanding of her feelings. It was a short silence that seemed like a life time of silence. In that instant moment of grief, Ted realized where he was; the Gerard house was second to a paradisiacal existence and he felt the great comparison and the bewildering existence in Linda's room.

"Ok" Ted paused unable to say anything interesting. "I understand your reluctance in joining the family for dinner."

She remained quiet and just fiddled with her food, didn't even look up at Ted. "I'll stay here and visit with you; if you would like that is but I think you shouldn't be sitting in here alone all the time."

Linda quickly glanced up and slightly met Ted's eyes and said. "Well I can't eat all this food by myself."

"Right so we won't talk about your troubles anymore tonight."

"That's fine with me." Linda acquainted herself with that instance and notion of a fresh start once her troubles got sorted out for her. "Mark has offered me a job in his hardware store and I'll be starting next month to help him with inventory."

"Linda that's excellent; you have good people on your side. They believe in your future and are lending you a hand up."

"Kelly is going to continue to work at the bakery after school and for a while in the summer. Then I am sure that after she graduates in a few months, she will dive right into working as a registered nurse." Linda stammered again. She wrapped her face in the palms of her hands while Ted reached out to her laying a supportive hand on her shoulder. He knew what a hard task lie ahead of her. A desperate quietness surrounded them. Linda's rehabilitation would not be easy and Ted knew it but he wondered if being so close to her was more of a hindrance in the steps of progress then being good for her. Although he realized that his support would be beneficial to her, he knew that he must be careful with her emotions. All along since he was reacquainted with her during this fragile time in her life he had been ready to flirt and to take her on a whirlwind romance; it was all as wishful thinking on his part. How could he attend to her in a romantic way with such gloom looming over her? Linda wasn't pushing away for any reason and the surroundings that she was offered and the support she had been given led her to be ashamed of the fraud charge. It was proving to be too much of a burden for her; a worry that would surely cause her to become ill. Her appetite was scares but her thirst made up for the nutrients she was not getting by not eating. As suddenly as her mood darkened she happened to find some sense and began talking to Ted candidly and even looked him in the eye when she spoke.

"Working in the store will be good for me."

"Sure it will. Have you ever worked in a store?"

"Yes when I was fifteen I worked for a family business so I have some experience. This will keep my mind occupied; don't you think?"

"I am glad for that Linda. I barely know what to say to you dear. I think I just need to keep my thoughts to myself to tell you the truth."

"Oh don't be, I'll work things out in my mind. Just stay with me won't you no matter what happens? Give me a hand in all this; I need you, really need you and want you for a close companion."

"Really?"

"Yeah I do. I just wish the circumstances were of a lighter nature. I'm the woman you have known, I've just—."

"Ted reached for her, held her and gently kissed her. Linda was grateful for his affection toward her. There was no need for restraint; they both knew where they were and dearly had respect in the moment. It was certainly a lovely move for Ted to make as Linda dreamed that he would take this action. Such a moment strengthened her feelings and gave her hope of a blooming relationship with him. The kiss ended but Linda lingered in his arms and he was only too pleased to have her close to him. All the while they were embraced they talked candidly about how they would find opportunities for future tenderness. Ted commented on his fondness for all the Gerard's and had no objections to having to be in their company for the chance to get acquainted with Linda and so on and on the two talked for hours without even realizing that time flew by so quickly. Linda finally found herself getting hungry so they went to the kitchen to raid the fridge while the family was away at a movie theater. And she did eat!

Saturday morning Kelly called home and Mary was in her office and had just finished a conference call. She ran to the phone as she expected it to be Kelly calling. "Good morning my darling girl, how are you?" Kelly reported that she and Mark were on their way home. They just landed at Pearson airport and are taking a bus home at approximately three pm. They will have a couple hours wait for the bus and planned on taking a little shopping excursion at the airport.

"The gifts are in the great room, I'll have your favorite supper ready for you and I'll bake some of the sour dough biscuits that Mark has fallen in love with. You'll have to rent a U-Haul truck to take the parcels home Kelly. George will take care of it he says this afternoon. Tell Mark that Elizabeth seems restless but is doing fine."

Mark and Kelly were home or rather back at the Gerard's at about two fifty pm. They were greeted by Mary, the twins, grandma and Aunt Barbara. Elizabeth had been sleeping but Mark went to get her and stopped in to say hello to Linda. Linda had escaped for the day on the internet with a long email from Ted and agreed happily to join the rest momentarily. While Kelly was excited about opening hers and Mark's wedding gifts, the twins ran around the room jumping on couches in noisy anticipation of having many pretty ribbons and bows to play with. Mary requested that the tree and evergreen be left up until the newlyweds returned from the honeymoon. It was a lovely sight for Elizabeth to watch Kelly's inspiration as she opened every gift. Every precaution had been carefully adhered to for Elizabeth's safe and uneventful holiday away from the rest home. Her health was good and her spirit unshaken throughout the week long stay at the Gerard's. She now had a beautiful daughter in law; one she would be proud to have as a friend and extended family member. Kelly was having a great time with her treasures when George arrived home from work. Ted accompanied him and with Linda and the rest of the family they sat down to a wonderful dinner; lamb, baked potatoes, scalloped corn and of course, sour dough biscuits. There was pumpkin cheese cake for desert and the festivities just seem to carry on and on at the Gerard household. Mary is always looking for an opportunity to celebrate. Linda was very upbeat and was feeling exuberant about having Ted there to celebrate with. She was also in hurry to get everyone to forget the she and Ted was there so that they could slip away to another room to be alone. However; it was not to happen this evening. Linda attended church with the family the next morning. She was uncomfortable because of the guilt she felt but did not protest. Mark and Kelly had some neighbors' drive the U-Haul truck for them to Kingston after lunch and George would drive Elizabeth and Linda in his car and would assist in the unloading of the truck at Marks house. Although Elizabeth was sad to leave the hospitality that George and Mary bestowed upon her, she would be relieved and grateful to be back in her room where it was quiet and familiar. The Christmas holidays and the wedding festivities, not to mention the detriment of the past months stress had begun to come to a restful end. For Mark and Kelly, life had become real again once they put their cloud nine away. The family went to church for the first session only so that Mark and Kelly and his mother and Linda could get back home after a nice brunch. "Carol, could you and Mellissa stay at our place for a few days to help unpack and straighten the house up with us?" Kelly wondered

"Yeah I will but I'll have to tear Mellissa away from Gregg. It'll be neat to see your new house, you're so lucky. I like how you made up your little apartment. I didn't like having to sleep on the floor though when I came over."

"Oh my little apartment, I had almost forgotten about it. We need to pack it up and move my stuff out too to make room for Patricia. That's first on the list. Mark and I can do that through the week after school."

"It's back to real life for the two of you." George said.

"I think we all better go to Kingston, we can get a motel room. You'll need all of our help, you both have a busy time ahead of you."

Kelly was relieved to hear that. There was an appointment booked for Tuesday with Linda's lawyer. Mark had to be with her and Ted was also going as support for her and to hear the evidence and to build her defense to ensure a lighter consequence. Kelly didn't have to go back to school until the twenty second of January so she could also be there for Linda to help her mood from plummeting. Elizabeth was beginning to fret because she was anxious to be back in her room so she could be with her things and see her counselor. That would be Mark's first stop. Mark ensured his mother's comfort in the car with George and Mary while Kelly sat in their own car waiting for Mark. They were all off for the ninety minute drive to Kingston. Kelly reached into her purse and pulled out a peppermint and unwrapped it while Mark suggested the perfect wall to hang their engagement picture on. "That would be perfect hung between our computer desks in the den."

"You were beautiful; I loved how you swept your hair across your forehead caught with a bret then the curls hanging down the side of your face. The way the curls hung against the yellow silk blouse was fabulous. Kelly I've never loved a picture of anyone more then I loved yours. I love you so much."

"I looked that way because I was pictured with you wearing your engagement ring."

"I never got the chance to ask you before but where did you get the wedding dress?"

"Would you believe that it was handmade in about three days? All the dresses were; six seamstresses worked around the clock until they were finished. Mom had to pay big bucks to get them to put a rush on the job."

"Your mom is amazing."

I know she is; do you know she had all the calls made before we got to Stirling last Friday and the whole wedding was in the works probably twenty minutes after she hung the phone with us. She lives to plan weddings and I think this one was her trophy." Kelly and Mark laughed in jest.

Mark got a little sheepish in asking the next question but he just had to know. "Kelly I was wondering since there wasn't really any time to for you to go shopping, where did you find time to buy that wonderfully splendid negligée?"

"Oh darling the bride doesn't buy that; her friends present that special item to her at her bridal shower."

"Well seeing you in that reminded me of a work of art; absolutely enchanting. I'm a lucky man. You are a beautiful women Kelly, did you bring that little item with you?"

"I did, I wouldn't leave it behind. I sort of thought you enjoyed it and I do have it packed my good man."

"Do you have any more lingerie'?"

"I don't but since you have mentioned your fondness for them I just bet I could find a little shop at the mall that sells it. Now that we are married I'm going to send all of PJ's to the Goodwill and I'll never wear them again."

"It is possible that you will never again need to wear PJs again. Tomorrow go shopping to fill your drawers with lots of those little lacy numbers."

"Ok we have our whole lives ahead of us now and I can try on a new negligée every night."

"MMM, we better change the subject." "I brought some bottled water, its cold, here's one for you too!"

"Anyway Ted is very good to Linda. I don't know what she would do without his friendship."

"Mom said she stayed in her room since they returned from the wedding. Mom brought her food to her room because she was so uncomfortable around the others."

"I still don't think anyone knows that she is under court supervision do they?"

"No. Only mom and dad knew. Mom told the others she has migraines. Ted snapped her out of her dark funk somehow. I'm surprised she didn't call me but I understand why she wouldn't want to."

"I believe with our support and Ted's influence we may be able to get her probation conditions. I think Ted is getting really serious about her regardless of the age difference."

"I don't see it as a conflict. I think he excites her. I couldn't believe the change in her when they first met at my parents' house. There is quite a contrast though in personalities; Ted with his military strictness and Linda with her changing moods. "It turns out it seems that they are just a pair of fools in love; you know, their eyes met across a crowded room with all that drama."

Mark laughed about how Ted and Linda have changed each other to suit their selves.

"Well keep watch over Linda's moods so that she does not jeopardize her chances for leniency. Court will be stressful and she could conduct herself contemptuously and destroy her chances for support. She has to be able to think clearly to get past this and adhere to her conditions."

The job you gave her will keep her busy and it's probably the best thing that has happened to her all year.

I'm so glad that you decided to help her when I was pessimistic. We'll get through this and I believe that Ted will ask her to marry him, would that be a dream come true? I know Ted, he's like a brother to me and I have never seen him act so flirtatiously around a women like he does with Linda; it's very unusual."

"He wants Linda near him."

"If you say so and I hope that's true for Linda's sake."

"In court I felt very strongly that there was much hope for Linda and that the court will take mercy on her because of her recent family problems, and she is sorry, it's her first offence and she has a lot of good support."

"She has a job with you and her lawyer said that was a positive factor in how severe her conviction will be."

"I think the lawyer will see that her case will have a positive outcome, I actually can't wait for the appointment on Tuesday. I am not looking forward to seeing Linda in her blue moods though."

"Yeah I've seen that in her" Mark sympathized. "She will learn from your positive focus, you are a good friend to her and I love you."

"I love you Mark, we have quite an adventure to start our marriage off with."

"Amen to that."

Amen to that! Neither Mark nor Kelly was skeptical that they were able to cope with the situation; they were team with one purpose. They had a big job ahead of them in opening the store and with Kelly graduating in the spring and helping Linda with her trials; they would need to walk hand in hand through it all.

They made it to Kingston and arrived first at the rest home to take Elizabeth back. Mark escorted her in and she didn't chat much with the receptionist, she told everyone she would visit after she rested. Mark carried his mother's baggage into her room and saw to it that she was comfortable. Elizabeth was pleased to see that the flowers Mary gave her at Christmas were not yet wilted and she could enjoy them a little while longer. She added some more water to the vase and cleaned up some of the petals that had scattered and dried on the table. The attendant brought her a tiny tray with a glass of warm milk and her favorite maple cookies in a little basket. Elizabeth even found a sweet little welcome home card signed by all the attendants on the tray. The gesture was accompanied by the beauty of the memories of her son's marriage to her wonderful Kelly and she felt cozy. Before Elizabeth knew it, she was asleep in her lounge with a crocheted shawl laid over her; she was in a peaceful rest and began to dream of her late husband. Elizabeth dreamed that he was standing before her, he was smiling and nodding. He looked so handsome, more so than she had ever seen him look before when he lived. He was speaking to her but she could not hear or understand what he was saying to her. She awoke speaking his name. “Gordon, Gordon where are you?” Before she could realize she was dreaming she looked around her room for him. She felt his warmth around her as if she had been sitting to close to a heater. The warmth was the warmth she felt inside because of the love they had for each other. She was neither afraid nor surprised but she wasn’t about to just sit there wondering what had just happened. Elizabeth walked over to her closet to see if there were any pictures of her and Gordon with her belongings. There weren’t any photos or albums anywhere but in a box she found a large envelope containing legal papers and one had a black and white picture of Gordon on it. This was the first time that she had seen a picture of any kind of her beloved husband and she indeed smiled and held it to her cheek. Elizabeth didn’t care about the content of the document; all she wanted was this time with her Gordon. The dream was pleasant for her; she had not been able to dream since she became ill nor could she taste her food. She only ate because she needed to. A vast amount of memories of her life before the accident had been blocked out of her mind since the trauma of his death had stolen most of her emotions and senses from her. Her memory of the day that picture was taken of him made her happy. She briefly remembered that the picture was taken the day that he dropped the puck for the men's league in a local sports arena. That's all she could remember about the photo. She thought she wanted to call in her attendant to talk about her feelings when suddenly she was distracted by a voice she knew to be Gordon calling her by his favorite pet-name; "Kitten-Beth". Kitten-Beth will you wear your hair today the way I love it, you know the way" Elizabeth was carried away by the need for her husband to walk through the door as she looked over toward it. She sat on the floor in front of the open door of her closet and tried to make sense of what was happening. She thought of this situation as actually being a phenomenon and she tried to remember how exactly to fix her hair in the style that made Gordon's heart flutter. She twirled a lock of her hair and placed it behind her ear when she remembered that she had no curling iron or rollers because she had her hair done by a care giver. She thought if she could find some more pictures that it would help her to remember how to fix her hair the special way that Gordon liked.

She didn't find any because all of the pictures were packed up and put away in storage for a time when Elizabeth was well enough to enjoy them. She sat there on the floor for a few more minutes, sobbing quietly and unsure of where to look next or what to do about the feelings she was having. Elizabeth whipped her eyes dry and started having a head ache while thinking of what a childish thing she was doing there sobbing like that. She shuffled her feet out from under her, put the picture away to get up and put her nightgown on to go back to bed to finish her nap. Her next meal would be along in an hour.

Chapter Eleven

Tuesday morning Linda almost had to cancel her appointment with her lawyer because of the amount of snow mixed with freezing rain. Mark postponed picking up his new car that the insurance company settled on. Reluctantly the three of them did go to see the lawyer and surprisingly Linda made it into the office. The receptionist actually looked disgusted at Mark for posting ten thousand dollars to bail out a person who would actually defraud and elderly woman out of her money; or it seemed so to Linda because of the guilt she felt. Linda could hardly breathe at that point. The truth was the receptionist was only just brief with the clients, was there just to do her job and not judge anyone. She prepared the new file, recorded the court order of the bail bond, her charges and custody release papers. Linda had applied for Legal Aid while in jail and signed forms for a continuance of certificate. Linda was the only client in the office that morning and with her moods spiraling the way they do, she knew she couldn't bear the embarrassment of being seen or noticed by others in need of legal counsel. The three sat quietly in the black patented leather chairs in the waiting room. The walls were dark paneling and the floor was of dark blue looped carpeting. The dark blue vertical blinds were pulled shut as if there was going to be anybody out walking past the window in such rough weather. The darkness of the room was dimly lit with cold stainless steel track lighting; it made the room feel very cold and there wasn't even any art hanging on the walls. The only brightness in the room was from the colors in some flyers placed in a help yourself display kit about domestic violence and a couple car magazines.

"Mr. Solmes will see you now if you'll take the second door on the right." The receptionist directed.

"How do you feel Linda?"

"Kelly I'm going to faint."

"You two go in and sit down; I'll see if I can get Kelly some water." Mark said.

"Good idea." And Kelly held Linda by the arm in case she did faint and hurt herself.

"I'm in a lot of trouble here, I can feel it."

"It's ok; I think it's just the coldness of the room and the weather. Here drink some water Linda and it'll probably be another few minutes before he gets here so try to relax."

"I'm trying." Linda sobbed.

Craig walked into the office, a short man with red hair, about thirty six years old and very professional and serious looking but with a certain warmth in his eyes which caused Linda to relax some. She immediately felt that he knew his job and the law well, a good judge of people and knew how to give counsel to his client's individual needs. Every inch of Craig was well groomed and his office was meticulous yet dark and glossy. He shook hands with Mark and Kelly and Linda and began to review the evidence that the Crown

Attorney had sent in to his office. The evidence was strong, complete and overwhelming against her. Linda was advised that the consequences for fraud under five thousand to eight years in prison unless the defense can argue and depending on the accused's evaluation, the conviction would be determined in trial. Then the lawyer interviewed Linda. An affidavit was prepared in her defense. I was in a desperate situation, my tuition fee was overdue and that portion of my student loan was late. I had not enough money for my rent which was also overdue and I had not eaten anything in three days. I could no longer rely on my parents for assistance."

"Your parent won't lend you any support even feed you?"

"No, my parents recently divorced and mother left father penniless. My mother received a large inheritance and turned her back on the whole family. I had no one to turn to and my roommate defrauds people by phone all the time and she has never been caught until now."

"Your room mate was the only other person involved is that correct?"

"Yes; in this case anyway."

"Describe the situation and the plans for the phone scam on December 19th, 2010."

"I don't know how Bonny decides who to call but she got the number of Martha Miller and knew the name of her daughter. Pauline Haslow. Bonny made the call and I was to pick up the money from Western Union because it was for my own use."

"So that's your involvement? Bonny planned the scam and the money was for you."

"Yes she does this all the time and has collected thousands of dollars last year from one scam or another."

"Continue."

"Martha Miller actually has a daughter named Pauline Haslow and Bonny pretends to be the daughter and said that she had been robbed and needed three thousand dollars immediately. Miller believed this to be true and wired the money. We drove to a western Union branch in Brockville so we couldn't be traced and the police were pretty much there waiting for us there to collect the money. I was arrested on the spot and so was Bonny as my assistant yet she was the one that planned the scam. I feel sick, where is the washroom?" Linda was very upset and crying and ran to the rest room with Kelly to assist her. While the two women were in the rest room, Craig spoke to Mark about the arrangement he had with the court and the state of the situation so far. Craig added in her file that she will be working in the hardware store and now would have the support of him and Kelly with extended support, meaning Ted.

"Well that would be an improvement and a positive situation to put before the court. Without your support Mark she would have remained in Jail until a trial date could be set. Fortunately this is her first offence; she is a very young woman and with rehabilitation I'm going to recommend six months house arrest with one year probation and rehabilitation with your approval of being her supervisor for the duration of the house arrest she will remain living in your home under the current conditions. Will you approve?"

Mark didn't hesitate. "Yes I am willing to abide by the current conditions."

"Mark! Mr. Solmes I'm sorry I have to get Linda to a hospital. She's convulsing, she is so upset." Linda franticly interrupted.

"Oh dear; call 911" Mark ordered. Mr. Solmes assisted and called 911 on his phone. The receptionist entered the bathroom and found Kelly kneeling over Linda who was lying on the floor shaking uncontrollably and was very pale. She began choking again and the women helped her to the commode where she vomited repeatedly. The ambulance had arrived within five minutes.

The attendants hurriedly put Linda on the stretcher, cleaned her up, gave her oxygen and tried to ask questions then rushed her to the emergency department where she was stabilized. Mark and Kelly were close behind and took care of the admittance forms then Doctor Meg Stevens attended to Linda and spoke to Kelly and Mark. "Do you know of any medication or acute illness or does she have a history of depression?"

"We have only been close to her for a few days, she is under our supervision ordered by criminal court and we are unaware of any medical conditions." Mark clarified.

"We were with her in her lawyer's office discussing her situation then Linda felt sick, ran to the bathroom and started convulsing as well as vomiting. We weren't expecting this."

"You say she has been charged with a criminal offence, what are her current orders.

"She is under our supervision until her trial and conviction; she does show signs of moodiness and depression."

"Is she taking drugs or prescription meds?"

"Not that we know of. We only see the moodiness. She has been going through some very rough times in the past year. I believe she doesn't know how to handle what's gone on but I would know if there were illegal drugs."

"Ok thank you for your co-operation; we are going to run some tests and have a psychologist analyze her and admit her. It will be your responsibility to inform the court and in the mean time she will be under constant supervision during her hospital admission."

"Constant supervision?" Kelly was very worried for Linda about her diagnoses. "Why is that necessary? Do you think she will try to hurt herself?"

The doctor explained that the tests could determine that she has serious emotional problems and under the Mental Health code she must have supervision. Kelly and Mark embraced, worried and suddenly shocked at the realization that Linda had some serious problems. As Mark held his frightened wife his thoughts wondered from the responsibilities of trying to be a mentor to Linda. How would they cope, would they even know how to help Linda? "You will be in contact with Linda's lawyer I trust."

Mark replied to the doctor. "Yes most assuredly, I'll phone him right away."

"I'll write the order for her admission. You'll need it to present to the court."

"Ok I see. Thank you doctor."

"When can we see her?"

"If you will have a seat in the waiting room a nurse will be in to see you shortly."

"Thank you doctor." Kelly said.

Kelly sat quietly for a few minutes while Mark made the call to Linda's lawyer. He was on the phone for close to twenty minutes. The call was supposed to just notify the lawyer of Linda's condition but it turned into an opportunity to advise Mark in these types of situations. Mark and Kelly were so bewildered as to how to deal with more complicated situations, sensitive as they were. With appreciation to good intensions, Mark followed the instructions given and used them to enlighten Kelly and to help ease her anxiety for having to care for Linda as well as Elizabeth.

"Kelly how do you feel about the lawyer's decisions?"

"I feel that he knows his job and he seems to be experienced in working for the psychiatric side of crime and will work to get Linda the help she needs instead of locking her up. I'm willing to work with Linda under professional direction. Maybe it's what we needed Mark to help us get through this because neither of us have the experience in these matters."

"Well Not with criminal mental health, mom's health condition is in a different category."

"Well yes exactly Mark. The professionals will walk us through and help us with Linda."

"Ted might want to know what's happened; I'll send him a text message now."

Linda was admitted to a room later that afternoon and although she was relieved to finally have some bed rest since her arrest, she was skittish. She was sure that these things only happened in the movies that strange and wild screams came ringing from the corridors of mental facilities where patients were tortured and poisoned. She was still nervous because of the unknown. Linda was given a hospital gown to wear temporarily but the attending nurse said she would be permitted to wear her own cloths as long as they were comfortable and had someone to provide her with something clean to put on each day. She was also permitted to have a TV. and books of her choice but visitors must be screened as well as phone use because of her situation and legal problems that could occur. With the admittance formalities out of the way she was allowed to have a couple visitors. Kelly and Mark were able to reach Ted and that evening he showed up in Kingston with flowers and a large yellow and white teddy bear and a shiny gold and purple box for Linda. Ted was terrified for Linda when he heard she had become so ill in the lawyer's office. He had come to Linda personally and he knew her heart and her plight. With that knowledge it was no surprise to Mark and Kelly that he responded with such concern and left work to be with her at the hospital with gifts and such in a very short time after hearing the news. Before he entered Linda's room, she had been sitting in her bed sort of zoned out; not from meds but from relief or helplessness, one or the other. She just stared at the window waiting for whatever would happen in the next moment.

"Hello darling lady."

""""Ted I may be here for days or weeks."

Linda began crying and reached for Ted. He set down everything he had in his hands for her gently at the foot of her bed, sat down beside her and embraced her. He cupped her face tenderly in his large hands and felt her tears dripping on his palms. Ted; the hardened soldier sat and caressed and consoled her with the tenderness and concern of a mother or new father holding their newborn for the first time. She held on to his caress and every one of his heart beats took each piece of her disintegrating emotions to protect them so that they would not be forgotten. He looked into her black eyes and the calmness in his dark brown eyes cradled her in adoring love and they were able to see the worth in their relationship. "I love you Linda; I came as quickly as I could and I left work as soon as Mark called me. I hope you don't mind but I stopped at the mall to get you some gifts."

"I don't mind, I'm so happy that you did."

"I was in the mall for only fifteen minutes believe it or not. Everything I bought was right at my fingertips like I was led to them.

"Thank you, that's amazing and I'm touched by your thoughtfulness Ted."

"Here these flowers are your favorites, I remembered that and this teddy bear is to comfort you when I'm not here. You have a hard time ahead of you but when you are well enough I want you to walk out of here in this—open it Darling."

"The fragrance of the flowers is like nothing I've ever smelled before. I don't want these to ever wilt. Thank you, I just want to sit here and hold them and my teddy bear."

"Life in here might be bearable for you now."

"Well I don't know about that but it does help to know that you brought these to me."

"Open the box it will give you incentive for getting better and to walk out of here very soon." Ted's eyes welled up with tears at the thought of that day that she would be released and wear the satin copper dress.

Before Linda opened the box she kissed Ted and told him she would be wearing the dress sooner then he thinks.

"I know you will be Linda, I want you to relax and heal though you have been through some tough times this year, and it's going to come to an end believe me."

"Can I count on you Ted to be here for me?" Linda's lack of confidence in herself was showing out of that request. She realized it after she asked it. Ted began to speak but she did not hear what he said until she had the nerve to look into his peaceful eyes. At the end of her pausing she asked to repeat what he had said.

"You know dear Linda that I will be here for you; with all my heart and mind I will see you through this indignity. You are a good person and a lovely lady. I'm going to make right everything that went wrong in your life these past months. You can count on me."

"I can count on you Ted! I'm beginning to heal already. I know that your love will be the foundation that I will stand uprightly with and I promise you this, I will walk out of this place with you wearing this beautiful dress. Thank you Ted; it's up to me now and I'll be alright."

He brushed her hair from the side of her face and he had tears in eyes, tears of relief. There was forty minutes left of visiting hours and Ted made the better of every second he had with Linda where ever they were. Linda finally connected with Ted and she seemed well. Linda's attitude never went this way or that; she remained happy and talkative throughout their visit. Just before the end of their visit, Mark and Kelly delivered some comfortable clothes, toiletries, some magazines and a large orange milk shake for Linda. Kelly was astonished at the change in Linda's' mood and she sat at the end of the bed and chatted. "Girl I am so relieved to see you smiling, there's color in your face and all."

"Well thank Ted for that. I'm so tired of feeling like a dirty old towel; it's great to feel happy."

"She's going to be alright, guaranteed. I don't think she'll need meds, and she will be out of here in a couple days." Kelly gave thumbs up and kissed Linda on the forehead before putting her things away in the closet. The announcement came over the P.A. system ending visiting hours. Linda had been sitting quietly for a few minutes when two nurses came into the room to talk to her prior to the doctor visiting. They commented on how much better she looked then when she was admitted a couple short hours ago. They took her vitals, spoke to her about the rules and left her some juice and cookies and a napkin and advised her that the doctor would see her shortly. Doctor Laura Sealy came into the room to examine Linda and found her resting comfortably in her bed.

"Good evening Linda. My name is Doctor Laura Sealy and I'll be your attending physician. You stay comfortable, you are here to rest and I'll pull up beside you and we can talk." Linda held out her hand to greet the doctor.

"I'm pleased to meet you. I'm feeling much better than I did when I was admitted."

"You do? Well that's encouraging, the nurses said that you have settled down and that you were looking better. Will you describe to me what happened before you fainted?"

"I was at my lawyer's office getting ready to discuss my case. I remember the darkness of the paneling, the grey ceiling and the dullness of the track lighting; my heart began pounding and I felt sick. I ran to the bathroom and was very dizzy. That's all I remember. I woke up in the ambulance and they told me that they were taking me to the hospital. I think at that time my heart started palpitating again and I began to feel sick again. I had oxygen and was lying down so I guess that stopped me from fainting because I stayed conscious the rest of the way here."

"Ok Linda I can see by reading your file we have ruled out a stroke. Had you felt ill earlier in the day?"

"I've been so very nervous about my situation and my head, I did feel some pressure in my head and felt a bit of dizziness a couple hours before the meeting."

"Linda you had a spike in blood pressure while you were in the ambulance and we need to get it regulated and observe your health both physical and mental for a few days. I'll prescribe blood pressure medicine and keep you on strict bed rest for a few days and we'll see if we can get you some help with your emotions. For now I am prescribing bed rest with visitation only once daily in the afternoon. There will be a therapist in to see you in the morning after breakfast. You be showered and dressed by ten am. and ready to speak to the therapist. Do you have any questions?"

"Is there a chance that I may be released earlier then the five day arrangement you spoke of?"

"It is routine for a blood pressure patient to be monitored and observed for at least five days. I'm sure you will be doing well since you have been able to rest already so don't worry; relax and concentrate on feeling better."

"Thank you doctor."

Sunday after church Linda Mark and Ted visited with Linda in the afternoon visiting hours relaxing with and pampering Linda. Kelly brought balloons and Ted brought about the twentieth bouquet of flowers and wonderful china doll wearing a Victorian dress with long brown ringlets. It adorned the cupboard of teddy bears already owned by Linda. Ted had babied Linda because the doctors ordered that she stay in hospital until Thursday. Linda's blood pressure and emotional wellbeing depended on it. Her lawyer had been to visit during her hospitalization and has submitted an application for leniency and mercy due to her situation prior to the arrest. She had no criminal record and was a gifted student before her unfortunate situation. The victim received her money back and a hearing may likely award her a pardon.

Chapter Twelve

"Good morning, I'm Mark Scott and I have an appointment with my insurance agent concerning insurance a payout."

"Come right this way Mark, Carmon will see you in the second office on the left."

"Thank you."

"You are welcome."

"Good morning Carmon."

"Good morning Mark, good to see you." He shakes hands with Mark. Well as for our conversation yesterday, Meridian Insurance has come to a settlement for you and we here at Creswell-Mavis Insurance Brokers are pleased to present you with this cheque for the damages to your 2010 Toyota Cameray in the amount of twenty four thousand, six hundred and nineteen cents."

"Good, right on."

"There is your cheque Mark and if you will sign these forms and initial by the green tabs as proof that this transaction is done."

"No problem." Mark endorsed the forms after taking a few moments to read them and enters in to small talk. "So I here congratulations are in order."

"Yes that's right; I married about two weeks ago. I feel I've known her all my life but it's only been since October."

"I wish you both all the best for a long married life.'

"It's for eternity. Kelly and I are sealed for eternity and we are looking forward making our married life together a rewarding experience."

"Mark I'm listening to you talk about your feelings and I feel inspired to take roses home to my wife, thank you for that."

"You are welcome. I hope the flowers are well received; actually I know they will be Carmon. Here that's done and I thank you kindly for the work you did on my behalf." Mark left the insurance office and made the short walk over to the photography store to pick up the wedding photos. He found a familiar figure silhouetted against the window and he entered the store. He walked behind the man and placed his hand on his shoulder to make his entrance known.

"Ted good day. Linda looked way better yesterday; you must be so grateful."

Ted turned around to greet Mark and he shook his hand. "I took pictures of her last night in every light and mood that I could capture her in. I'm viewing them now."

"I like the gleam in her eye Ted; it's for you. You have done wonders for Linda. She'll heal easier now;

Kelly and I didn't know what we were going to do to help her."

Hey Mark; you and Kelly have nothing to feel guilty for concerning Linda. You have done more for her then anyone has."

"Yeah, physically we have done much but watching our blessed life has not done her any good I think by the way her moods change so quickly. We have been worried and very grateful for your intervention."

"Where is Kelly today?"

"She is with my mother. They are at home unpacking wedding gifts and she has taken this week off from school. There's not much going on yet with her classes and she quit working at the bakery."

"Oh did she? Well marriage will be good for her; you were so worried about rushing because of her busy schedule. She can concentrate on her marriage and graduating now.

"She has always given one hundred and fifty percent in everything she does; she puts me to shame because of the amount of ambition and drive she displays."

"Thanks Ted, I know she is more rested now. She just real worried about Linda's case."

"I've been in contact with Linda's mother, did a bit of investigating and found the witch and I'm going to meet with her."

"You're joking!"

"No way Mark; if it wasn't for her mother's selfishness and bitterness, Linda wouldn't have got into trouble. I'm going to turn that women's thinking right around and she is going to make it up to Linda."

"Oh I have no doubt that you will change her mom's way of thinking. Linda's lucky to have you in her life at this time. You genuinely care for her."

"It feels good to be needed especially by Linda. I've known her for a while you know and the first time I laid eyes on her I knew that I was going to be close to her. I'm getting anxious Mark; I want her out of the hospital and the trial to be over so we can concentrate on building a relationship and getting Linda back to feeling normal."

"I agree she'll be in frail health for a while. She and Mom get along well; Linda feels sorry for her and so they can relate to each other. They share the guest rooms and Kelly's parents' house and so they spent a fair deal of time together. When she comes home Mom will probably be a great support system to Linda."

"Oh yeah; she has to stay in Kingston, that's a sudden downer."

"She bound by court unfortunately Ted."

"Oh—; I had forgotten, I have been getting so close to her these past few days and it will be difficult to leave her here. I am going to be busy with her mother I guess that will be a consolation. It's time to set her straight on her priorities."

"Ted you be careful; supposedly her mother really turned vicious and has turned against her whole family. There may deeper problems, more vendetta then just selfishness which caused the rift between the family."

"I'll deal with it. Linda is my priority; I'll deal with the dirty work."

While the men finish their conversation Kelly and Elizabeth are back home unpacking.

"I have a text message Elizabeth. I'm going to look at it, be careful please; don't lift anything heavy."

"You go ahead Kelly. I'm going to read the manual for this four sliced toaster."

"Oh it's Mark. He met Ted at the photo shop and Ted knows where Linda's mother is; he's actually going to contact her and take action on Linda's behalf."

"Good for him, Oh my goodness! If anyone is going to reach that women and deal with her, it's Ted."

"Elizabeth this is juicy."

"Oh you're awful!"

"I know, but—oh I wonder how this story will unfold. I can't believe Ted is actually going to step in between them like that. Legally she had the right to her inheritance why did she turn on and abandon her family; oh it was just malicious Elizabeth."

"Ted will turn the table on her if he has to. Mary says he has some education in law. He studied it in military college. I don't think she scares him."

"He says Linda doesn't know and we mustn't tell her; Ted will. Oh I feel my own blood pressure rising right now. I wonder how this will affect Linda when she knows about it."

"She isn't well right now; Ted will have to be really careful with her. OH Kelly what a situation. I'm sorry that you and Mark have to begin your married life like this dealing with someone else's problems."

"Yes I know Elizabeth; it's been a real trip. I'm glad Patricia is doing ok. I don't think I could handle another trial. She has the support of her parents and I actually haven't heard from her since before Christmas. There are obvious problems between Patricia and Linda; I may not see her until I go back to school. Mark is coming home with the wedding photos so I'll do your hair if you want; he wants to go out shopping for frames."

"That'll be great; the curling iron is plugged in Hun." Elizabeth became very quiet and her face was radiant as she closed her eyes and imagined her own little paradise where she had to make no effort to have peace. She breathed a cleansing sigh and Kelly didn't speak either while she brushed or styled her mother-in-law's hair as if she were secretly led into a dream. Kelly fussed and primped and curled as if the two women were together in the same dream but the silence was broken when Elizabeth cried. She browsed into the mirror with recollection. Startled, Kelly placed one hand on Elizabeth's shoulder and the other on the side of her face and beckoned that Elizabeth not be upset or cross. Elizabeth's face still radiant and moistened with tears, she clasped Kelly's hand in assurance that all was well.

"Dearest Kelly, my hair." She exclaimed in love. Elizabeth recollected her husband watching her with adoring eyes as she presented herself to him with this exact hair doe. Both Elizabeth and Kelly looked in the mirror at each other unafraid but feeling his spirit with them. They existed with a calm assurance that it was his instruction that Kelly took to give his wife the hair doe that he loves most for his beloved wife. Kelly knew not about this secret. Elizabeth was in love again and the memories of love came flooding back, good memories of her marriage and she felt comfortable with them.

"Kelly The other day I was trying to remember, oh anything about life before my husband's death and I looked in the closet at my room and found a picture of Gordon; it was as if he were there asking me to wear my hair in this style because it was his favorite. It was so wonderful Kelly. I tried to find more pictures but they are in storage away from me because of my trauma. Now here today you have done my hair in that exact style for me. I feel him with us dear and he has inspired you to style my hair this way, the way he loves it and I feel his love again. Thank you Kelly." The two embraced.

"I believe I was inspired by your husband to do this for you. I've never done it this way before. I love you Elizabeth and you are—we are all going to be fine."

"Thank you, he has been looking for a way to tell me that he is here for me.' Elizabeth began to cry; she was able to feel emotions again and even able to laugh happily at this realization. Elizabeth and Kelly began to pray in gratitude for the gift they had just received. They had both been involved in that great moment of healing and then they started to get ready to go shopping with Mark and now had a great story to tell him.

Meanwhile on that same morning, Ted arrived home with those lovely photos he snapped of Linda. He had a variety of frames and pocket albums to place them in and decided to look at his emails first. "What's this: pond.dove@yahoo.ca: AW! This is just what I needed." It was an email; a reply to his note to Linda's mother Sinew Lee.

> To Ted
>
> I don't know why YOU should interfere in a personal family matter the way you have. The relationship that you have with Linda is yours and her business. Unfortunately for you both, I am not responsible for her current problems. As far as any further contact between you and me or Linda is concerned, the matter is closed.
>
> Sinew Lee.

To Sinew

If this is the only response you can give to a request for assistance to your daughter's plight, then I must reward you with the prize for indignity imposed upon a member of immediate family. Now you listen to me, Sinew; Linda is in need of moral and monetary support you can provide. I will proceed farther and suggest to you that this matter not be neglected. No harm will come to you, I assure you of that. It is important that you take heed of what I say. With this and the knowledge you have from my first email to you, I will be expecting a positive response from you in a timely manner.

Ted.

Four days had past and Ted did not receive a reply from Linda's mother. Therefor it occurred to Ted that he had not reached Sinew or made any kind of impression on her. Sinew was most assuredly not shaken up by Ted's stern request for help for assistance on Linda's behalf. Now failed as a positive stand of authority, he referred to his law books for a renewal of his confidence on a matter that he could not put aside. He learned that he could make an effort to investigate Linda's family medical records. These would be crucial in determining whether her poor health was treatable. Ted gathered this vital information as assistance to the doctors who were treating her illness with blood pressure medicine. He sent another email to her mother and explained the problems wither daughter's health.

Mark and Kelly's home had become in the short time since they were married, a world onto their own. The memorabilia of their great day spanned the rooms and corridors. At every glance and turn of head could be found symbols of a relationship stable and supported by threads that interlock one memory to another. Elizabeth although not fully released from the rest home, was spending most days with Kelly unpacking and arranging the treasured parcels once tagged with colorful ribbons and bows. Parcels which are now a part of a home that furnishes the beginning of a marriage and partnership in life abounding in blessings true. For most of the day Kelly and Elizabeth were answering phone calls and making calls to Mary for advice on arranging articles around the house. When the phone rang one certain time it didn't occur to them its seriousness and importance. Kelly answered casually and did not recognize the nervous woman's voice on the other end. "Hello is this Kelly Scott I'm speaking to?"

"Yes, who am I speaking with?"

"You are looking after—." The woman's voice turned emotional as she had begun sobbing.

"Excuse me is there a problem? May I help you please?"

"Kelly my name is Sinew and you have been looking after my daughter for some time and you have been courageous in taking on such a serious job."

"Oh Sinew! Elizabeth it's Linda's mother calling! Ma'am I'm so happy you have decided to contact me and please be assured, I mean no criticism against you. I know that life isn't always fair to us but when we reach out to each other in times of fear and uncertainty, much good can be accomplished; I thank you so very much for calling me about Linda."

Sinew was startled by Kelly's understanding as she was nervous and very skeptical that her intervention would be well received. She nearly didn't call at all after five attempts to dial the phone, she just lept into it. "I see that you are very wise for such a young women, it will be a pleasure to make your acquaintance."

"Then you have decided—, Ted told me that he had been in touch with you and it has been my prayer that somehow we would be able to reach you concerning Linda's health and situation. This is all we ask ma'am and maybe there would be a chance for you to reconcile with your daughter."

"I understand you are conscientious. Reconciliation will definitely take some time Kelly but I want you to know that I can appreciate all that you are doing for Linda and I truly feel guilty for all you have been through so far with Linda. It can't be easy for you and your husband yet you must be commended for your efforts."

"Oh thank you, we are committed to helping her with at first much trepidation but Mark was impressed that she was reaching out to us and believe me with help and support and rehabilitation, Linda will come out of her troubles a better person Sinew. Her health is first priority though and the court case is in remand court until her blood pressure has stabilized."

"Really, I hope Linda is grateful for all you do for her, you see there is a lot of—."

"Sinew, I want to praise you for calling me' I know it wasn't easy. I hope you will take your own time with this and when you feel comfortable enough, we would surely appreciate anything you are willing to help Linda with. I know that she wishes she could see you again."

"I live in Washington but I am in Ontario right now, In Toronto exactly."

"Ok—well um; that's great. I'm willing to come to Toronto to talk to you."

"Actually if you could do that; I've flown here and would appreciate a ride there to Kingston whenever you would have the opportunity."

"My husband and I will be there later today Sinew, I can't thank you enough. I'll locate Mark right now then get back to you about a positive time of arrival."

"Good enough Kelly. Thank you."

"You are most welcome; bye for now. Elizabeth did you hear? I have to find Mark right away."

"I suppose he's at the store Kelly, text him, I'm sure he'll drop what he's doing and run back here."

"I know he will and there has been such a delay in getting the store opened because of all that's gone on but I'll need him to go with me to get Sinew. Oh my gosh; I'm walking in circles; look at me." The two women laughed.

"Kelly sit down and collect your thoughts. I'll call him, just relax for a moment."

"Ok, go ahead."

"Kelly lie your head down on the table and put one arm over your head and try breathing calmly. He is on his way home now. Do you know he dropped the phone when I told him he was to pick up Linda's mother?"

"He is as nervous as I am then."

"That appears to be the case. He was at the store and he's going to drop everything and come home to get you."

"Oh so often he has had to drop everything and go, poor guy will never get his store open I fear." Elizabeth laughed charmingly.

"He is far better now than he used to be; he used to be so focused that he wouldn't know at all what was going around him and everybody else would be completely drowned out."

Kelly laughed out loud. "Do you know the way we met he was walking over to the store to unlock the door. He was late and he bumped into me nearly knocking me on my back and kicked my back pack off to the road emptying it and ripping the strap loose."

"That's Mark, looks straight ahead using tunnel vision or something; clearly an accident waiting to happen. Is that really how you met?"

"That's how it all began but I'm finding that he is more careful these days." The two women hugged after sharing affectionately their comments about Mark.

"I'm going to change my cloths. I imagine Mark will too so I'll go and pull something from the closet for him too. See you in a while."

Elizabeth was slow to decide what to do with herself now, they would be gone for hours and Kelly and she were unpacking together. How would she know where to arrange the countless gifts that were showered upon Mark and Kelly? Elizabeth began to feel confused as she does, which is not that often anymore. She decided to lie down because it seemed to be what she needed to do now. Elizabeth thought for a moment about something else to do because she knew if she went to bed, she would be there for hours. Elizabeth tried diligently to keep her mind focused and busy and knew she would be sluggish and have her sleep habits disturbed if she did take a nap.

Linda sat timidly on the side of her bed listening. She was accustomed to the sound of Teds footsteps on the corridor floor before he enters her room. She had been waiting for the doctor's visit to release her while her new dress lie across her bed beside her ready to put on to walk out of the hospital on Teds arm. Her blood pressure had been stabilized by medication in the quiet sanctuary of her room. She felt well but much excitement lay ahead of her on the arrival of her mother from Toronto. She would have the reconciliation between her mother as well as the court case to deal with. It all could cause her to be too anxious and set her back in her recovery. She sat a moment longer and looked at the remnants of her snack when suddenly she felt the warm flesh of Ted's lips caress her cheek along with a tiny fragrant bunch of lily of the valley. Linda quickly turned and reached for him, as he spun around to greet her lips with an extra and slightly more personal kiss, she wondered why she didn't hear him come in her room and she asked him. "Why didn't I hear you in the hall? I always hear you then my heart flutters, it actually does when you turn into my room."

"I know it does my sweet, I walked quietly, wanted to surprise you. You look especially bright today, brighter and with more color in your face then I have noticed in two weeks since you became ill. Please say you are going to put the dress on today."

"It is ninety eight percent possible, the doctor was leading up to it yesterday since my appetite has been good for the last four days. The meds are working for me and my blood pressure is stable.

I'm bored, very bored I might add."

"I heard the nurse say that you have been extremely quiet, just kind of looking off somewhere."

"I know. Kelly brought me books, I pick one up, turn a couple pages then put it back down. I feel too lazy to concentrate. I'm worried about having to go to work at Marks store."

"Why, because of lack of energy?"

"Yes, no energy. I'm not really moody though and I miss talking to Elizabeth. I feel sometimes like I have been some support for her or like I need to be that therapeutic shoulder for her."

"She reaches out to you because you understand what it feels like to be alone in the world. You two can relate to each other. That is the way to be, Elizabeth is home more now. There has been quite an astonishing breakthrough in her own recovery. She has opened up and can remember people, events and situations surrounding the tragedy back in Alberta. She has a great love in Mark and Kelly. It's just marvelous, the change in her health."

"I think Marks' marrying Kelly has given her a lot of hope and positive structure to build her healing process upon."

"There you go Linda spoken truly from your heart and from intelligence with you are bestowed with. Linda dear you have no reason to fear consequences. Oh there will be some formalities to deal with in your case but believe me; it's all going to be over so quickly it will make you laugh." Ted held her face lovingly in his hands and gently kissed her on the forehead and then on the cheek, just with the right passion to allow her to feel just comfortable and to know of his warmth and support.

"I'm going to get showered and fix my hair and makeup and put on the dress for you to see. I know that the doctor will be releasing me today."

"Ok Linda that's positive thinking and some definite action to get the wheels in motion."

"For a better tomorrow Ted."

"For a better tomorrow Linda."

"Linda started singing the theme song form the musical "Annie" Tomorrow. Ted picked her up and spun around the room with her singing the lyrics along with her because he was genuinely willing to react to Linda's happiness even if it were with childish anticipation. While Linda showered Ted flipped through the pages of some of the books on the shelf near the window when the doctor came into the room with a less concerned appearance then the days before her recovery. Ted explained that Linda was showering which prompted the doctor to reply that he would return when Linda burst out of the shower, shampoo dripping from her hair and tussling a bath robe around herself.

"No! Don't leave please doctor. What's the prognosis today?"

"You know it as well as your nurses know, but the question is do you feel like being released?"

"Yes please, I promise that I'll be ok and I will be careful with my blood pressure medicine. I'll watch food labels and do exactly whatever else you prescribe to the "T"."

"Ok Linda you get in touch with you sureties and you can leave whenever you please. I've signed your release form."

"Well this is great Linda. I can take you home, Mark and Kelly don't have to be there with you but I do have to take you straight to their house. I'll cook you a nice dinner after I get you comfortable. Now run and finish with your shower. I can't wait to walk out of here finally with you on my arm wearing that dress."

"Please wait right here; I promise you I won't be long at all."

As were Ted's wishes he escorted his love out of the darkness of ill health. The hour was there's and the glow from the shimmering soft satin dress reflected on her skin and dazzled the walls of the gaunt corridor. The timeless lines and the sleekness of its style made Ted proud of how fabulous she was wearing it. The drive home was a rather confusing time; Linda was enjoying her brush with freedom and had desire to heal and be well enough to have courage to take responsibility to deal with her consequence but the thought of all these things left her felling overwhelmed. Ted was somewhat afraid of his feelings; he was finally able to be alone with her and she looked lovelier then he had ever seen her look before. He was puzzled by her sudden timid mood. The departure from the hospital was not all he had hoped it would be—in his wishes and thoughts. There was a short pause at the stop light when Ted looked out his window. He did not see anything but had hopes that the silence would end. He heard the rustling of Linda's coat and caught the soft scent of her perfume. He looked over to where Linda sat beside him and could see the burden on her shoulders and the tears of unbearable times ahead of her. He then felt the reality; he was living in his dreams of Linda and him wondering away in romance and comfort. He was there alone with his friend, a woman who looked upon him for strength and support. That's all he could hope for from her at this time.

Elizabeth received Ted and Linda at the door and she pardoned Ted for being alone in a house with two women because he was a close friend to Kelly's family and a welcomed guest of Linda's. Although Elizabeth was startled to see Linda released from the hospital into Ted's care, she was relieved that she chose to come directly home. Mark would have a heavy bail bond to pay if Linda rebelled and so this was a definite concern of Elizabeth's. She didn't comment about it, she was just relieved that all was well with Linda, for the time being. Elizabeth didn't have the nerve to reveal the plans for Sinew to arrive later that evening in hope of trying to reconcile with Linda. She was most afraid of her reaction that such a shock would have her back in an ambulance with a spike in blood pressure. She decided that Mark and Kelly had better deal with her. Elizabeth took their coats and commented on the sweetness in Linda's demeanor and how classy she looked wearing the dress that Ted gave her which made them both feel welcomed and put Linda at ease. This allowed her to be more relaxed and receptive to Ted. Ted enjoyed time alone with Linda whenever he could find it. They found the back den to be comfortable and there they could sit and talk and try to reflect on how quickly events happened over the last few days and how the next few weeks would likely bear a tremendous load of uncertainties in Linda's future. She felt safe in the warmth of the room and in Ted's company which would prepare her to cope and find courage to seek assistance through the dreaded trial. One thing that Linda learned by what she had done wrong was that she need not attempt to take her burden lightly and to also not try to endure it alone. She confessed this to Ted and he felt the closeness to her at that moment that he had been hoping for. So of course Linda was fully prompted to show Ted that she was willing to devote her heart to him and relate to him affectionately. She did so when his cues were appropriately offered and the two followed each other's gestures in perfect rhyme.

Later in the afternoon Elizabeth met Mark and Kelly and Sinew at the front door. She was so excited she could barely speak clearly, with hands on her head then across her mouth then she extended her hand to greet Sinew. Sinew was about fifty years old with long black hair pinned at the back of her head loosely and she was tall for a Korean women. Her skin was delightful in its olive shade, clear and wrinkle free. Sinew was quite and an amazing looking woman. Her daughter matched her beauty however she was petite in frame.

"How do you do Sinew? Welcome to our home; come in we are going to eat in about a half an hour."

"Thank you Ma-am."

"Mom did you cook dinner yourself?"

"No dear, Ted and Linda are in the kitchen finishing up, I was just sitting at the table. Come in and sit down everyone. I'll tell Linda you are here."

"Are you alright Sinew?" Kelly asked as she noticed Linda's mother nervously rubbing her hands together.

"I'm worried about her reaction of course; she must be pretty hurt."

"Mom you and Kelly go and get her and sit with her."

As everyone waited in the living room, Kelly and Elizabeth entered the kitchen and softly broke the news to Linda that her mom was in the next room and wants to reconcile with her.

"She wants to now help you Linda, it's never too late." Kelly persuaded.

"I didn't even know where she was for almost two years; she left us, didn't tell anyone and we've all been so angry. Is she in the living room right now?" Linda began crying uncontrollably and Elizabeth sat and held her, her face began to get very red. Linda turned to stand up but couldn't; she collapsed and fainted across a chair and may have hit her head but Elizabeth caught her and Kelly jumped between her and the table. Kelly hollered to Mark to come quickly; get an ambulance for Linda!"

"Oh no! Sinew sit down please, please be calm and let me get an ambulance here for Linda.

She is taking meds for high blood pressure and this is not a good sign if surprises like this are going to cause her to collapse." Mark dialed 911 and ran to the kitchen to give them a report over the phone. "Kelly they are saying to elevate her head and cover her, keep her comfortable and watch for vomiting." Elizabeth grabbed a large terry towel to cover her with from the hall linen closet and a small cushion from a kitchen chair. Sinew did as Mark asked and Elizabeth decided to sit with her since Mark and Kelly waited there in the kitchen for the paramedics. Sinew fidgeted in her discomfort and whipped the perspiration from her forehead and neck with a Kleenex and nervously commented.

"I shouldn't have come here like this"

"Like this? What do you mean?"

"I could have written to Linda instead of just showing up in her life again after two years. This was ridiculous she was just released from the hospital. Oh Why have I done this?"

"Sinew please calm down, please. Any way you choose to present yourself back into her life would prove to be difficult because of her weekend health. Let's just get Linda to the hospital and play this by ear. We can get you two back together once the doctor gets her stabilized. Is there anything I can get you sinew to help you feel more comfortable?" Elizabeth asked her.

"If you have anything for headache-actually I have something here in my purse so if I may have a glass of water Elizabeth then maybe I had better leave. I shouldn't have come here I tell you."

"Please—I'll get you water and I won't tell you what to do." Replied Elizabeth. "But my concern lies with the unexpected responsibilities that have been placed on my son's shoulders. He is completely and financially responsible for Linda. Now with health problems, we don't know if she will be able to work and Mark is preparing to open his store in the middle of all this upheaval. Please Sinew; consider all that I have said."

Sinew said nothing for a few moments just sat quietly and drank the rest of her water after taking her aspirin. The paramedics were not long showing up at the kitchen door and began taking her vitals, administer and I.V. with meds to stabilize her blood pressure yet again. Linda had not regained consciousness since she collapsed. This episode actually put Linda's life in danger as her vitals peeked its highest. Mark and Ted and Kelly stood helpless as they watched the paramedics put Linda onto the stretcher and strapped her on to get her ready to be put into the ambulance. Mark shook his head in bewilderment. "Kelly what are we going to do?"

"It's Linda who faces uncertainty. We will pray for her and for Sinew, that's what we will do!"

"That's what we will do; right there my dear lady is why we are partners. Let's go; we'll get to the hospital in time to admit her. Ted went into the kitchen to inform everyone that Elizabeth would stay at the house.

Within twenty minutes Ted, Mark and Kelly were at the hospital. Their worrying was well justified; Linda had a heart attack and was rushed to I.C.U. No one would see her for hours.

The doctors and staff worked on her and finally at nine thirty pm. Informed Linda's supporters that they were able to stabilize Linda and there was minimal damage to her heart. Her condition warranted continual medication and perhaps weeks of hospitalization to ensure recovery so that surgery would not be done on Linda's heart. "She needs to be comforted now and her depression monitored very closely."

"We are attempting to bring her conviction down to a minimal conviction." Mark assured the doctor.

"I have no doubt there. I have met all of you and I am familiar with the support and effort made on her behalf and that's good to see." The doctor made his encouragement know.

"I don't know how I will reconcile with my daughter; I believe that my coming here has triggered her heart attack. I mean no harm to Linda." Kelly stood up and walked over to Sinew and offered her comfort in her despair over her daughter.

"I can't say if the worse is over Ma-am; we are working to monitor her depression and to observe her wellness and stress levels. Every day there is a new ordeal to learn from which why she needs further hospitalization. With that and the support system she has in all of you we will work together for the better of Linda's health and wellbeing."

"When can we see her?" Mark asked.

"I suggest that you and Kelly go in first; see if she is comfortable with meeting her mother. The nurse will be with her at all times in case of traumatic symptoms occurring."

Kelly hugged Sinew before leaving the waiting room to enter the I.C.U. department. She whispered, "Have faith." She anxiously left her with Ted and left to ring the nurse at the I.C.U. desk to enter through the doors. When they entered Linda's room they saw her ill, pail and Linda's eyes welled up with tears upon seeing her friends. The nurse explained the purpose for every machine and that they monitor her vitals which can be viewed at the nurses' station; they are not to worry about the sounds and beeps being made. Kelly spoke to Linda as a concerned big sister would speak to her younger sibling.

"You be calm dear; know that we love you and will keep a constant visual on your health and progress here. You can ensure that one of us will be here at all times Linda."

"Thank you, I'm so scared. I don't know what's happening to me all of a sudden."

"You are not healthy right now and we are going to concentrate on your wellbeing for as long as we have to. The doctor will keep us informed and you don't have to worry about anything at all except trying to get healthy for your own good, no one else's, just for your own good.'

"Linda, really, all you need to do is rest and don't worry about anything. We will do all the worrying for you at this time." Mark added.

"Is Ted here?"

"He is here, you bet he is. He can visit. The doctor advised us to come in here first as encouragement for you." Mark offered to leave to allow Ted to come in and she agreed. Kelly stayed and continued to talk to Linda when a very tall, muscular and extremely manly figure caused Linda to hush and her gaze suggested to Kelly that she wanted to be alone with Ted. She patted Linda's hand and snuck out. During Ted's visit with Linda in the I.C.U. there was a clambering of anxiety as Mark tried to encourage Sinew to stay at the hospital and eventually go inside to see Linda. She did prefer not to for Linda's own good.

"Linda is scared and ill; she doesn't know what's happening to her. It is in Linda's best interest that you do not go in there just yet." Sinew finally seemed offended and was lost for words and sat and wondered what the change in Kelly's attitude was all about. "I'm sorry; I have seen what a complete mess she is in there. She still is unsure of her consequences, we all are and she is still ashamed of what she has done. Linda was alone pretty much, in this world and her brother and sister although being a great support to her during the family rift have not been able to be reached. To this day she does not know why you turned on your family."

Mark interrupted. "Oh Kelly take it easy."

"Don't worry; she's exactly right. You see Linda always seemed to be afraid of me, I never knew why. I had always ordered her older brother and sister to step up and tow the line for me. I never did that to Linda because of her gentle nature. I fear that I pushed them to rebellion but they always looked after Linda; always. I saw the closeness my children shared—" Now crying almost uncontrollably, she added. "I was hurt in that I felt that there was nothing that my children wanted from me and I believed there was nothing I could do to win them over. I supposed I should have been grateful to have children who actually enjoyed each other's company. Then my parents died in an accident and I could barely realize what life I had left; how could I be of support to anyone? I just snapped I think and turned into someone I don't like very much then I left everyone. Why, oh why did life hand me this to deal with?" At this time and at the end of her vent, Kelly was holding her and handing her tissues.

"Mark will you get her something to drink please?"

"Right away."

"Oh dear I'm so very sorry for everything that I've done and how it has effected Linda's life. It's something I never would have expected Linda to do."

"I know that, I was shocked. I didn't know Linda personally but I was still shocked just the same because of what I did know of her character. She actually requested that Patricia, her roommate who by the way was also shocked by Linda's actions, ask her parents to bale her out of jail. Mark felt strongly that we should help her out. We don't think Linda will rebel against us or the courts."

"Oh I'm not surprised that this situation has put her where she is. I know that everything about her legal matter is driving her crazy—I'm grateful for the support she has, I can't say where she would be with out you on her side."

"Her shame is extreme Kelly insists."

"I'm not going in to see her until she is willing to reconcile with me. I'm going to write her a letter. I will stay in a motel in the city until then."

"Thank you for understanding; Sinew, I am glad you are no longer offended. The two women sat quietly; it had been a long day and they put their heads back and closed their eyes longing for a few moments of rest and peace.

The nurses were not far off but Linda and Ted were able to talk to each other alone for a while. Linda was relieved to have her handsome Ted in with her; he kept her calm according to the monitor. She kept her hand on his heart and he stayed very close to her and gazed into her eyes steadily and sent his concern for her though his closeness. She confided in him her fear that every dilemma would be cause to be stricken with heart failure and have to be hospitalized. "No one is going to rush you into anything; no court, school, family member, no one. I want to have you by my side Linda. I need you well. I need you to be strong and no one will cause you to be vulnerable again. I want to care for you."

Linda got the glow back into her cheeks and the beauty back in her eyes in the dim soft light of the room. She looked into the large boned structure of his face as if it were a wonderful piece on a museum wall. "I have felt the beating of your heart and I know you mean what you are saying to me."

"Soon we will be whole and complete and at peace with each other. Linda, marry me; dear let me be yours. I'll care for you, no one will ever abandon or hurt you again, and I love you."

"Yes, Oh Ted yes. Thank you, I'll marry you as soon as you want to."

"Let's get you well enough to walk down the aisle without fainting, but we should keep it quiet; no big deal, it will be too stressful for you."

"Ok, we could concentrate on a great honeymoon instead."

"Indeed! Don't worry about the court case, we will deal with it one step at a time and I know for a fact that you are not going to jail. I am hoping that if the court knows you are married to me, you will be able to live apart from Mark and Kelly and you will not be able to break the law. Since they paid your bail they will remain your sureties. If we can't work this out to the satisfaction of the courts then we'll have to wait until after the trial is over."

"Well I'm going to do everything the doctor and nurses tell me to do and I will recover quickly. I want to be a strong bride for you. I can hardly wait; I love you Ted. Please hold me until I'm well and I can walk out of here for good.

Chapter Thirteen

With all the love that Ted shared with Linda combined with the dedication of Mark and Kelly's strong support, Linda couldn't help but to survive her illness, estrangement from her mother and the anxiety of the court trial. Linda finally reconciled with her mother and learned to understand Sinew's feelings of rejection from her children that caused her eventual isolation and rift in the family. How often misunderstandings dishevel bonds and lack of communication and neglect of family values lead us unable to engage with respect to family. In regards to Linda's conviction, being a first time offender, she was granted the mercy of the court and was ordered to participate in a counseling program for six months. She was given a one year peace bond and if she did not break the law during the one year, she would have her criminal record erased. Linda was released from the hospital within nine days to the care of Mark and Kelly at their residence. She and Elizabeth always had a fondness for one and other. Their gentle personalities embraced and there was never awkwardness between them, only peace and understanding for each other frailties and the two women lifted each other's personal constitutions. Linda was at least company for Elizabeth while Kelly completed her final semester before graduating nursing school and Mark with the opening of his hardware store kept him away from home quite a few more hours daily than usual.

On Valentine's Day, the day before Linda's twenty second birthday, a delivery man brought a large package to the door for her. Ted and Linda had been sitting by the fire place snacking on cracker and cheese and drinking mulled apple sider when the doorbell rang. Ted unfolded his arm lovingly from around Linda's tiny waist while she opened the door. He knew who would be greeting her by the time of the day it was. There standing with fourteen of different variety of size of heart and flower balloons and a large pink parcel was a delivery man from Childress's bakery. The box was creatively adorned with a gold chiffon ribbon with dangles of candied red hearts and white feathers. Linda's smile was marvelous and Ted's heart couldn't stop pounding. He knew what gift lie inside and a bobble for his true love. It was a surprise for her and this day of romance and love would find a peaceful Linda and grant her continual success in love and in life and assured that she is cared for. The delivery man extended his best wishes to Linda and handed her the gift as Ted assisted with the bulkiness and size of the box. She took the balloons, hid behind them and kissed Ted. The passion with which she kissed him embarrassed the man standing at the door who waited for the signature. He was prompted to then just lean against the brick arch that framed the front door and looked off to the next yard where two children played in the snow. Of course Linda was anxious to tear into the box guessing that there were sweets inside because a hint came to her by the way of the bakery name on one corner of the box. Linda laid the box on the dining room table while Ted took care of the delivery man and thanked him very much with a large tip. He joined Linda who was happily waiting for him to join her to watch her open the box. She opened the box and laughed so uproariously she cried.

There inside the box was a two tear heart shaped cake adorned with Tarzan and Jane hanging from the vine of a tree. The little figures were imitations of Ted and Linda posing as Tarzan and Jane. She tried to talk and tell Ted how amazing the figures were but she laughed and he laughed because he realized her appreciation. The gift was very well received.

This Valentine's day, the first for Mark and Kelly did not go ignored. The two newlyweds left home early in the day to attend Temple sessions. Today would be the first time they had been back to the temple in the few weeks that they had been married and couldn't think of a more loving way to spend Valentine's day. It was a lovely mild day, clouds were clearing and the sun was beginning to warm up the earth and hearts of those awaiting spring. Bounteous treasures and gifts for Mark and Kelly would be bestowed upon them this day in the house of the Lord. The Elder at the front desk extended a welcome to them on their first time as husband and wife participating in Temple ordinances and wished for them a beautiful experience.

In the Temple that day they found true peace and clearness of knowledge to that purpose of Christianity; to redeem all mankind, to exalt all who are faithful to the Lords commandments in Jesus Christ's name.

During a certain quiet time in the temple, Mark and Kelly sat peacefully and after their prayer, they were overwhelmed with the gift of the Holy Ghost. Both, a little startled at the intensity of their feeling, as Mark looked into her eyes and she into his, they received an answer to their prayers. Their eyes welled up with tears and their hearts swelled with the truthfulness of what had been revealed to them. Together they gently placed their hands on Kelly's abdomen and felt the life that was protected there. In a marvelous moment of joy they embraced and the Lord and the angels that surrounded Mark and Kelly were witness to the surprise and added to their blessing of love. Mark and Kelly were lifted up to a higher level of spirituality for their marriage has been blessed with a baby.

Before Mark and Kelly left the temple to go to their car, they met a couple that Kelly knew and they conversed for a few moments. They shared with their friends their experience, the wondrous revelation that was opened up to them and congratulatory comments were given. The couple took pictures of Mark and Kelly as a reminder of the occasion and experience they shared. The other couple had partaken of ordinances once with a group of young single adults and was strongly impressed that they will marry. Blessed are these two young couples for the Lord had revealed to them their most precious desires for they were obedient to God.

Mark was at his best today, just on top of life and life was surely moving forward and the sorrow that was deeply embedded in his soul did not cripple him. His mother was recovering nicely thanks to the love of his dear wife and his choice to move after the death of his father. He was sealed to the most beautiful and wonderful lady he could ever dream of. She was in love with him and was carrying their baby, the Lord so testified. "I love you Kelly, I have to find a good restaurant. I have to really take care of you now."

"Somewhere romantic please, it is Valentine's day."

"Hey isn't there an Amish restaurant about twelve miles South; George and Mary eat there."

"OK, yes take the 210 south to Miller county road and drive about five minutes to get there.

"It will be very quaint."

"Yes, they will feed you well too, that's my motive." Marks eyes continued to show his emotions as he looks over to his pregnant wife.

"I trust in you Mark as a care giver. I know that you will give us the best and you are the best that we could ever hope for. Thank you; we love you."

Mark could barely hold onto his emotion then and Kelly smiles so brightly at him. The baby beamed at him through the loveliness of Kelly's eyes and they held hands the rest of the way to where they were going to have their lunch to celebrate their celestial blessing that Valentine's Day. They had their wonderful lunch traditional to the Amish setting; very simple, delicate and warm and filling. Mark made a couple of stops along their way to the next destination, George and Mary's house. It was nearly supper time when Mark drove up in the driveway. George and Mary had not returned home from work but Aunt Barbara and Grandma were there to greet the happy couple.

"Grandma it smells so good in here, meat loaf right?"

By the way Mark and Kelly walked into the kitchen, both beaming with maternal glory, grandma knew instantly. She saw the baby in her eyes and excitedly yet quietly pulled a chair for Kelly to sit her down and served her a nice glass of milk. Kelly wasn't surprised by her grandmother's instincts; she was just grateful for it and felt like she was home. She felt like grandmas little girl and told grandma and Aunt Barbara all about it. Dad walked into the kitchen through the great room carrying a dozen red roses and looked for an appreciative vase to make best of the beauty beheld in it so it would adorn the front table at the door side. His love would see them first when she enters.

"What a nice surprise. Didn't expect the two of you to drop in, I thought you would have been swept away on cloud nine together." George greeted them.

"I wanted to come home dad and I can hardly wait until mom gets home."

"She'll be home any time now, probably stopped at the store first."

"We went to the Temple dad, our first time since our wedding."

"Great. You need a break from all that's been happening in the first weeks of your married life. I hope everything is calming down and more of the responsibility in being put on her mother."

"It has." Mark intercepted. "The hearing has passed and Ted and Linda have gotten really quite close and

Sinew has been reconciled with Linda, thanks to our Kelly."

"I was only a vessel for the Lords work; they and the Lord have done the rest for their own good."

"Well I've been worried. You two need a better chance to begin your marriage and work together for each other. How's your mother Mark?" George asked.

"She's very well George. Linda and mother have been a comfort to each other, their gentle personalities mesh and they are very good company for each other."

"Oh good mom is home. Mom come here please, come here hurry." Kelly was exuberant in seeing her mother. Mary first hugged and kissed her husband for the roses and asked for the where about of Cindy and Sheila. She greeted Kelly and Mark with hugs and invited everyone to be seated in the dining room for supper. The twins came running down the back kitchen stairs to show mom and dad their basket of Valentines. They presented the cards to their parents that they had made earlier in the morning before they left for work as part of the center piece on the dining room table beside Mary's roses. Grandma and aunt Barbara served the supper and luckily had prepared enough incase company came and were no left overs for sure. After everyone had finished eating grandma entertained the thought of having everyone take turns sharing a bit of good news for everyone to here. The twins started and they were sitting beside their big sister Kelly; they talked of all their favorite little shows they got to watch on TV. that day and about their favorite Valentine cards.

Sheila pointed to Kelly and said. "You have your turn now, do you have special news?"

"Why yes I do." Everyone anxiously listened because Kelly wasn't home often and it was known to everyone now of all the excitement going on in her life at that time. "Well we went to the temple today and had a celestial experience where God revealed a special gift and a blessing for us. It was so intensely beautiful and mom and dad, we stopped a drug store along the way home."

With that said everyone listened intensively with their jaws dropped.

"I bought a pregnancy test to be sure and it was positive; we are pregnant and couldn't be happier."

The silence broke into joyous laughter. The family was exuberant with their congratulatory comments and hugs then the women gathered in the kitchen to tidy up and talk more. Grandma made Kelly comfortable in a big arm chair with a nice cup of homemade hot chocolate. The twins resorted to the great room to play with their dollies and dishes. By the time all was tidy, the family met in the living room where grandma presented Kelly with her very first baby gift; a white and green layette set. She had one made for all the older girls when the Monique got pregnant with her first child. This excited Kelly and she couldn't stop touching the softness of the knitted garment and in amazement imagined what her little one would look like wearing it. Kelly promise to bring the baby home from the hospital wearing the set.

"Well Kelly it's time we left for home, we need to tell my mother and your grandparents our news then you need to get your rest."

"Sounds good Mark. I need to see my doctor by the end of the week and decide on an O.B.Y.G."

"Stop in at a drug store on your way home and buy some prenatal vitamins." Mary demanded.

"I already did mom when I bought the pregnancy test and I bought lanolin cream also for my skin.

"Aw, that's thinking; it's never too early to start treating your skin. It has a long way to stretch. Listen dear, you're going to be great, you are tall and thin and fit and healthy but most of all you are patient and caring. You care for everything you have. Most of all, you have a caring husband to walk with you throughout this journey. I want you to be rid of all the stress in your life from the past few weeks."

"Meaning Linda I suppose. As we told dad the hearing is over, she did well and I expect that Ted will marry her within months. All is going well mom. Linda is saving money so that she can help herself. She thought of moving out already but could only afford to rent a tiny unfurnished room. We told her to stay comfortable in our house for the time being."

"Will her mother help her? She can afford to do something for Linda."

"Her mother is trying to move here and is getting a job transfer which is not going to be easy since she has only been posted in her position for just a few months."

"We will pray for Linda and her mother to have an easier time and that Sinew can get a transfer in a timely manner. I believe that if we have a family prayer tonight before you leave, we will see results." Mary declared.

George led the family in prayer on Linda and her mother's behalf. The Holy Spirit touched the hearts of everyone in the family because of their charitable service to Linda and Sinew.

Mark returned home with Kelly and before getting her comfortable for the evening they happened to chat a while with Linda telling her about their blessed news. Linda also had news of her own to share.

"I have been inspiration and good feelings since attending church with you and I have become so close to Elizabeth. Her faith in God and her sweetness is so wonderful. She has helped me by teaching me how to pray and most importantly, I know that God hears my prayers. He understands that I'm sorry for mistakes I've made. With this understanding I now feel more comfortable about being able to move forward with future plans and that I need to forgive myself. It's a tremendous load off of my shoulders and I am feeling healthier."

"Linda we are so happy for you." Mark told her and he was touched by her testimony and could see willingness in her to except the things in her life that she could not change. She could now move forward positively to achieve her goals. Happiness for Linda was just around the corner; just a prayer away. Happiness would finally be hers. Mark, Kelly and Sinew would be beside her and witness the changes for her future.

The phone rang while Linda and Kelly were talking about pregnancy and Mark answered it. "Linda its Ted on the phone, he wants to talk to you."

"Oh good I hope he is going to take me out; he said he wouldn't likely be around for Valentine's Day." She ran to the phone excitedly hoping that she would have a chance for a late evening drive and a chat.

"Hi Linda, happy Valentine's Day. I have three hours free and I just happened to be in Kingston; I want to see you and I'll be there in five minutes."

"I've been ready all day just in case you happened to call. I'll get my coat on and will be watching for you at the door." She hung up the phone and ran back into the living room falling back wards onto the couch. She wrapped her arms around herself and sighed. "I'm in love. My soldier man is going to walk away from battle just to be with his true love, oh Heaven loves me." With that she jumped up to get ready and Mark and Kelly watched on with approval at her excitement and walked off into the den to sit by the fire.

In exactly six and a half minutes from the time Linda hung up the phone her love knocked at the door and the two of them were in Ted's car and on their way to a surprise destination. Ted had plans for Linda; he chartered a helicopter to fly her over the city for a romantic evening ride. The lights over the water were a special treat and a favorite sight of Teds. He figured that Linda would enjoy and relax with him in the evening sky. When they arrived at the landing strip the owner of the craft was there and had the surprise already for Linda. Ted was still in his work uniform which pleased Linda and now she was going to ride beside this great figure of a man while he flew a helicopter and it added to the fascination of this great spell he had on her. It was a typical February night; the sky was clear and the stars were bright and it was as cold as a Canadian night could be. Linda wore a large hooded down coat with large parka and fluffy fir mittens, blue jeans and Eskimo boots. Although she was bundled up in full winter attire, she yet posed a very petit' frame and a soft interior light of the craft caught the glimmer in her dark eyes. She smiled very sweetly at Ted to profess her child like enthusiasm for the amusement ride. With the conviction of Ted's plan he flew the craft stalwartly and devoted his attention to the loveliness of the women of his deep desires. There sitting beside him that pretty silhouette against the darkened sky; he reached over to lay her parka against her shoulder to allow the stars to shimmer against the blackness of her hair and there they were in love. Linda was well on her way to recovering from her heart attack and was now accepting the blessings that God would bestow upon her through trusting relationships. It was a peaceful evening and heading onward to ten thirty pm when Ted landed the helicopter. In a little more than an hour he would have to leave Linda and go back on duty. He chose to take her on a helicopter ride because of the wonderment of the sights at night and he knew the sight of having her sit beside him would be breathtaking. He knew that she showed interest in what he did as a military officer; she found it to be very alluring and he wanted that attention from her. She knew by his glances that he enjoyed her flirtatious attention. A few strands of her hair blew across her eyes as she looked up at him, she had to look up a fair ways to meet his eyes as his large chest was actually at her eye level. She could smell the thick fabric of his military winter jacket which broadened his torso. She wanted to be nearer when he tenderly pulled her into his caress and the manly warmth of his entranced her. The bitterness of the icy winter night was also controlled by him in the vibrancy of that passionate moment. Ted picked Linda up and she remained committed to his gaze, she quietly surrendered with love and he carried her to the car where he would end the evening and ask for her hand in marriage. He was serious with his intensions but Linda felt playful. She told him a Valentine joke but he didn't get the punch line until she pulled the Valentine from her purse and gave it to him.

The Valentine held the answer to the joke and he appreciated the pun by kissing her on the forehead. They were out of the cold wind and the car was beginning to warm up so he candidly took her mitten off of her left hand without her really noticing what he did, she was still chatting about how she found the joke. She felt the heat pulsating from his large hands when he held her petite fingers lovingly and kindly he held her hand to his lips. This caused her to pause from being playful; she looked at him; smiling and not taking her eyes off of his as to wonder what he had been feeling just then and what his intensions for the next enchanting moment would be. His military demeanor suddenly softened and he told her that he was in love with her. He pause from what he was about to say because of the fullness in his heart and with his other hand he reached into the inside pocket of his coat. He took her left hand in his and placed a gold and diamond ring on her finger and asked, “Linda with all of my heart and soul I ask you please, and I would be honored if you would agree to be my wife?”

“Ted I hold this moment in our lives most dear to my heart. This is the moment that memories will hold the kindest of feelings for us throughout our lives as husband and wife. I love you for giving me this special gift. Yes Ted, I will marry you, I love you.”

In mellow tenderness they looked into each other’s eyes, the love radiated and they had been released from doubt and their destinies were meant to meet. The sweetness in her face sealed the knowledge for Ted of the truth of their love and spirituality of marriage. They talked at this time candidly that a spring wedding in May would set the tempo for the path of their lives together. In spring it’s warm and colorful and life begins its fresh start as Linda would begin a fresh start to her life.

Ted’s spare time was flying by too quickly and he decided that taking Linda home would give him about five minutes to get back to the base. Mark and Kelly would have turned in for the night so he would just leave her with a hug and a kiss with plans to go snow mobiling on the next weekend. Linda returned home and quietly got undressed and prepared herself for a warm bubble bath so that she may lay in the softness of the bubbles in the glow of candlelight and watch the fire flicker in her marvelous diamond ring. The house was quiet and all that could be heard was the popping of the bubbles. She lay there still and the happiness of her thoughts mildly led her to the fantasy wedding in May of hers and her soldier man. She dreamed of having her father and her mother walk her down the wedding isle and although that would be a tough task to pull off, it's a goal that would be worthwhile perusing. Would she marry in a church or decorate the Gerard's gardens with white trellises and chairs and a long white carpet leading to and outside alter? Would her brother and sister find this marriage to be the defining event that would reinvent the family bond that was ripped away and shattered just a couple short years ago? While she wondered about all of these blessed hopes she glanced at all the candle which began to burn brighter to give her thoughts and dreams truth and purpose. In the peacefulness and tranquility of the moment she heard her grandmother's voice say, "Go forward in Faith." Her grandfather's voice followed, "Be with the one who delights your soul."

She laid still there, her eyes filled with tears, not from fear but with the comfort of knowledge that was just given to her. Linda was looking toward a blessed life and feared no more for her future.

The weekend came and just as Ted promised he picked Linda up and they and Mark and Kelly fueled up the snow mobiles and headed to Stirling to ride the country trails. Kelly packed a good lunch and filled the thermoses with hot chocolate but stayed behind at the house so as not to hurt herself. She would instead accept babysitting duties for her niece and nephew so that Monique and Brian could go along with Mellissa and Carol to head up to the trails also. Before leaving George suggested that everyone meet up later at the Two Loons Lodge. Mary would make reservations for a winter party of sorts. It would be part snow mobile party and part engagement party for Ted and Linda. George and Brian knew of about seventy miles of trails that they could travel on that day. It was a perfect winter day for outdoor activities; there was a fresh snow fall almost every night and it happened that this Saturday was clear and bright and perfect for a fun day in the snow. Ted was almost a permanent fixture around the Gerard household on his off duty times and Linda was getting closer to the family. She was learning to relax and was in weekly contact with her own mother. They were both enjoying the rebuilding of their mother and daughter relationship and there was plans for Sinew to come to Kingston for two weeks to in part pay for and assist Linda in making her wedding plans for May.

George and Brian led the group of snow mobiles onward. Kelly stood by the back kitchen door and listened to the numerous engines, the tracks brushed the light top snow around while the cleats on the tracks dug into the crustier snow underneath to give traction and speed as the group followed the leaders off the property. She joined the twins, grandma, Aunt Barb and the children in the great room to read a story. Mary sat close by and knitted for her new grandchild that was expected in October. Linda found the outdoors and the cold fresh air relaxing and although she road on the back of Ted's machine they talked constantly over the noise of the engines. Linda enjoyed his company, the beauty along the trails and most of all holding tight to Ted. This was her first time on a snow mobile and was amazed and hoped for many more of these winter outdoor activities and spending more time together in the future. They would not be seeing each other during the week days except for the pleasure of the odd impromptu hour here and there when time permitted. The group stopped among a grove of evergreen trees to have a warm cup of hot chocolate. George stopped to tell the new members of the group that it was the grove that the girls and the 4-H club planted and they continue to plant yearly as a project in learning and replacing trees that were taken. Linda was so talkative here on the beauty both of the nature and of the story of the work and experience and memories brought forth from that grove. The Gerard family extended their gratitude for Linda improvements in health and spirituality. They began to pray there in the grove and related to her inspiration to go forth in faith and to rely on the Lord threw the charity of those who care for her. She and Ted grew in love more on these kinds of experiences spent with the Gerard family as well as with the truth in their destinies. After some frolicking in the snow the group carried on throughout the miles on the trail where George led them and they ended the trip at the lodge where the rest of the family and some friends would welcome the chilled snow mobilers. Much to the surprise of Ted and Linda, the gathering was planned to be an engagement party where Sinew, Thom, Jack and Tanya Lee would reconcile for Linda. Kelly was instrumental in bringing the family together and to determine that the rift was not important anymore and didn't really hold substance in the first place. A small part of mistrust was able to tear apart and make each of their minds toil with paranoia until the family grew apart. This hurt Linda the most. When all involved were given the chance to realize the wrong that had happened for little or no reason, it was easier for the Lee family members to look upon one and other again with mutual understanding and trust. The family had not been together in the same room for almost a year. Linda got to have all of family members under one roof; although she was scared at first Mary and Kelly greeted her for support. It had been only a month since Linda had the heart attack but she is now able to control her blood pressure with medication and did not fall ill with nerves. Everyone at first remained seated and gave Ted and Linda a chance to gradually socialize and greet everyone personally. The meeting with her father, brother and sister was awkward but still rather sweet and Linda looked at Ted and nodded. "Well I think everything is going to come together nicely for us."

"I'm sure it will, this is all for you dear."

"Let's go to the front of the room and announce our engagement and wedding date."

"Ladies and gentlemen. Linda and I find this day to be the second happiest day of our lives. The first was earlier this week when I asked this wonderful lady to marry me. She said yes in the sweetest way that I could imagine. Although I knew that we would be meeting some people here after our day in the snow, it is a surprise to us that it has been made into a party for us. Thank you all of you for your kindness and I believe Linda has a wonderful announcement to make."

"Thank you, and thanks all of you for sharing this special day with Ted and me. My heart is beating so rapidly I can hardly stand. It is a pleasure to see my family all together because I have not seen them all in months and that make this a joyous time for me. I guess I would like to announce that we will take our vows on May 12th. Arrangements have not been fully made yet but if the Gerard's have their way I won't be waiting long for plans and arrangements to be completed. Since they have pulled this elaborate party together in two and a half days I want the party to begin and ask that you all have a great evening. Thank you on behalf of Ted and me." Mark escorted them to the head table and they feasted on a chili and garlic bread dinner, the perfect food for winter enthusiasts.

Cinnamon hearts floated in the punch as a symbol that Valentine's Day was still being celebrated and was on the minds of all couples attending. A live country band crooned for those in love and everyone actively participated in line dancing and country boogying. Echoes of stomping and clapping were sent to the outer wind and a glee filled evening air.

The party went on to the wee hours of the morning so the Gerard's opened the guest wing to Ted and Linda and her family for the night and for those who wish to attend church with the Gerard's and the Scotts. George and Mary of coarse were always looking for missionary experiences and were prepared to invite Ted and Linda to visit with President Cassidy regarding holding their wedding in the church. Mary was anticipating an outdoor reception on her lovely lawns to give her another opportunity to shower another bride with princess like attention. Truthfully if Mary gets the need to nurture, Linda will not have a chance but to let Mary have her way. It wouldn't hurt anything and the bride would be treated like royalty. Mary would afford Linda the opportunity to fully reconcile with her family before the big day and that would assure that the family would have a comfortable experience.

During the wee hours Linda and her mother sat together in her bedroom at the window and shared a tender moment. They talked and reconciled and made a commitment to put away their troubled past. Linda opened up to her mother, listened to her mother and began to understand Sinew's feelings and breakdown due to her parents dying. Linda initiated reminiscing about her grandparents. Sinew openly but with a heavy heart spoke of her parents pride at her giving birth to each of her three children. Sinew commented about the year her parent immigrated to Canada; she and her siblings were children and it was the happiest day of their lives. Their sponsors were two wealthy sisters who had no children and they spoiled Sinew and her two brothers. "We felt as though we had moved to a whole other world from literal rags to riches. The sister provided English tutors for all of us. They trained my father so that he would know how to manage their restaurant."

"Momma they went far in the business didn't they? Florence and Victoria could never have held that business together in their golden years without your parents and they certainly provided well for their family."

"That they did; I miss them terribly Linda. I continue to morn. I did not seek professional help, I just let my mind suffer and I can see now that it has hurt you. I am so sorry."

"Mom I'm the one who is sorry, I thought and so did the others that you took the money out of selfishness; we didn't consider your anguish at all. Oh mom I'm sorry for the kind of pain that took you from us. Can we at least try to end the rift and find pleasure in family life?"

"Well whatever family life we experienced wasn't the loving bond that the Gerard's share as far as I'm concerned. But we have the opportunity to start over and build on whatever family situation we have."

Linda sat quietly and looked away from her mother. She was right about having a strained relationship with the family. There wasn't much to build on however the Gerard's could be a good example for them to follow. Sinew noticed the unhappiness in her daughter's expression and she cupped Linda's face in her hands. "Linda I am truly sorry for everything that has happened to you." With tears streaming down her face she continued. "I promise to commit to be the kind of mother to you and to your brother and sister that you all deserve. Please don't feel any more pain on my account."

Sinew held her daughter for a time and they decided that they would start fresh on a new day tomorrow.

Chapter Fourteen

Sinew and Linda woke up together and went down stairs to an empty house. There on the dining room table they found a little note form Mary telling them to help there selves to breakfast. Their breakfast was in the food warmers still hot and smelling irresistible. Linda's father, sister and brother left early in the morning but had made plans with Linda to spend the next weekend together at Mark and Kelly's house. Ted was on duty and the rest went to church so Sinew and Linda had a couple of hours to eat and talk alone together. Sinew was still nervous about talking to Linda about the trouble she got into so all she was interested in was talking about plans for the wedding in May.

"Linda, are you planning on getting married in the church that Kelly goes to? I know that they are not of our faith; I know you trust that they will make arrangements for some spectacular over the wall lovely wedding but I think you should consider marrying in a church of our own faith."

"If that's what you want mom—."

"No Linda you ultimately make the choice, it's yours and Ted's day. I wish only that you make the proper choice. We could book a banquet room at the country club and this would ease any stress and burden from the Gerard's. I know that Mary enjoys this stuff but she has many daughters and I think she is just being nice in offering you her assistance."

"Do you believe that? You know they have beautiful property and I can only imagine it to be like a tropical garden in the spring or a colorful English garden when I try to picture what it would look like here. I have dreamed all week long of walking through the rose gardens wearing my wedding dress."

"I suppose Mary will make your dress too."

"Mom, what's wrong with you?"

"OH I know that Mary and Kelly have been very generous but are you going to let them rule your thoughts until they are living their lives through you? Yours will be the first marriage of my children and I feel I should be helping to plan your wedding day."

"Mom you are depressing me; I don't even want a wedding now. If it keeps up I'll tell Ted that I just want to run away and the sooner the better." Linda got up and walked away from the table. Sinew followed her daughter into the kitchen and stood close to Linda and with her hand on her shoulder she spoke to Linda.

"Dear I regret upsetting you; let's leave it alone for now, really. You and Ted decide what you both want to do but please include me will you?"

"Thank you Mom, I accept your apology."

"Maybe you both will have made decisions by next weekend and we can talk then."

"Well I don't know mom." Linda continued to feel the strain on their relationship. She had not gained enough trust in her mother or her family to yet include them in personal aspects of her future.

"Linda I am willing to work with Mary in the planning of your wedding, I'll be in touch with her through the week."

"You will what?"

"I mean I will be happy to have her help, I want to make you happy Linda."

"Oh mom that's fine but please let me have time with Ted to discuss our plans, to decide what it is that we would like to do. Gosh maybe he would like me in a yellow or an orange dress, I don't even know this yet. I am going to be his bride and I will be what he wants me to be on our wedding day. Please mom, understand this."

"Well I can't understand you; you are offended at everything I say." Linda quietly left her mother standing in the kitchen and she went to the den to use the computer. Sinew was hurt by Linda's reaction and didn't hide her feelings about it. She got her purse and coat and car keys and left the Gerard house.

Linda was no longer bound by the court to live with Mark and Kelly. They eventually began to enjoy each other's company and Elizabeth was fully released from the rest home and also living with Mark and Kelly. The hardware store was open and Mark would hold the grand opening on the twenty eighth of February. Linda was already on the pay roll but did not yet have enough money to rent her own apartment. Ted would soon be Linda's house mate so they held to their living arrangement for the time being. Ted would be in the North West Territories until Thursday night on emergency military duty. Linda planned on working at the store; make a guest list for the wedding and she would talk to the Childress's about designing her wedding cake. She was not sure where to hold the wedding but she was leaning toward Mary's garden. Linda had only heard about how beautiful the gardens were and was hoping that Mary and Kelly could show her pictures when they returned from church. She had thought of holding to tradition to wear the magnificent gown her mother and grandmother wore. It is an exquisite silk, chiffon and lace gown with a fourteen foot train. The veil is four layers of embroidered chiffon. The problem with the dress is that Linda's mother and grandmother are taller then she is so Mary's assistance would be helpful. Linda wondered how she would make the wedding arrangements without her mother being offended at any suggestion that didn't run by her first. She grew tired of worrying and went back upstairs to soak in the tub until the family came back home after church. She enjoyed being alone mostly but the peace was broken by the sound of the twins running up stairs to their room to change their cloths for lunch. The happy sounds in the Gerard home especially on Sunday Is a break in Linda's boring yet stressful existence. The girls through their dresses out into the hall and Linda noticed it and picked them up and greeted Sheila and Cindy. "Are these dresses dirty girls?"

"No they're out of style." Cindy commented.

"We have new cloths mom bought for us yesterday. They are for occasions but mom said we could put some on today." Sheila added.

"Well that's nice. Do I get to be the first to see you wearing your new cloths?"

"Will you help us find what matches?"

"Yea, help us pick out what to wear." Sheila and Cindy asked.

"Right on; I can do that." Linda gladly replied and she entered their room and the girls were jumping on their beds in excitement and Linda sat at their desk chair to wait for the girls to show her their much sot after fashions. Linda helped them choose the floral embroidered blue jeans and the black and white cotton blouses with musical notes trimming the sleeves and bodice. Linda brushed their hair and accessorized the hair with floral combs. They looked so sweet.

The girls invited Linda to lunch. "Come on down stairs with us, we are having cake for desert. Mom said." Linda escorted the girls downstairs for lunch, one holding on each of her hands and they joined the family. After lunch the ladies helped aunt Barbara and grandma clean up then Mark, Kelly and Linda headed back home to Kingston.

Elizabeth is now completely released for the rest home but she still continues to tire easily and she rested right up until supper time. Linda sat at the computer for a little while because Ted had some free time to chat and she kept busy there for over an hour while Kelly prepared supper. She made pizza and salad and had ice cream to go with the pie that grandma sent home with her. Linda's brother and sister decided to drop in; they decided to really keep a better watch over Linda. They had both been away with friends over the Christmas holidays and were unable to be reached. Their mother needed to relax; there had been family skeletons rattling and she needed the situation between her and the children before the social event at Mark and Kelly the next weekend to even out. Mark met them at the door and escorted them into the den where Linda was visiting Ted on the net.

"Come say hi to Ted we are video chatting. He is in the North West Territories. He got there at eight am this morning. He left the party last night and he and some of the other officers flew through the night to get there. Isn't he amazing? Look at him."

Ted began the conversation. "Good to see you both again. I'll be done here in the North on Saturday morning and I won't have another chance to communicate again after this afternoon." Jack was interested in his work in the North.

"Will you be taking pictures at all? It would be nice to see pictures of the scenery there."

"I won't be its strictly work this time but I can email some interesting pictures that I have on file; hold on a few minutes, I'll send some now."

"Ted I'm having Tanya as my maid of honor; do you have a best man?"

"I haven't yet but I had considered George. Would you like Jack to be the best man?"

Jack intervened. "Hey Ted don't you worry, you barely know me. It would be more appropriate to have George stand with you."

"That's fine with me Ted; isn't my brother nice?"

"It is considerate of you Jack and it makes planning easier for Linda."

"We'll help Linda however she needs help if she wants it. We have always been close, the three amigos you know?" Tanya laughed. "Yes I know, Linda is fortunate to have you both near her and I can concentrate on work easier knowing you are available for her."

"That's great Ted. Hey I still feel the wind in my face from you passing me on your snow mobile." Jack joked.

Ted laughed. "Was that you? I saw something out of the corner of my eye; I was going to stop to ask you if you needed a push or boost because you seemed to be sitting still." Ted replied in jest.

Linda got in the joke. "Jack was slacking back like he was afraid of putting tracks in the snow or something."

"He doesn't have to worry about messing up the snow; he can ride on my tracks." The four of them had a great laugh and carried on together for another few minutes until Ted had to say goodnight and he would see them all next weekend. The three of them adopted Ted as the fourth amigo. Linda's spirits were very high. She had no more black moodiness. The conviction was minimal, her health was gaining momentum and she had the love of her live along with her brother and sister by her side again. Although she was grateful for her job in Mark's hardware store it was below her expertise but she was willing to give it her best effort.

Monday, Tuesday and Wednesday the last shipment would be received by the store. The merchandise would need to be entered into the computer and arranged on the shelves. That would mostly be Linda's job and the store would unofficially open on Thursday afternoon for business. She would then be working in sales and cash. Mark instructed her to be quite efficient in her job. Linda is very smart and learns easily. Mark tells her something once and she knows what she is supposed to do. Mark told her that he appreciated her and that training her was a pleasure. Her assistance actually made the job of securing the scheduled opening of the store no task. Wednesday afternoon Mark, Kelly and Linda were in the store working along with Jack, Tanya and Thom, their father as extra hands. There was still much to do to have the store ready to open the next day but most assuredly, they would be ready. Mark was impressed with Thomas Lee. He was very responsive to his kids and experienced in retail because of managing a restaurant all of the years that he has lived in Canada. Mark and Kelly had a very good crew and enjoyed the good company that came with the help. Linda received a cell phone call; it was her mother and she wanted to see Linda. Linda asked Kelly to take a break with her and meet her mother across the street at the diner. "Linda I didn't know you would be bringing Kelly with you, don't you trust me?"

"Mother why are you being rude to us?"

"Linda if your mother wants to speak to you alone I understand, you don't need me there Hun. She hasn't seen you since Sunday, don't worry."

"Mom I can't believe you did that to Kelly; you've made me so mad."

"Linda I've asked you to meet me, am I wrong to want to see you?"

"That's fine but you were extremely rude in your attitude. I just find you to be miserable sometimes and you had no reason to do that to Kelly, She has been so kind to me. What is it that you want?"

"Please I'm sorry Linda; calm down. Have you had your lunch dear?"

"Yes quite a while ago."

"Ok sit down with me and I'll order something, I haven't eaten yet. I wanted to talk to you before I go back to Washington. I'm leaving March seventh and I wanted to leave a cheque with you to help you to pay for the wedding."

"Oh I see Mother; does this mean you are not going to move back to Kingston?"

"That's right, I've made my decision. I think you and the rest of the family will be all right. You don't need me and I have made a life for myself there."

"Ok whatever you want but I don't think you have given reconciliation much consideration mom. Are you upset with me?"

"Linda you are recovering now and you have a good future ahead of you with Ted. I'll be at the wedding, just send me an invitation and I'll be there for a few days to celebrate with you."

"Oh I see so away you go on your own again. That way you don't have to engage or actually reconcile with your feelings. What about the family learning to relate to each other again?" Linda got up to leave, she was shocked and hurt and as she stood she fainted. She had a rise in blood pressure caused by the confrontation with her mother. Sinew called 911 and told one of the patrons to go across the street to the store to tell Kelly what had happened. People rushed over to Sinew to help her in the care of her daughter and to wait for a few short moments for the paramedics to arrive. Linda did regain consciousness but she was incoherent and began vomiting. She was very ill again and would need hospitalization. Mark and Kelly discussed the ordeal with Jack and Thomas. They wondered how Linda would survive being married to a military officer and make light of the stress of planning a wedding if she could not keep her blood pressure in check. They feared that the illness would leave her disabled for the rest of her life. Sinew rode with her daughter in the ambulance to the hospital.

The rest would meet them there shortly afterwards. Mark, Kelly, Jack, and Tanya met in the waiting room and Sinew and Thom attended to Linda in the emergency department while the doctors and nurses worked on Linda. Ted was unable to be reached. Mark and Kelly would have to wait until he returned to Ontario on the weekend to tell him of Kelly's setback. As a military officer Ted is often called to duty on a moment's notice; it is a great sacrifice to personal time and obligation. This responsibility has been second nature to Ted but Linda as his wife will not have the comfort of a flexible schedule and lifestyle that she is accustomed to. She now has to deal with using medication to stabilize her blood pressure condition. Ted was attracted to the gentleness of Linda's personality and her delicate and natural beauty but now it may seem that his desire for partnership with her would be selfish because of her ill health. There may be too much strain put on her as a military wife. Thomas and Sinew's concern for their daughter left them feeling skeptical that there should me a marriage between them. Thom and Sinew had a very serious conversation regarding this and it was decided that Sinew would stay on in Kingston for what mattered; the family and Linda's recovery. Linda is in love with Ted and is ill at this time so her parents wouldn't confront her too quickly about postponing the wedding. They would first discuss the matter with Mark and Kelly since they have been such an example and support to her. After talking with Thom she realized and agreed that the confrontation was not the cause for Linda's attack; it was a reaction to her illness and it will take time for Linda to learn how to work on problem solving. Sinew also realized that it will take time for her and Linda to be comfortable in each other's company and that she would have to pull back and wait until Linda reaches out, she would be willing to except Linda's need and desire for a relationship with her. For now Sinew will be counting on Kelly to convince Linda of what's best for her wellbeing.

Linda was admitted to a room and was being observed. Thom and Sinew asked Mark and Kelly to meet them for dinner so they could all talk. It was decided that they would meet at Mark and Kelly's house where the atmosphere would be comfortable. Mark called ahead and asked his mom to prepare some food for them and Linda parents. Elizabeth had dinner on table when everyone arrived. She invited them to sit down, eat and be comfortable. After eating Mark and Kelly, Sinew and Thom met in the living room while Elizabeth cleaned up. Thom began to speak. "Mark, Kelly; we need your help to try to convince Linda to postpone the wedding."

"Yes and we are hoping that because of Linda's health she will decide against marrying Ted. He is much older than her and she will find it to be very stressful being married to a military officer."

"I agree with Sinew on this matter. Sinew is not going to leave and we aim to break the rift in our family. This will make life easier for Linda." Since Kelly has been closer to Linda, she replied fist to Linda's parent's request. "I don't know—I'm literally shocked and . . ."

"Kelly we know that Ted is a family friend of yours but our concern lies with Linda's wellbeing and we know that his duty will take him away from her often. We know Linda better than him, he hasn't known her for more than a few weeks and it just seems to be a disaster waiting to happen." Sinew made her distrust in the situation know.

"That's right and how can he have her wellbeing at heart? Look at him, he is very regimental and she is sweet yet moody and now she is ill. Please Kelly consider her condition and see our concerns."

Mark attempted to defend Ted's motives. "Let me talk to Ted I've gotten to know him fairly well. Leave this with me and please don't confront Linda directly with your concerns. Kelly will keep her eye on Linda; she will have a R.N degree in a couple of months. She knows what to do with Linda's health issues." Mark concluded.

"Ted will do right by Linda. They have had a spark for one and other for quite some time so the engagement isn't really as big of a surprise as it seems to be. I would only imagine that their marriage would be good for her; he can provide very well for her you see, and that alone would be much of a relief for her health. Kelly also came to Ted's defense.

"Please consider what we ask" Sinew pleaded. "We are not trying to upset anyone's life' we have been confronted with hard times these past two years and have not known how to cope with everything just blowing up in our faces."

"She is right. I do not hold Sinew responsible. She didn't know how in her mind to deal with her parent's tragic death and so she left us thinking she ran off with the money out of selfishness, needed to start fresh. We all know that she regrets it now but it will take time and much work to reconcile the family."

"Do you two feel that you will remarry? That would be wonderful and I will support you all in any way that I can." Kelly offered.

"We don't know that. We won't necessarily reconcile as husband and wife but we are a family that has fallen apart. What we desire is to pick up the pieces and carry on as a family should." Sinew replied.

"We are not asking you both to take full responsibility in persuading Ted and Linda to sort of slow down or back off; we will talk to them both when Ted returns and Linda is feeling well." Thom said.

"Linda is very happy being engaged to Ted. I think you are making a mistake but time will tell. We can't predict how Ted and Linda will react to your concerns. I will say that we will support whatever Linda decides either way." Mark declared.

"I didn't think you would make this easier for us." Sinew complained."

"We simply disagree with you. However maybe Linda will take your concerns to heart and postpone the wedding after she had a chance to talk to you. Mark and I wish all the best to you and your family during the next few weeks. I know that after a two year separation there will be a lot of stories to catch up on." Said Kelly.

"Please accept our thanks for all that you have done for Linda.

You are good people; caring, trusting people. We can both see that. Kelly if it was not for your kindness and understanding that first day that I spoke to you; believe me I would not have come here to help Linda. There was sweetness in your voice; your disposition drew me to want to be able to trust you. I could hope that there would be some chance that the wall of contempt would be taken down if I but took the initiative and open up to you."

"Well thank you Sinew. It was always my intension to do the best I could to help Linda get the assistance she needed. She really felt like she had nowhere to turn and I felt so bad for her in spite of the decision she made."

"I know your feelings, Ted told me all about in an email. I felt very intimidated by his bluntness. He made me feel like I was in more trouble and it scared me; that's why he got a negative response from me. He did do the right thing by giving me your name and phone number. I was very frightened about calling to talk to you but I see I did the best thing for Linda in calling you."

"Sure you did Sinew. I'll tell you my heart jumped right into my throat when I picked up the phone and heard you introduce yourself." Kelly's encouraging words relaxed the tension between the two women.

"Now you see Kelly why I am concerned that Linda is marrying someone of Ted's bluntness. He can be very intimidating."

"I agree with you Sinew. I am beginning to understand your concern and hesitation a bit better now." Mark said. "We will talk to Linda to appease your concerns; again we will support Linda in whatever she decides to do."

"I disagree with your pessimism. I've seen how Linda comes to life when she is with Ted. He would provide a wonderful life for her. Marrying Ted would be a God send to Linda." Mark concurred. Mark and Kelly talked a bit more about Linda to her parents and Sinew and Kelly joined Elizabeth in the kitchen for some Herbal tea. They said good bye after tea and supposed that they would meet at the hospital the next day. Elizabeth went upstairs to bed to read and Mark suggested relaxing in the den to watch their wedding video. Mark made a fire and the two of them curled up on the floor in front of the TV on a soft warm fake fur rug to watch their blessed event. Mark presented Kelly with her favorite massaging lotion and sat behind her to apply it to her back. She pulled her hair to the front of her shoulder in anticipation of feeling his warm touch. While he massaged her tenderly she sang to him the song that was playing on the wedding video and by the time she was finished singing she was completely released of any tension of the day's events. She was relaxed and answering to his advances. Very quietly he turned down the volume of the TV and made his wife comfortable on the carpet and large cushions. They were alone together like that until the fire dimmed down. Mark put the fire out and softly helped Kelly up. They retreated to their bedroom to watch the rest of the video and go to sleep.

Thursday morning came upon them; it was the grand opening of the hardware store and when Kelly woke up she felt nauseous for the first time. "Mark I feel really pregnant now, I am feeling morning sickness"

"You look pale too; do you think you can make it to school?"

"Oh sure, I'll have a light breakfast and take lots of water to school with me today. I am sorry that I can't make it to the opening."

"Jack and Tanya will be helping me today, they told me so yesterday."

"That's excellent and I'm glad of it. I'm going to check in on Linda about two pm. then I'll be in to help."

Jack and Tanya did indeed show up for work at the store. It was to be a temporary situation. Mark hired five other employees other than Linda so the day went fairly smoothly. Thursday seems to draw senior citizens out to shop and the employees were busy with extra service. Kelly felt well for the remainder of the day and wondered how long it would be before she began losing her breakfast in the morning. However she was happy to be experiencing the nausea in the knowledge that she was carrying Mark's and her little baby and she was radiant. She made it to the hospital just in time for visiting hours to see Linda and found that her parents had been there with her for the day. She entered the room to find Linda crying and her parents consoling her.

"Linda, hi sweetheart, is there anything I can do for you?"

"Can you contact Ted?"

"We don't really have his contact information while he is on duty but I'll email his personal inbox from my blackberry in hopes that he checks soon. I'm afraid that's all I can do Hun."

"Ok, I'm just miserable without him and I feel so sick."

Kelly realized then that Thom and Sinew could be right about Linda being unhappy married to Ted. She just didn't want to believe it. "Linda I emailed him just now. Honey have you considered that you'll miss Ted so badly during a deployment when you are married?"

"Oh I don't care, Kelly can you just email him please?"

"Ok sweaty just relax, I did and I told him that you are sick again and to call the hospital if he can. How is that?"

Thom and Sinew informed Kelly that Linda has not eaten and Kelly also expressed concern for that. "Linda I'll do my best to contact Ted but it really isn't going to do any good worrying him about you. He can't leave his post to come to you so I want to be able to tell him at least that you are eating; Linda will you please try to eat?"

"Yes you are right; could someone find me some salad and chicken soup?"

"Oh thank you Kelly. I'll get you some, I'll go to the restaurant to get it and I'll be back as soon as I can." Said Sinew.

"Linda honey let's talk." Her father requested. "I know that you are lonely being in the hospital and Ted can't be here for you. That shows us that you are in love with him."

"Yes I am dad; he doesn't know I'm sick and he is so far away. I hate that he can't be reached."

"Now dear he'll be away quite often. I don't think that you have considered this when you entered into a relationship with him."

"No dad I didn't but I don't care. I love him and he very much wants to marry me."

"I know he dose dear but try to consider how much it's going to bother you when he has to go away. Please Linda, see how miserable you are right now. Consider the amount of time he will be away from you and how you are going to feel before you actually marry him."

"Dad, what are you saying?"

"Linda your parents came over last night to talk to us about your cancelling because of your illness. It may be too much for you to deal with."

"You what?" Linda protest fiercely.

"Last night I disagreed with your parents but I now see your distress and my opinion is leaning toward what your parent suggest; that you don't marry Ted."

"Oh you are all crazy now! Why do you want to ruin my chance of being happily married to Ted? Look at you, you got your happily ever after story. Are you afraid that I'll have a better wedding than you or something?"

"No Linda, honey please don't be angry; I just want you to be well." Kelly in fact was terribly hurt by Linda accusation but realized that Linda wasn't able to understand their reasoning. All Linda could see was Kelly being jealous.

Before Kelly could say anymore, Linda's hospital phone rang. It was Ted. Kelly was sitting closest to the phone and answered it. "Kelly I just had a terrible feeling that I should look at my mailbox and I read your email. I don't have long to talk; can I speak to Linda?"

"Yes here she is; she's in bed. Linda its Ted."

"Oh Ted are you coming home? I'm so sick again but I am not in I.C.U. I'm so miserable and I don't know why I'm getting sick every time something happens to upset me. Please can you come home?"

"Linda I'll be right by your side on Friday night when I get home. I love you Linda.

Remember our helicopter ride? It was in between jobs and honey; I'll always make time for you. I'm busy yes, but if I have a half hour here or there I'll be with you. Are you good with that?"

Linda smiled and said. "I'm good with that. I'll take a half hour here or there and I'll make it worth your our while Ted."

"That's my lovely little soldier girl. Where's the teddy bear I gave you? If you have it there you use it to snuggle with and that's an order; darling."

"Yes sir babe."

Thom sat straight up in his chair with a shocked look on his face and Kelly hid her face; she was laughing so hard. Sinew walked in not knowing what just happened to change her mood so quickly. Kelly sat there just beaming and watching the change in Linda and Kelly spoke. "Do we need to say any more?" She directed her question to Linda's parents.

Although Thom and Sinew acted like they were relieved their concern remained with their daughter's wellbeing. They did not continue to press the issue of the relationship ending. Linda assured Ted that this attack was not as serious and she would be released in a couple of days as long as she was stable. She anticipated a quiet weekend though; no partying. They said goodbye to each other as Ted was on duty and would have to finish their conversation when he returned home to Ontario.

"I feel better already. I love him very much. He will always know in his heart if I'm not well; he has made it part of our bond. I'm in his heart and he is in mine. The fact that he had a feeling that he should check his inbox proves that this is true. I will marry Ted on our scheduled May date. Now if you will all understand that I am as sure as I can ever be, I am going to recover and plan my wedding. I am going to be very busy working and making my wedding plans and building a stronger relationship with Ted. So you see I won't have time to be getting sick anymore."

Kelly approached Linda and kissed her on the head and bid her a good day and much rest for recovery. Mark gave her a few days off, as long as she needed with the doctor's permission to return to work. Thom and Sinew stayed a few minutes more and were relieved that Linda had straightened up and talked for a bit more.

Chapter Fifteen

As Linda stated she was released from the hospital two days after she was admitted. Thom and Sinew picked her up and drove her home. Ted was back from the north but wouldn't see her until Sunday evening. Mark, Kelly and Elizabeth were not home; she figured that they were all at the store so Sinew made some of Linda's favorite herbal tea. Kelly introduced her to it and she often relaxes with a cup of peach and ginger tea. They sat in the living room and Thom and Sinew were very careful to listen to everything Linda had to say to get to understand her feelings and desires in order to avoid upsetting her at this fragile time. Linda realized her parents concern for her and in appreciation, she accepted Sinew's cheque to pay for the wedding. Soon after her parents left she wrote an email to Ted and then went upstairs to take a relaxing hot bubble bath. There she drifted off to sleep for a couple of hours. Elizabeth returned home while Linda was asleep in the warm bubbles but Mark and Linda didn't return from the store until eight o-clock in the evening. At that time Linda was on the internet busily looking for bridal gowns and ideas for floral arrangement and invitation designs on a bridal website. Elizabeth had a meal already for Mark and Kelly when they got home, Linda had already made herself something for dinner so she did not join them. She was very happy and relieved to be home and have a week off of work and was hoping that Ted would have a couple days free to spend some time together alone and help with ideas in the wedding planning.

Sunday morning Mark, Kelly, Elizabeth and Linda joined together for breakfast and they were able to talk Linda into going to church with them. They had a little while to talk and the topic was Kelly's pregnancy. "I'm only one month along and I'm surprised that I'm already having morning sickness. I'm eating lightly at breakfast but expect it to soon get more severe."

"Have you been to the doctor yet?" Linda asked.

"Unfortunately I haven't had time. I want Mark to come with me and we have an appointment tomorrow."

"I have hired a young lady, Janice and I trust her to run the store If I'm not there for a while anyway."

"I agree; Janice seems to be on the ball." Linda commented.

"We are going to a maternity clinic so that we'll be able to have an ultrasound without delay. Gosh I can't wait to see the Scott child." Kelly boasted as she rubbed her tummy.

"While I was looking for bridal websites I came across some maternity fashions and with your height and slender build, you are going to look fantastic in the newest styles."

"Oh thank you Linda. I've already been massaging my abdomen, hips and thighs with lanolin; Monique started preparing her skin right away and it greatly reduced stretch marks. She got a few marks on her lower back because she didn't think to massage that area."

"Well good luck." Linda said.

"I imagine that you have already started knitting." Elizabeth commented.

"I actually have not but I have stuff already made in my hope chest that I've made."

"You have a hope chest Kelly? I didn't think girls did that anymore; collecting thing for their marriage."

"What you mean you don't have one?" Linda laughed with her answer.

"No not a chance. My parents were always so busy with the restaurant to show interest in marrying off their daughters. The restaurant became our lives too until we got into to college. I think it's only been the past year that Jack and Tanya had any social life at all. Mom and Dad rarely let them out of their sights and I think that's the reason for all the hard feelings."

"How's that?" Mark asked.

"Oh I know family closeness is most important but we forgot that we had lives of our own and when we started learning that there is something else to life besides working in a family business, my parents didn't like it." Linda vented. "My dad stayed with managing the restaurant but had some bad times after mom left. He worked day and night and Jack and Tanya helped when they could which made them angrier at mom for leaving. I'm very surprised that they had anything at all to do with her since she has come back to Kingston."

"Well it's fortunate that they have put their feelings aside for your sake."

"Yes that's right but it's going to take some time for us to all grow together again as a family."

"It's not impossible Linda. You are right; it will take some time." Kelly said

"You come to church with us today and we'll pray together."

"Have faith Linda, we all do." Elizabeth said and Mark and Kelly agreed.

"Ok I'll get ready. I'm glad you asked me to go, it will make the day go faster until Ted comes over tonight."

They all left to go to church together and arrived fifteen minutes before the service began and found Jack and Tanya sitting together in the chapel. Linda was so happy to see them and felt right at that moment that Mark and Kelly were right about faith playing the part in her family reconciling. They quickly went to sit with Jack and Tanya and spoke quietly. "Are mom and dad coming to church?"

"I don't know." Jack said. "The missionaries came to the store while you were in the hospital." Tanya answered.

"We told mom and dad about talking to them and mom said she might come but I don't know whether dad will. He'll be at the restaurant doing prep work." Said Jack.

"Listen you all sit here and I'll wait in the lobby to see if they show up. They'll feel more comfortable if someone they know is there to greet them." Mark said.

The chapel filled up with people in the last ten minutes and Mark entered with both of Linda's parents. None of the other members of the Lee family had been to church but Linda and she was thrilled to see them yet puzzled that they would attend the Sunday services. It was a very social experience for Linda's family. The pastor was certainly glad to see Linda's whole family and also to know how well Linda was getting along since the first time he met her. He praised Mark and Kelly for their service of all they had done for Linda in her time of need. Mark invited the Lee's over for lunch and they feasted on a variety of sandwich wraps, fruit and yogurt. It was a nice light lunch and was a usual occurrence for Sunday brunch. After eating lunch the missionaries who invited the Lee's to church made a surprise visit and brought a religious video to view and visited with the Lee's for a while. The family needed that type of encouragement at that time. They needed to be associated with people who would support and encourage forgiveness and the importance of the family circle and most importantly now, reconciliation. While talking to the missionaries Sinew praised Kelly for charity towards her daughter. She referred to Kelly as an exemplary member of the church and in God's Eyes. In so many words, Kelly was their angel.

Mark and Kelly took Monday morning off to go to the maternity clinic and Elizabeth accompanied them. She couldn't sleep over the excitement of getting a view of her first grandchild. "Mom, why don't you stay home and try to get some sleep; we can bring home a photo of the ultra sound to show you."

"No there will be time this afternoon to sleep. I couldn't live with myself if I missed this day." It was a twenty minute drive and Elizabeth did rest then. At least she had a tiny bit of energy for the excitement of what she was about to see in the ultrasound picture. Elizabeth waited in the waiting room while the doctor examined Kelly. The doctor was of course impressed with Kelly and what great health she is in and for the healthy habits she displays. She knew enough to begin taking prenatal vitamins and to prepare her skin for the inevitable stretch marks. It was time for Elizabeth to be called into the ultrasound room. This was a new experience for Elizabeth; ultrasounds were not done on a regular basis when she was pregnant with Mark. She entered the room eager to know how Kelly is. "How are you dear?"

"I'm just great and everything is moving along on schedule; I'm one month along."

"And you are beautiful Kelly." Mark glowed and he held Kelly's hand while the technician prepped her.

"You have a good size uterus and an abundance of amniotic fluid. Oh now look at what we have here my dear girl." The doctor enticed.

"What? What are you looking at; I can't tell what it is you are looking at." Mark said.

Kelly knew though and the look on her face was priceless, then she grinned from ear to ear.

"Do you see these two dark circles side by side?"

"Yes is that the baby." Mark asked.

"It's babies Mark." The doctor reported.

Marks eyes were as big as saucers and Elizabeth gasped, covered her mouth with her hands then sighed.

"We have twins Kelly! Look at that; an instant family." This discovery was a jubilee for Mark.

"This is quite a surprise." Said Kelly.

"I think the front bedroom will be suitable for our little ones." Mark observed.

"I think you are right; with the two closets and a long narrow room, there will be plenty of room for two cribs. The carpeting will make it warm and quiet in there for them. It's faces the street but it is a quiet street and we will be able to open the widows so they can have fresh air while they are sleeping." Kelly answered.

"Mark and Kelly they look good, congratulations. I'll snap a few pictures and give them to you."

"There we go Mark; our first baby pictures to put in the babies first scrap book."

"Well that's awesome. Mom you didn't expect two grandchildren did you? There's the proof mom; twins!"

"Isn't that lovely and I'll be living there with you to help with the babies. It will make things easier for Kelly and Linda will be married to Ted by that time and living with him." Elizabeth commented.

"Ok Kelly you can get dressed and see the receptionist on the way out of the office to make another appointment for four weeks' time. Usually at twenty weeks we do another ultrasound and the sex can determined. Unless there is suspicion of complications we wouldn't do another one until that time but since you have twins we will do one more ultrasound at twelve weeks." The doctor would be pleased to see them at that time.

Mark talked to the receptionist about getting another appointment for early April and Kelly busily called her mother's cell phone. "Mom hi can you talk for a moment?"

"Yea but just for a minute; how did you do at the clinic?"

"Well mom I'm having twins!" Long pause.

"Mom are you still standing? She heard her mother sobbing before she began to speak.

"Oh God bless you Kelly now you take good care of yourself dear and those precious little ones. If they are boys Mark might like to name them after his father and uncle."

"That would be a wonderful tribute to them mom; I'll mention it to him. I love you too Mom, I wish you could have seen the look on Marks face and his eyes, my goodness I thought they were stuck in one position; wide open."

"Kelly dear you'll have lots of help when you bring the babies home; you won't have to lift a finger. Oh I can't wait to give you a baby shower for our little ones."

"Ok mom I can't wait either. I especially can't wait until I can feel them, moving around."

"That will be interesting. You know you'll have to put them in the same crib for a while."

"That's right mom I will. They will need to feel close to each other."

"I have to go now dear; talk later and I love you Kelly."

"Bye mom; talk later and I love you too." Kelly and Mark took Elizabeth home and then they headed over to the bakery to tell the Childress's and all the employees. They parked in front of the store and when they got out of the car they stood on the side walk holding hands.

"Well Mark it was right here in this very spot where this all began just four short months ago." Kelly reminisced. She glowed while she smiled thinking about her memories of that day in November when they met in front of the bakery.

"That it was my love; the day my life began. Thank you for letting me stumble into you."

"The pleasure was all mine."

"Really?"

"Why yes, it's not every day a girl gets in the way of a man as handsome as you are."

"No you are the catch of the century Kelly. I must have been crazy to want to keep an appointment with a bunch of guys instead of getting your phone number."

"Well let's go inside to get a donut and tell my grandparents the news." They went inside and the Childress's happened to both be behind the counter.

"Hi grandma and grandpa."

"Hello Kids, how was the doctor appointment?"

"Well give me three donuts and sit down with me and I'll tell you."

"I'll have a donut for myself." Mark requested.

"What?" One for you and three donuts for the new momma?"

"Yes three for me please."

"You're kidding! Do you want one for you and one for each baby? Is that what you are getting at my dear girl?" Cried Grandma.

"That's right and hurry will you, we're hungry."

"Oh my dear! Bob get her a whole box of freshly made donuts."

Bob laughed and shook hands with Mark and grandma ran from behind the counter and kissed and hugged both Kelly and Mark.

"Kelly so much has happened for you in so little time and the next big day is your graduation in a couple of months. Honey I'm so happy that you came in here looking for a job instead of trying at Wal-Mart. I never would have had knowledge that I'm going to be a great grandmother of twins."

"Thank you grandma, I love you so much. Listen I was wondering if it wouldn't be too much to ask; could I have a couple pictures of your daughter? I'll be curious whether the twins look like her at all."

"Sure sweaty I'll bring some over tonight. That's a good idea Kelly."

"Are you sure you don't mind?"

"No it's not a problem. If someone else wanted the pictures of Heather I may feel defensive but I don't with you. You are my Darling girl."

"Well thank you for the donuts. We'll save some for tonight when you come over to see us and bring photos. We have to get back to work and school; we'll look forward to seeing you both tonight." Mark said and they left.

They made their way home so that Kelly could get her own car to go to school but they saw Ted's car in the driveway and saw it as an opportunity to spread their doubly good news. They walked in to see Ted and Linda embraced. Ted had just arrived and brought lunch for Linda and him. There was enough for everyone so Mark and Kelly took a lunch break with them and shared their fresh warm donuts. Kelly started the story of the days blessed events.

"We brought donuts from the bakery that grandma gave us. I joked with them that I needed three donuts and Mark spoke up and asked for one for his self. They got it right away." Said Kelly

"You asked for three donuts for yourself? Are you saying you need one for each baby or you were just extra hungry?"

"I believe it would be the first Linda." Mark proudly announced.

"Twins! Kelly you'll be sprouting in your dress at my wedding in May. I want to ask you to be my maid of honor but I'm just elated Kelly. Ted, what do you think about that?"

"Double the fun, double the diapers, double the garbage at the curb; no I'm just kidding. I'm truly happy for you both. You be careful Kelly with your schedule the way it is. You could find yourself spread very thin."

“Oh Ted you sound like my mother.” Kelly said gleefully.

Ted hugged his close friend Kelly and shook hands with Mark.

“Linda as for your request that I be your maid of honor, I would be proud to but shouldn’t you ask your sister? Now don’t get me wrong I’ll do anything I can to help you but your own sister should do the honor and Yes I imagine that I’ll be showing quite abundantly by May; that will be the four month mark.”

“Well ok we’ll eat now and I’ll give it more thought later.”

“That’s a hefty good idea. I’m starved and happy to be eating something decent after being away for a week.” Ted commented.

As the months went by Linda polished up her wedding arrangements and called the members of her wedding party. She was worried about stepping on toes since Ted asked George to be his best man. It would seem more appropriate to have partners stand up together but both Sinew and Mary told the future bride and groom to do what was pleasing to them for their happy day. All the plans went smoothly once they considered that reasoning. Linda’s health had improved and all that were close to her were kept aware that stress could be dangerous for her blood pressure and much was done to accommodate her. By this her family realized the blessing of being able to engage in one and others commitment to trusting, compromising and working together in harmony; all for the benefit of Linda's recovery. Since the family saw and agreed that Linda cannot stand on her own and she needed to develop skills for problem solving. With this unfortunate weakness, Linda could have hurt her chances for a good future. Fortunately Mark and Kelly saw the disadvantages that she faced and took the initiative lead by God's grace to help Linda. Sinew provided generously for Linda wedding of her dreams. Ted was the man she loved and she had his heart to hold. She was free from the bondage of guilt and would move forward with her own ideas of the reality.

Ted and Linda decided to have the ceremony in the chapel that Mark and Kelly attend. The reception was to be held in Mary and George's garden and precautions were taken in case of bad weather. Beautiful canopies were placed along the lawns and a large white tent would be on hand in case of a weather emergency. Linda did not have the option to wear her mother's wedding dress because of the difference in their sizes; she was much more petite' then her mother. Mary arranged for a designer that she knows to meet with Linda and Sinew and they designed a very delicate gown. The chiffon skirt was caught by and empire waist line at the bodice with a floral lace back and a "V" neck gathered with an arrangement of pearls at the shoulders. Monique and Mellissa created the floral arrangements and the bouquets. Tanya was the maid of honor and George, the best man with Carol as the bridesmaid, Jack as the groomsman and the twins were flower girls. The food was catered again through one of Mary's connections which made the wedding planning much less stressful for Linda at the approval of Sinew and she was never offended by Mary's participation and ideas.

On the last weekend in May Ted took his bride Linda to the chapel and there took their vows during a wonderfully sacred romantic ceremony. Linda looked healthier then she had in months and was like a china doll in her white chiffon, lace and pearl gown accessorized with a feather, silk and pearl head piece. Ted dressed in his formal military uniform accessorized with his medals and white gloves and he glorified in his bride as she made her way up the isle to his side and carrying her bouquet of white roses and lily of the valley. Her future was now stable in health, family and marriage and in Teds testimony to the guests, he thanked Kelly for her sweetness and Mark for his faith in God and to Linda for trusting him with her heart.

Chapter Sixteen

Mark and Kelly were grateful to have been such a support to Linda and to have seen her succeed in life. They kept in close contact with her and Ted and Kelly reported her doctor visits and even invited Linda to the ultrasound in June when they would learn the sex of their babies. Linda was thrilled to be one of the first to know and promised Kelly to take her shopping afterwards to buy little things in the colors appropriate for the twins. Ted had been living in an apartment on base and before the wedding he and Linda went house hunting for a rural property. They found what they wanted about five minutes' drive from the base and there they set up housekeeping. Linda continued to work at the hardware store until the wedding and then quit since a ninety minute drive would be hard to handle every day.

The everyday events were smoothing out and Mark and Kelly were happy in their marriage and Elizabeth had an emotional time during the week of the one year mark that her husband and his brother died. It was a comfort to her though, knowing that Gordon was with her in spirit and was influencing her wellbeing and was close always. Linda's moods evened out and her relationship with her mother improved. Although Sinew moved back to Ontario to be with her family, she and Thom did not reconcile in marriage. They decided to support their three children as a family and built a finer bond then they ever knew before.

In June Mark, Kelly, Elizabeth, Mary and Linda were present for the ultrasound. They were pleased to find that

Kelly was carrying twin boys and the little ones were growing and thriving normally. They were expected to be born late in October. Kelly graduated in May with honors and has a registered nursing degree but as plans sometime change, hers did for the time being because of her forth coming career as a mother. Through the summer Kelly helped Mark in the store which thrilled the Childress's; they could see every day the progress in Kelly's pregnancy. Mary and George decorated the baby's room with all of the finest furnishings and wall art that would please the new parents. Elizabeth gave Kelly a wonderful summer baby shower on their back patio. Everyone that Kelly knew was there and they showered her with the latest in style little blue, purple and green tiny outfits and sleepers and baby toys. The women presented Kelly with maternity nightgowns, robes and slippers and a new suitcase and Lamaze kit for her trip to the hospital. On weekends and in spare time, Mark, Kelly and Elizabeth barb-b-qued and pic-nicked, planted gardens of new flowers around the yard of their new home. With the babies on the way the Scott's home was becoming just that; a real home and just not four walls with a roof for Mark and Elizabeth to merely just exist in. The business was starting to flourish, although it took a couple of months, business was great. Mark was rewarded sufficiently for his many hours of hard work and dedication to making a new home for him and Elizabeth and now for Kelly and his children.

Saturday October seventh, Mark Kelly and Elizabeth had just finished dinner with the Gerard's in Stirling when her seemingly constant Braxton Hicks cramps began to bother her. Kelly had been at her parents' house for three days so she could relax. She had been very emotional that week and no one but her mom could sooth her and make it better. She was in close contact with her Abdulla and mid-wives; the three of them were on call for Kelly. Mark made a call to them because of Kelly's anxiety and closeness to the October, twenty fourth due date. Mary ran a nice warm bath in the Jacuzzi and turned the jets on low for Kelly and lit some fragrant candles to relax her daughter. She brought her some flowers and put on the soft quiet music as additional way to pamper her.

"Kelly this is good. What new mother wouldn't be relaxed in here?" Mark stood behind his wife and massaged her shoulders.

"Did you call Marlene and the mid-wives?"

"Yes babe, they are on their way and they should be here in about an hour. Do you think you are in active labor now?"

"I'm not sure but the cramping is different now, it's very low and acute and it's difficult to straighten and stand. That's why I got in a hot tub, to relax the muscles."

"Marlene will tell you more when she gets here and examines you and the mid-wives are bringing the birthing pool and bed matts just in case this is it."

"Ok, that's good to know."

"Kelly, are you frightened now that the pains are feeling different?"

"I don't know really what to expect so I can't speak about hard labor yet. Open that window and bring that tree branch in here so I have it to grab onto later."

Mark laughed at her and continued to massage her shoulders and back while they waited for Marlene, Valarie and Anne the mid-wives. The ladies arrived and Mary escorted them to the room where Kelly was still relaxing in the tub.

"I'm glad you are here Marlene with the mid-wives. I've been having pressure and pain in the lower area. This is not the usual tightness in my abdomen."

"Ok Kelly if you would move to your bed we have it prepared to examine you and we'll cover you with your robe. Oh Kelly the bath water is murky; your water has broken. You are in the early stages of labor. We'll examine you and get you walking to bring the contractions on stronger and to bring the babies down." Marlene instructed. Kelly moved to the bed with Mark escorting her lovingly. She was unaware that her water broke since she was in the tub when it happened she didn't know when it happened. Marlene examined her internally and it caused her to have a very strong contraction and the pains continued after that every fifteen minutes. Valarie and Anne helped her to get dressed so that she could walk around the house. It was then eight in the evening and too dark and cold to walk outside so she joined the rest of the family downstairs and walked from one length of the house to the other.

Monique and Brian had arrived with their children and were prepared to stay the night in anticipation of the blessed event. The twins collected all their baby dolls and made beds for them in the great room.

They pretended that they were nurses working in the hospital nursery and had two of their best cradles prepared for the new little ones. They even made up a waiting room all accessorized with magazine to look at during the long wait and juice boxes in case the family got thirsty. The whole family was there in the Gerard home and it was expected that they would miss going to church the next morning because Kelly would labor throughout the night. Grandma and Aunt Barbara got together and made herbal tea, warmed up mulled sider and made sandwiches and a fruit and cheese tray for every one; it would be a long evening. George and Brian lit all the fire places to make the house cozy and everyone gathered in the great room to watch videos of Kelly and the girls while they were growing up. Kelly labored and walked throughout the occasionally stopping to watch the video of her child hood in that wonderful house, the very home where she was about to deliver her sons into the world. In the early evening all was well and Kelly was fairly comfortable and Marks nerves were still at ease with Elizabeth dozing off in the big cushioned chair by the fireplace. She would get a bit of rest and participate in the excitement to happen in a few hours. President Cassidy and his wife came by at ten thirty to assist Mark, George and Brian in giving Kelly a blessing. They prayed that God be with Kelly and ease her labor that she will stand to deliver safely and that the mid-wives would be guided by His divine direction while caring for Kelly and the babies.

Most of the family went to bed around midnight. Elizabeth, George, Mary and Aunt Barb slept until four o: clock and then joined everyone in Kelly's room. They found Kelly squatting on the bed bent over a soft large ball with the Abdulla holding a warm herbal sack over her lower back and Mark massaging her temples. Mary went to her daughter and rubbed her back while quietly singing to her relaxing Kelly in the middle of a contraction. Kelly enjoyed the sweetness of her mother's voice while she vocalized the baby's down. Mark looked up and noticed his mother standing at the door and he smiled and when Kelly finished he walked over to greet his mother and invite her into his wife's birthing room. "Mom the contractions are five minutes apart and are getting intense. All is moving along well and she's half way ready at five centimeters dilated, she is fully effaced. So far she has been able to breathe through the contractions and just came out from another relaxing warm bath."

"Oh that's wonderful; it seems that the warm water is working for her."

"They're going to have her walk for another hour if she can than they will examine her again. I'm so proud of her mom, she's stronger even then she thought but there's still a ways to go and I don't know how well I'll hold up; I'm getting quite emotional already seeing her in this much pain."

"I know honey; I bet you are feeling for her because you are such a loving husband just like your father was. Let me get you some herbal tea."

"Thanks mom I could really use some right now."

"I'll make a pot then."

Mark and Marlene guided Kelly downstairs so that she could walk some more without waking anyone up. Elizabeth had some refreshments ready and Mark stoked the fire in the great room and joined Kelly for another walk through the house.

"I'm surprised that I can still walk; it feels better for my back to be up and standing."

"You are starting another contraction" Marlene said.

"Yes I am and it's a hard one, the hardest one yet; oh dear, I think I'd better sit down."

"Ok Kelly that was less than three minutes from the last pain. Breathe through it sweetie."

The contraction brought Kelly to her knees and it worried Mark terribly. He could stand no more and became very emotional, so much so and he was unprepared for it. While Kelly suffered Elizabeth tried to comfort Mark and reminded him that he needed to be a strong coach for Kelly and put his feeling aside. "The babies have to come out dear and it's going to hurt; please go to her and hold her."

You're right mom I'm sorry, I feel so ashamed of myself. Well here it goes; you're looking at King Kong here all the way until she gives birth."

That pain subsided and she walked for twenty minutes more having nine contractions each more intense then the last. She had to get back into the tub and Mary had it all ready for her. Mark carried her up the stairs and Marlene examined her before letting her back into the tub.

"Oh my! Kelly you are doing wonderfully. You are about seven and a half centimeters. You can sit in the tub while Anne and Valarie get your birthing pool ready."

Kelly was beginning to lose control and Mark wasn't feeling much better. She clung to him and wouldn't let him go so he got into the tub behind her so she could rest against him while he supported her and held her throughout every contraction. He was so wonderful, he cried with his wife and held her lovingly and massaged her tummy.

At around six in the morning the rest of the family was beginning to stir. Kelly and Mark moved to the birthing pool, now ten centimeters dilated and with the dramatic urge to push, Kelly began to deliver her babies with her husband holding her. All the women were present and George and Brian were close by to welcome the babies. Monique and Mellissa were on hand with the camcorder and at seven twelve am. the first baby boy was delivered to Mark and Kelly's joyful arms. After Mark cut the cord they sat there in the warm water and caressed and sang quietly to their precious little one. Anne took him to weigh him; five pounds, eleven ounces and nineteen inches long with black hair. Elizabeth held him all swaddled in his first little nighty while his mother delivered his brother. At seven thirty am. Kelly gave birth again. The two were blessed with another little boy, six pounds and three ounces, eighteen inches long. He lay in the warm water with his parents and never took his little eyes off them as he cooed softly to them.

"He has come straight from God's arms to ours."

"We'll name him Gordon after my father and his brother will be Geoff, after my uncle. I feel my father's presence." Tears shot from Marks eyes and his heart was overwhelmed by the blessing of having his father's comfort.

"It's an honor to have these children Mark, I feel like I know your father right this moment. OH thank you. Thank you Jesus."

The mid-wives bathed the babies and got Kelly comfortably in bed to rest and nurse. They were wonderful. The boys had their first feedings and then drifted off to sleep; they had a big day and needed their rest so they could receive guests later. Mark and Kelly nestled with the babies and slept while they could. The Childress's got word of the births and made their way to Stirling to visit the family. Ted and Linda were also on their way as well as Linda's family. The Lee family was also very interested in the arrival of the twins and would also go to greet the babies with little gifts. By supper time Kelly felt very hungry and well enough to receive her guests and introduce her twin boys, Gordon George Scott and Geoffrey Mark Scott. The Childress's brought pastries from the bakery and the Lee's brought Chinese food from the restaurant for supper. The four families spent the evening enjoying the blessings of love, freedom, friendship and the bond of family and it was a testimony of God's hand in their lives.

THE END

CPSIA information can be obtained
at www.ICGtesting.com
Printed in the USA
LVHW080422290621
691443LV00015B/312